TEASE

a novel by

Alexis Anne

This book is a work of fiction. Names, characters, places, and incidents are the product of the author's imagination or are used fictitiously. Any resemblance to actual events, locales, or persons, living or dead, is coincidental.

Tease Copyright © 2014 by Alexis Sykes

ISBN-13: 978-1539475668
ISBN-10: 1539475662

All rights reserved, including the right to reproduce, distribute, or transmit in any form or by any means. For information regarding subsidiary rights, please contact the Authors.

Cover design by Alexis Anne
Cover Photo: Adobe Stock by tverdohlib

Manufactured in the United States of America
Second Edition October 2016

BOOKS BY ALEXIS ANNE

The Storm Inside
Reflected in the Rain
When Lightning Strikes
Never Let Go
Tease
Stripped
Tempt
Burn
5 Dirty Sins
6 Dirty Secrets

Undressing Cara
Kissing Owen
Filters

PRAISE FOR *THE STORM INSIDE* & *TEMPT*

The Storm Inside

"It was one of the best love stories I have read to date. The writing at times was so descriptive you could feel the love, pain, confusion and desperation between the characters."
-*Books Unhinged Book Blog*

"This book starts off with a BANG! Literally!! Their scenes together were so intense and the sex scenes were so hot, my whole body felt on fire." -*Lustful Literature*

"The sex was HOT! Jake melted me with his words."
-*Miscellaneous Thoughts of a Bookaholic*

"I loved the writer's portrayal of what life can throw at young love." -*Brenda's Book Beat*

Tempt

"Very erotic" –*Cosmopolitan.com*

"This has truly been an awesome book and an amazing series." –*Books of Past, Present, and Future*

To N~
For whom I write all the dirty things...

Chapter 1

Sunday Night

"Your usual?" Mitch asked without looking up.

"Please," I huffed as I threw myself down onto the barstool and slammed my purse on the countertop. Mitch grabbed the bottle of Wente Cabernet Sauvignon, my favorite, and filled my glass generously, just the way I liked it.

"How's it going so far? You aren't lonely yet, are you?" His forced smile told me my unhappiness was obvious.

"I'm up and down." In the short time since we moved to the South Carolina town of Calhoun Beach, Mitch had become a friend and sometime confidante—most likely because he was the keeper of the alcohol. "I'm sure I'll get used to it."

I wouldn't get used to it.

The problem was my entire world consisted of two people: my little sister, Lily, and my best friend from college, Allison. Both of whom, as of two days ago, had left me. Lily was back at Yale for her last year of college, and Allison was on a project with the London branch of her architectural firm for the next six months. Except for a group trip to London for the Thanksgiving break, I wouldn't see either of them until Christmas.

I'd been abandoned, or at least that was what I told them (only half-jokingly) as I put them each on their respective planes.

Mitch shook his head, "They'll be home before you know it and the three amigos will be back here for drinks with me, yet again."

"I need to make new friends, don't I?" Somehow I couldn't see spending the next six months sitting at the bar as a healthy option, no matter how desperately I wanted it to work.

Mitch nodded. "Pretty much."

"Ugh." I grunted and laid my forehead down on the cool surface of the bar. "But I don't like people."

"Thanks."

I didn't move. Instead I spoke directly into the lacquered wood, the vibrations of my voice bouncing back at me. "Not you, you're awesome. But most people... they kind of suck."

"Look, give it a try. You might be surprised. You've only been here a few months and you've barely scratched the surface on all that Calhoun Beach has to offer."

I sat up and shifted back against the barstool with a grin. "You mean there are places to eat other than

Seychelles?"

Seychelles Bar and Grill was the restaurant on the ground floor of my apartment building. Inside was dim, but elegant. Dark wood was the main architectural feature and white tablecloths covered every table. The bar was situated so that guests had a view out the back window of the beach.

It meant we had food downstairs nearly every night, a bar any time we needed a drink, the beach out our back door, and a huge, gorgeous apartment that had been refurbished, along with the rest of the historic building, ten years earlier. I thought I'd died and gone to heaven when Allison and I did our first walk-through.

"As much as I love having a job...yes, there are other restaurants in town," Mitch snorted.

"I eat at the diner across the street..."

"You're hopeless," Mitch agreed, shaking his head like I was a lost cause.

I would have punched him in the arm if there hadn't been a bar between us. "Fine, I'll start getting out more. Sheesh."

"That's my girl." He pushed my wine glass closer and I took a sip. "Know what you want to have tonight? I can get your order in before the dinner crowd hits."

"Scallops, please." My stomach started growling at the mention of food.

"Coming right up."

While Mitch busied himself with my order and the other two customers at the bar, I pulled out my Kindle and dove back into the book I'd wasted most of the day on: a ridiculously over-the-top romance. It wasn't my usual fare, but with my friends gone, no life, and absolutely no desire for a relationship, it was actually kind of liberating to live vicariously through a fictional character. Love belonged on the page and as far away from my real life as possible.

I had zero interest in relationships or anything else that resulted in broken hearts. People were users—my parents taught me that early on. Every time I became attached to someone it became a way for them to manipulate me.

If you really loved me...
I just need some help...
This is the last time, I swear...

I'd had enough. Calhoun Beach was my chance to start over and this time I was in charge. I'd made a few rules for myself, but the most important was to never get attached to anyone. I had fun, but on my terms. And when it came to pleasure, as long as I followed my rules, I somehow always managed to find satisfaction.

By the time Mitch brought me a water I'd plowed through three chapters of my book. "Dinner should be right up—" Mitch stopped mid-sentence as something over my shoulder caught his eye. "Hey Adam, It's been a long time!"

I glanced back as a tall man strode up to the bar and enthusiastically shook Mitch's hand. He was gorgeous.

Incredibly, perfectly, gorgeous.

My heart jumped and I had to swallow to stop a sigh from escaping my lips. Tan skin, chiseled jaw, straight nose, bright brown eyes, and a muscular body. The immediate physical reaction I had to the sight of *Adam* was embarrassing.

And much to my delight and fear, he grabbed the seat next to me. Only inches away. My skin crackled with electricity.

Why was he sitting so close to me when the bar was nearly empty?

Except the bar was packed. Sometime while I was zoned out in my book, the restaurant had filled to capacity and the only empty seat was the one next to mine. *Lucky me.*

"How's Germany?" Mitch asked, leaning against the bar with his arms crossed. There was genuine curiosity on his face—this wasn't small talk, they were friends.

Adam leaned back in his seat and clasped his hands behind his head, giving me an enjoyable view of his long, lean body. My pulse quickened. The black t-shirt was fitted enticingly around his biceps. This was a man who took care of his body and I could only imagine what else that t-shirt was hiding.

Or I could find out for myself. I adjusted slightly on my stool as my body roared to life and heat pulsed between my legs.

"Man, it's awesome. I'm having the time of my life. It's been a real pleasure to see it all come together like this. I never would have imagined."

"I'm so jealous, but happy for you. I always knew you'd do great things..."

"Thanks, I appreciate that," Adam replied with a proud grin on his handsome face. "Glad to be back home for a couple of weeks, though. How are things here?"

Mitch chuckled, straightening up. "Same old stuff, nothing really changes. Can I get you a drink?"

"You still got that Golden Goose Ale on tap?"

"Sure do."

I sat there pretending to read as Mitch and Adam continued to exchange random information. I couldn't help but wonder how Adam and Mitch knew each other, why he lived in Germany, or what brought him back to Calhoun Beach.

Or why he was so damn sexy.

For the first time in two days I wasn't whining about Lily and Allison—heck I was half glad they were gone. Mitch was right, I needed some fun in my life and Adam seemed like a perfectly a good way to start—if I could form coherent thoughts while looking at his delicious body.

My phone vibrated against the countertop, startling me from thoughts of stripping the stranger beside me naked. Allison's name was emblazoned across the screen along with a picture of the two of us on the beach. An hour ago I would have been ecstatic to talk to her while I waited for dinner, but things were different now. I had a man to seduce.

I tapped out a message letting her know I'd call

her later, when Mitch grabbed my glass and started refilling it. "Thanks."

"No problem, Elizabeth. I just got the signal your dinner is ready. I'll be right back."

Mitch disappeared and Adam and I sat there, side by side, neither of us with anyone else. It was that awkward silence that comes when you are both fully aware that the other one is also fully aware.

"You like the Wente? It's a favorite of mine as well."

My heart skipped a beat. He was talking to me in a deep, smooth voice that was softer than when he was speaking to Mitch.

"Yes, it's very nice. I get it every time I'm here," I answered quietly, flashing a small smile and making eye contact. *Sweet Jesus...* his eyes were amazing.

"You come here often then?" he asked, cocking his head to the side as he turned to face me.

I blushed and suddenly wished I wasn't wearing a sun dress. My telltale nervous flush extended all the way down my chest and I realized I wanted this man more than I was prepared to admit. "Yes, I actually live upstairs," I pointed up towards my apartment, hoping to distract him.

It didn't work. His gaze was locked on me. It was steady and curious, with just a touch of confusion. "Really? How is it that we've never met before? I've been eating here for years and Mitch is a childhood friend."

I took a steadying breath and tried to relax my nerves. It was scaring me how attracted I was to Adam.

My mind was filling with images of his hands against my skin, roving over my breasts, down my stomach, and between my legs. I wondered what it would feel like to have his lips on my body with his cock buried deep inside me as I rode him.

The images were so real and insistent. I felt like I needed a cold shower just to sit beside him. "I just moved to town about four months ago."

He stroked his stubbled chin and I couldn't stop focusing on his long fingers as they brushed past his lips. "Makes sense then," he replied. "I've only been in and out of town briefly over the last few months. So what brought you to Calhoun Beach?" He leaned his elbow on the bar and I got the distinct impression he was genuinely interested in hearing about me. Which felt weird.

"Work. I'm an assistant professor at the college," I answered his question but I didn't want to talk about myself. I wanted to hear about him. "And what brings you to Calhoun Beach from Germany?"

His eyes didn't move. "My family lives here. I come visit every few months." The corners of his lips turned up slightly in a half-smile. "Where did you move here from?"

I fought my instinctive need to flee when his questions turned toward my past. I never talked about my childhood, I avoided all questions related to my parents, and I never told people my real name. But there was something compelling about Adam, so instead of asking for my check and ducking out the door, I searched for an answer I could live with. "I'm not really from anywhere. My family moved around a lot...the longest I lived anywhere was during college."

"And where was college?"

"New Haven."

Adam nodded thoughtfully, "Yale? Good school. And what are you teaching at the college?"

The questions were hard and fast. This wasn't a normal, casual conversation between two people stuck at the same bar. This was an interrogation. Why Adam felt the need to question me, I hadn't figured out, but I was hoping it was because he was as attracted to me as I was to him.

"I'm in the Historic Preservation and Community Planning department." Being a professor was the only thing I ever wanted to do. It was the furthest thing from my childhood I could imagine, and it gave me the power and control I so desperately needed.

Adam's eyebrows shot up. "Wow, you sure picked the right town for that."

Calhoun Beach was pretty much one giant historic district, with buildings from nearly every era. The College of Calhoun Beach had one of the most prestigious departments for historic preservation in the country. Landing my job at my age was a coup.

It was at that moment that Mitch returned with my dinner. "Bon appetit, darling. Enjoy!"

The scallops looked amazing and the smell alone made my mouth water. "Thanks Mitch." He had an odd smile on his face, giving me the distinct impression

that he was amused, then walked away to serve another customer.

"Those look delicious," Adam murmured. "You'll have to let me know what you think. I was going to order the steak tonight, but I think I might change my mind."

I could swear his eyes were twinkling. Were they twinkling at me? I took a bite and the perfectly prepared scallop practically melted like butter in my mouth. I barely suppressed a groan.

A strange look of pleasure crossed Adam's face, but he shook his head and closed his eyes, erasing it.

"They really are wonderful tonight. You should get them," I said between bites, curious about his reaction. I was almost positive Adam was just as attracted to me as I was to him.

He looked away from me as if he couldn't stand watching me. Something had suddenly shifted and Adam seemed almost as uncomfortable around me as I first did around him. He downed the remainder of his drink, clinking the glass against the counter as he waved at Mitch, indicating he'd like a refill.

It was my turn to ask the questions. "You don't have much of an accent. Are you from here?" Adam had a faint drawl to his words, but not the distinctive accent I was used to hearing from the locals.

Adam glanced at me warily, but warmed after a moment and his smile returned. "Funny story, actually. My family moved back here when I was fifteen. I finished high school here, but that was it. This is home now because it is where my folks live, but I didn't really grow up here."

"Where is home, then?"

His brown eyes looked a little distant and sad for a moment, "It used to be New York, but I guess it really isn't anymore."

Before I could press him for more information Mitch reappeared, interrupting our conversation, "Did you decide on dinner, Adam?"

"I'll have what Elizabeth," he paused glancing intensely at me, "it is *Elizabeth*, right?"

I nodded, feeling a little thrilled that he just made the obvious effort to make sure he knew my name.

He smiled broadly, "I'll have what Elizabeth's having. I certainly can't pass it up after her rave reviews."

Mitch glanced from Adam to me, and back again. "Not a problem, coming right up."

We sat quietly, sipping our drinks for several moments. The silence was comfortable but full of anticipation and I wasn't sure what to think of the stranger beside me. He was very handsome—my physical reaction was evidence of that. I'd gone from lonely and cranky to nervous and horny in a matter of moments. But he was also asking a lot of questions.

I ate my scallops very slowly, giving myself as much time as possible to feel Adam out.

"What are you reading?" he suddenly asked, startling me from my thoughts.

I glanced down at my Kindle, feeling exposed again. "It's just a romance." I waved my hand in the air

in an attempt to dismiss his interest.

"What's it called?"

"Why do you care?"

He grinned. "Why won't you tell me?"

I tried not to blush all over again, but he'd gotten me. It was like he could see my vulnerabilities and knew he needed to concentrate his efforts if he wanted to get under my skin.

Which he seemed pretty hell-bent on doing.

"I'm sure you've never heard of it."

"I bet you I have."

What was with this guy and his romance novels?

"Or," he asked, leaning just a little bit closer. Close enough that I could feel the shift in warmth from his body. "Do you assume as a man I have no interest in romance novels?"

"Well, yes." Why were we even having this conversation? Hot guys on vacation did not talk about romance novels over drinks with strangers.

"What's the name of the book, Elizabeth?"

Demanding. Adam was incredibly demanding for someone who'd known me all of twenty minutes. But compared to the other men in my life, this seemed fun, not intimidating. It wasn't a power tactic; it was Adam pushing at my boundaries to feel me out.

"It's called *The Summer of Us*."

"By Robin Green. It is number two on the *Times* best-seller list right now."

Ok, so I was honestly, truly shocked. "I think I'm impressed."

Adam bounced his eyebrows and took a sip of his beer. "I read a lot and I don't restrict myself to any particular genre. I read whatever is hot or piques my interest. When I travel I usually grab the books on display at the airport."

A reader. A genuine, in the wild, reader. If I thought I was attracted to Adam before... "I read everything, too."

Somehow the stupid grin on his face grew and his eyes lit up. "Kindred spirits."

My heart skipped a beat.

This was trouble.

Thankfully Mitch placed an identical plate of scallops in front of Adam and I got a break while Adam ate. His brow was slightly furrowed and his brown eyes were staring at some imaginary object in the distance as he chewed. His dark hair was just long and wavy enough to be perfect for running my hands through. His hands were large and capable looking. They were properly manicured but also showed signs of use. *I wonder what he does with those hands......*

His phone buzzed, startling us both. He frowned and tapped a quick reply before standing abruptly and waving at Mitch who made his way back over.

"I've got to go," Adam said, looking annoyed. Then he dropped several bills on the counter, glancing at me sideways as if he were having an internal debate.

"Not a problem. Have a good night Adam. It was good to see you." Mitch grabbed the cash and slid it into his apron pocket before moving a few feet away to help another customer.

Adam stuffed his phone and wallet back into his pocket and gulped down the last of his beer before turning to meet my gaze. "It was very nice having dinner with you, Elizabeth. Will you be here tomorrow night?"

His eyes were locked onto mine so intently I could feel him everywhere and my entire body heated again. If all it took was a look from Adam for me to respond like that, I'd spend another evening at the bar. "I usually am."

"I hope you are. Have a good night," he murmured as he left.

"Good night," I replied with the last of my breath. Adam had taken the rest.

"You enjoyed your scallops?" Mitch asked with a goofy grin on his face.

I nodded as he took my empty plate, "Mitch, who was that guy?"

He laughed, "Hey, I told you to find someone to hang out with. I just didn't think you were going to settle on the first person who sat down next to you." He leaned in and spoke lightly under his breath, "You could do a lot worse than Adam. He's a good guy."

And that was what hurt. That right there. Adam was a *good* guy. He was probably looking for a date or two. Maybe he was just up for some fun, but it was also just as possible he was the kind of guy who wanted more. The kind of guy who asked insightful questions, held open doors, and cared about the woman he was kissing. "Perhaps you should warn your friend about me then."

Mitch paused, staring right back at me before sighing, "Lizzy, you really shouldn't be so hard on yourself."

I raised a speculative brow, "I'm not kidding, Mitch. I think the one you should be worried about is him."

He simply shook his head, his good-natured smile returning but not quite reaching his eyes. "I'm not going to say a word to him. He can handle himself."

I pushed my wine glass around in a circle, studying the grain of the wood beneath it. "What does he do in Germany?" Maybe Adam's life was so tied up on the other side of the world he was too busy for more than a fun night or two.

Mitch set down the bottle he was holding and leaned in. "He's got the coolest job I've ever heard of. He designs those crazy futuristic prototype cars for Mercedes. You know? The ones you see in magazines and stuff?"

"I don't think I've ever met anyone who actually did that..."

"I know, right? He was always building stuff when we were in high school. He built his first car all by himself. I'm not really surprised that Mercedes snatched him up."

It sounded like Adam was pretty set up in Germany. He had a life and a cutting edge career—family or not, he wasn't going to be spending much time in Cal-

houn Beach. "Thanks Mitch. See ya tomorrow night."

"Thanks Lizzy. Have a good night," he called after me.

I threaded my way back through the busy restaurant to the door that led upstairs to my apartment. My feelings were divided between an intense desire to have Adam any way I could get him, and a need to keep this guy, and his questions, as far away from me as possible.

Chapter 2

Monday Evening

I pushed the last student out of my last lecture and locked the door. The entire day had been shit. Complete, utter shit. I could tell by the glazed looks in my student's eyes. I usually tried to keep my classes interesting with debates and questions, but today...I'd droned.

It was all Adam's fault.

All I could think about were his eyes and the way they'd locked on to me. Like he could see me naked. I was turned on and the need was growing, not shrinking. Seeing him tonight would only make things worse.

So the question was: did I want to take a chance? Satisfy some needs that clearly needed some satisfying, or steer clear of potential complications?

Based on the little flutter of heat between my legs, my body wanted to take a chance. Unfortunately, my brain wasn't completely on board. Adam and I had clicked. This wasn't just a physical attraction—it was also mental and emotional. Adam was the kind of guy I could have a conversation with.

But I didn't want that kind of guy. I wanted the kind that would fuck me senseless and leave me satisfied for days. No questions, no complications.

The walk from campus back to my apartment was a short ten minutes and I was so deep in thought I almost jumped off the sidewalk when my phone rang.

"Hey."

"Hey!" my sister replied. "You sound out of breath."

"My phone scared me."

She laughed. "Sorry to terrorize you. Howya doing?"

"Good. Headed to dinner. How's school?" I could picture her smiling face with her perfect blond ponytail and brilliant blue eyes. She was a classic beauty from her nearly six-foot frame to her athletic, but slender, body. She always had a camera-ready smile and equally friendly personality. The beautiful girl you could never quite bring yourself to hate because she was so damn nice.

"Good. I'm all settled in." I was nine years older than Lily and more her mother than her sister until the last couple of years. Protecting her from our parents meant that I usually took the brunt of their poor choices while Lily remained blissfully unaware of how bad things could be. This was why she was still speaking to our parents and I avoided them like the plague.

"Having fun?"

"Always. Look," the sudden change in her voice stopped me in my tracks. Lily was calling about *them*. I could feel it. "Mom and Dad are supposed to drop in on me tomorrow before he heads out on his new lecture tour thingy."

"Tell Cybil and Roger I said hello."

Lily sighed. "Do you really want me to?"

"No. It just seemed like something I ought to say." The last thing I wanted was for Lily to mention my name in their presence. The less they thought about me the better.

"Mom just did a round of promos for her new season. You should watch an interview or two for information's sake if nothing else."

I rolled my eyes and wished I could scream, but instead took a deep breath. It was impossible to miss the news that another season of reality television had hit the airwaves. I saw my mother's face staring back at me while I checked out at the grocery store and in every other online ad. "Just email me the links. I'll watch them if you ask me to, but I'm not tracking them down." I had absolutely zero intention of watching a second of my mother acting like an idiot in front of the camera for a living.

"I already sent you two. Knowing your enemy is the best form of defense," she gently reminded me.

So was moving as far away from them—and their three-ring circus—as I could imagine. Calhoun Beach wasn't the other side of the world, but it was the exact opposite of Hollywood in every other way.

"Good luck with them tomorrow. Better you than me."

"Good night Lizzy," she sighed.

I slid my phone back into the pocket of my bag and tried to erase Cybil and Roger from my thoughts. Just thinking about them sent a shiver up my spine. *They* were the reason I never let anyone into my life.

I'd built a new life that had nothing to do with my childhood. Instead of paparazzi chasing me, it was students. Instead of long hours at parties, I read studies and wrote papers. I lived a quiet life in a quiet town. It kept me sane, but it was also keeping me stuck.

After we settled into our apartment in Calhoun Beach, Allison started in on the suggestions. She wanted me to build a life here. A real life. She said it was 'time to stop running'.

Only I didn't know if I knew how. That was why I was stuck on Adam. I wanted to see him again but he was so much more than my usual fuck buddies.

I was getting close to my building. All I had to do was walk past the restaurant and up to my apartment—grilled cheese for dinner was as good as anything. But my legs weren't listening to my head and, before I knew it, I was stepping inside Seychelles instead of the door to my apartment.

My heart was thudding in my chest like a drum, making my cheeks flush and skin burn like I was out for a run. I wanted this. It scared the crap out of me, but my attraction was so strong that it wasn't worth fighting.

I stopped at the window and checked my reflection, smoothing down my dark hair and unbuttoning an extra button on my blouse to expose some cleavage. But then I turned toward the bar and realized it was empty and I was an idiot. Adam wasn't there.

Of course he wasn't there. What was I thinking? It wasn't a sure thing and yet...I was positive Adam would be there, waiting for me with a wicked grin.

"Elizabeth?" It was Hannah, the hostess, approaching me from her podium.

"Hey, sorry. I thought I was going to grab dinner real quick, but I'm not feeling great. I think I'll just make a sandwich and go to bed."

She cocked her head and the corner of her lips turned up a little. "Actually, I was coming over here because someone wants to see you."

I froze somewhere between mortification and anticipation. "Who?"

"Adam Callaway. He asked me to show you to his table when you arrived. Unless—"

I held up my hand. "No, it's fine." Now I really was an idiot. Hannah had probably seen all my primping.

Her smile turned into a full-blown grin. "Right this way."

I followed her through the restaurant, weaving through a smattering of tables filled with quiet couples grabbing a quick dinner after work, and into the darkest corner. Adam was looking down at his phone and I got a chance to study him for a moment. His dark hair was brushed back, but loose and a little messy. He wore a light blue button-up and grey slacks. He looked like he'd just come from a meeting and not at all like he was enjoying a vacation.

The moment he saw us approaching he pushed back his chair and rose to his feet, a dazzling smile playing on his lips—not quite the wicked one I was imagining, but close. He was just as sexy as I remembered him.

Actually, that was a lie. He was even sexier. His broad shoulders pulled at the seams of his perfectly tailored shirt and suddenly I was wondering what they'd look like straining as he moved inside me.

"I'm glad you came."

"I'm glad I came, too," I replied with a smile. The kind that usually gave guys the idea I wasn't using that word lightly.

Adam chuckled, catching my hint. He kissed me lightly on the cheek before we each sat. Hannah was gone by the time I looked up, but I could hear her giggle from across the restaurant.

Subtle was not the word of the night.

"I hope you don't mind, but I thought a table would make conversation easier."

"Who said I wanted to talk?" I was going for the obvious. It would be better for both of us if I made my intentions clear from the beginning.

Adam coughed a little. Perhaps my forwardness was a bit much. I tried to dial it back a little.

"Well I guess I don't have to ask if this is a friendly dinner or not."

I grinned. "I'm glad you brought that up. Can we lay all our cards on the table?"

"Can I drink first?" he asked, picking up the glass of red wine in front of him.

"Absolutely. Mind if I share?"

"Not at all, that's why I got the bottle." He picked up the Wente Cabernet Sauvignon I'd been drinking the night before, and filled my glass half way. "Now, what did you have in mind?"

It was make or break time. I needed my terms to be clear or I'd have to walk away. I was ridiculously attracted to Adam, but I couldn't risk this being anything other than sex. "If I understood our conversation last night, you are only in town for a short visit?"

He nodded slowly, his eyes locked on to mine. I couldn't tell if he liked what I was saying or not.

"Good. I'm not looking for a relationship, just some fun."

He swirled the red liquid in his glass studying me, then it, before he took another sip and set it down carefully on the white tablecloth. "Does that mean I can't enjoy dinner with you?"

My nerves fluttered. Something in the cadence of his words told me Adam was pushing me again. In a weird way it was like he already had my personality—and my desire to stay out of relationships—pegged. But that couldn't possibly be true, this was only our second conversation. "I'm sure we could have a meal or two, but I want to be clear: I'm not looking for anything."

"We can't be friends *and* fuck buddies?"

"No," I snorted. I could only imagine the fifteen different ways that would implode on me.

But instead of throwing Adam off, he took it as a challenge. "Really? Now, that seems wrong. If I can fuck you, I can certainly enjoy hearing about your day over a glass of wine."

My breath caught in my throat. I wasn't expecting that response and I found it far too attractive. "You see," I leaned forward on the table and clasped my hands under my chin, "that kind of thinking tends to lead to caring and feelings. I don't have time for either of those."

"But you do have time for sex."

"Priorities," I replied with a smile, just as I felt something brush against my leg.

"Sounds to me like you might need to revisit those. I think I can make you scream my name *and* bring you coffee without ruining your life." His foot moved up my leg and pushed my knees apart.

I swallowed. The contact of his body against mine was electric. Even with distance and clothing separating us, it turned me on. "I wouldn't want to take that risk." My words were softer, breathier, than they had been a moment earlier.

"I don't see where the risk is. I'm only here for two weeks. How can you lose? If you don't like me, I'm gone. If you *do* like me, I'm still gone."

Adam leaned back lazily in his seat, which gave him a better angle to move his foot up my thigh. That was when I realized he wasn't wearing a shoe. Just a sock. It was soft and supple against the sensitive skin that led from my thigh to the hot, throbbing taking place between my legs.

If he just pushed, the pressure would feel so good.

But he didn't. Instead, he pulled back, tracing a trail down my thigh and calf, and then left me alone.

The loss of his touch was shockingly overwhelming. Almost as overwhelming as having his foot so close to my core. Adam had a gift, and he knew how to play me.

I should run.

"Two weeks, Elizabeth. Think of how much fun we can have."

"Two weeks?" I asked. It was like I was under his spell. He'd given me a taste of what having him in bed would feel like, but only a taste. It left me unsatisfied and ready to combust. How could I possibly think straight when all I wanted was to drag him upstairs and rip off his pants?

"Two weeks. I won't butt into your life unless you ask me to. I just can't stand the idea of fucking you without getting to know you. We had a good conversation last night." He huffed under his breath and sat back up. "It isn't very often I meet someone I actually enjoy talking to."

And that was what did it. I'd said the same thing to Mitch. I hadn't wanted to go looking for new friends because it was so hard to find any I liked. I liked Adam. He was smart and funny. He listened as much as he spoke.

I wanted to keep talking to him.

And just like that, I let go of my first line of defense. "Let's see what dinner holds and go from there."

Adam held my gaze. He looked confused and intrigued. I'd done this before—caught the passing interest of a good guy with my cold distance. The one comfort I still had was knowing that all I had to do was show Adam my real life and he'd be gone in a heartbeat. The curiosity was only there because of the mystery. Once my secrets were out, there was nothing left to hold them.

So this would be ok.

"We should order," I offered, opening my menu.

"I figured you had that thing memorized by now."

I glanced over the familiar curving fonts and snapped the heavy binder shut. He was right, again. I didn't need to look, I was using it as a distraction. I wanted to escape from the reality that I was making a massive mistake.

The waiter took our order and the next thing I knew, Adam was leaning back in his chair, smiling and drinking. "So, Elizabeth. How was your day?"

The bastard. The sex had better be earth-shattering. "Surprisingly boring compared to last night."

"Same here. It's amazing how 'relaxing' seems boring when you'd rather be doing someone else."

It was my turn to cough. I took a swig of wine to tamp down the urge to skip dinner and move straight to sex. "Well, at least we're clear on how you feel."

After that, conversation was actually pretty easy. Adam steered clear of any questions about my past or personal life, sticking with sports and my job instead. He told me about his work and how much he enjoyed living in Germany.

One thing was clear: Adam was passionate about cars. Once I got him started he barely stopped to breathe. "I've been building them since I was five. My granddad helped me build my first go-kart during a summer trip to Calhoun Beach."

"You visited often?" *Why did I ask that?* I didn't need to know stuff like that.

He nodded. "Every summer for a month and every Christmas. Granddad eventually gave me my own space for a workshop. We'd wander the junkyards looking for rare and unique parts." He shook his head, his eyes unfocused with memories. "I was done for after that. I became obsessed. One of my teachers had a friend who was an engineering professor. He hooked me up with some tutoring on the side. I learned all the ins and outs of modeling, software, design...Mercedes drafted me right out of college and I've been on the concept team ever since."

Adam was fascinating to listen to. Maybe it was his passion or his excitement. Not many people were so enthusiastic about work. Whatever it was, it had my attention and it wasn't until our waiter quietly placed our bill on the table that I realized we were the last customers in the restaurant. "What time is it?"

Adam's brown eyes were no longer bright or relaxed. He glanced at his watch. "It's eleven fifteen. They are probably more than ready to get us out of here."

Eleven fifteen? We'd been sitting there for hours. How was that possible?

He grabbed the bill and opened his wallet.

"How much is my half?"

"Dinner is on me." He stacked several bills on top of the check and stood up. "C'mon. Let's get out of here."

I looked at his outstretched hand. It felt like a turning point. I could still walk away. But taking his hand somehow seemed final. Like I was sealing the deal. His fingers were worn and rough, probably from working on his cars, and all I could think about was how amazing they would feel against my skin. I took his hand.

Adam yanked me up out of the seat, sending an electric current up my arm.

Was that excitement? I hadn't felt that in a long, long time...

"Good night, Hannah. Thanks for letting us stay so late," Adam called as he ushered me out of the restaurant, onto the street and the ten steps to the door that led up to my apartment, never releasing my hand.

"Thanks for walking me home, I know it was terribly out of the way," I joked, looking up at him and smiling softly. How was it that we still hadn't kissed?

I wanted him to kiss me.

He chuckled. I liked (far too much) that I made

him laugh. "You like living here?" he asked, looking up at the building.

"What's not to like? Food, beach, walking distance to work." He was close, but not close enough. It was like the game he played at dinner. *Teasing me*.

It was time I played back. I stared him directly in the eye and let him hear my altered breathing. He was affecting me and I wanted him to know it. I licked my lower lip and took a deep breath, letting my breasts rise and fall seductively.

Adam's gaze dipped to my lips and then to my chest exactly as I suggested. He may be in control of me, but I was in control of him. I could feel the electricity building between us. The anticipation had me lightheaded and wet.

To my relief, he stepped into me, grasping my free hand so he had just my fingertips held lightly inside his. It was the only part of us that was actually touching and the pressure built up behind that touch was explosive.

With the wicked smile I'd been waiting for all night, Adam gently tugged on my hand, pulling my body flush against his, and kissed me.

And oh sweet Jesus—Adam was a phenomenal kisser. His arm came around my waist, pressing my hips into his, while his other hand fisted at the nape of my neck, tilting my head back and opening my mouth to him.

His tongue was foreign and strange, but I loved how it felt to have his soft tongue stroking mine.

My body melded against his, seeking more contact, more friction. God, I needed some friction.

And then—his fucking phone rang. I hadn't heard the damn thing all night. I just assumed it was off or on silent. But no, it chose now of all times—when I was just about to yank my new fuck buddy upstairs—to finally ring.

Adam looked at me, startled. "Um, I'm really sorry, I have to take this." But he didn't move. He kept me pressed against him as he slid the clamoring electronic device out of his pocket and shoved it against his ear. "What?"

I liked how strong Adam was. His arm was wrapped firmly, possessively, around my waist. I ground my hips slowly against his thigh and hips while he talked, a dark curtain falling over his eyes with each rock of my hips.

Maybe I didn't really need him after all. Just his arm and his leg...

"No, I'll be right there."

Adam shoved his phone back in his pocket and his jaw flexed. Angry Adam was hot.

"Bad news?"

"There is a problem and unfortunately, it can't wait."

I pressed against him again, flexing my fingers into the firm muscles of his biceps. "Not even fifteen minutes?" *What kind of problem could possibly be more important than sex?*

Adam flushed, pushed me against the brick of the

building, and kissed me hard. His body arched into mine and I felt the telltale firmness of his erection. "Fuck," he swore as he swallowed and leaned his forehead against mine. "I can't. This can't wait and I can't do you in fifteen minutes. I need more time than that."

"Please?" I groaned. It was sad and desperate, but I was so turned on. He'd been on my mind all day and I needed a release.

"Fuck," he swore again, "Do you have your key?"

I grinned. *Yes, this was happening.* I handed him my key and he yanked open the door. Just inside was a small foyer and a set of stairs. It was empty and quiet. He shut the door, dropped my keys, and pushed me against the wall. "Keep an eye out, gorgeous."

I swallowed as he ran his hand over my clit. We weren't going up to my room? "I'm just one floor up..."

"No time," he gasped as he nuzzled my neck and worked my clit some more.

"No time?" I asked, throwing my head back against the wall as Adam lifted my skirt. "Oh fuck it. I don't care."

I felt his grin against my skin a split second before he kneeled in front of me, hooking his finger around my panties and pulling them to the side. With two fingers he plunged deep and I cried out.

Dear god it felt good to have part of him—any part of him—inside me. I'd take what I could get. Warm, firm, insistent, just like Adam. He moved his fingers in and out of me slowly, then, just as slowly, his warm tongue made contact with my clit. The combination of sensations was overwhelming and my knees went weak.

Adam reached up with his free hand and held my hips in place. I wasn't going anywhere. But we were out in the open. Anyone else could come home at any moment and Adam had some stupid emergency he needed to get back to, so I needed to find that release fast.

His fingers curled, his tongue stroked, and I reached inside my blouse, caressing my breast and moving my sensitive nipple against the fabric of my bra until it was free. I pinched lightly at first, then rolled it between my thumb and forefinger.

That did it. The buildup hit me all at once—there was nothing slow about this climax. I released my nipple and clapped my hand over my mouth to quiet my moans. Adam didn't let up. He worked me inside and out, fingers and tongue, until I sagged, panting against the wall.

If he was this good in five minutes in a foyer, I was going to love a full night in a bed.

He withdrew his fingers then moved my panties back into place, sliding my skirt down my legs, and adjusting my blouse before taking the lapels in his hands and looking down into my eyes. "Call that a preview of the next two weeks."

I nodded. I was completely speechless.

"Have breakfast with me?" His voice was soft, but insistent. "I don't want to wait until tomorrow night."

Yes. Breakfast. My foggy mind was willing to do anything for more of what Adam Callaway was selling.

"Where?" he asked. He sounded breathier now, too. The bulge in his pants was straining against the seams.

I pointed behind me. "Diner across the street."

He nodded. "Ok. Six?"

"Six," I agreed with another nod, just in case I wasn't actually speaking.

"Good," he replied, dropping several soft kisses on my lips before he pressed my keys into my hand and left.

Chapter 3

Monday, late

I didn't sleep. Not really. Mostly I lay awake staring at the ceiling fan as it swirled overhead. What the fuck was I thinking?

I knew exactly what I was thinking: sex. Adam sex, to be specific. I wanted all of it. There was something special about him that my body responded to in a way that it had never done before. Sex was always easy for me. All it took was a guy I was attracted to who had a modicum of talent. If he wasn't up to the task I was more than happy to take control, get what I needed, and get out.

But Adam sex wasn't like that. It was easy, intense, and satisfying...*and we hadn't actually had sex yet*. Which was precisely why I was lying in my bed counting down the minutes until six o'clock. He'd left me satisfied, but wanting more. As I shifted, my sheets grazed across my naked body. I was hyper stimulated from my earlier encounter and it didn't take much to arouse me all over again.

But did I wait for Adam, draw it out so that I was wet and waiting in the morning, or did I give in and satisfy my craving in order to give myself a level head?

I gave in.

It was as much fun to fantasize about what Adam would be like as it was to feel his mouth on my clit and his fingers inside me. He was tall and muscular, which meant he'd be heavy on top of me. He'd be firm in all the right places.

I spread my legs and arched my back, the sheet dragging along my nipples until they broke free. Tiny spikes of pleasure shot through me. That was going to be number one on my list: I wanted Adam's mouth on my nipples.

It was dark and quiet. My breath was the only sound in the room as I slid my finger down and touched the same spots Adam had touched earlier.

He was good. Normally I needed to guide my lovers the first time. But not Adam. He didn't need any coaching—he just knew.

I froze, one finger on my clit, one stroking the entrance to my sex. *He knew me.* Adam just seemed to know what to do whether it was talking or touching. It was natural. Too natural.

I banished the thought, squeezing my eyes shut, pinching my nipple with my other hand.

Pleasure. This was all about pleasure. Nothing else mattered. If Adam was as good in bed as he'd been earlier, then the next two weeks were about pleasure and nothing else. If I was lucky, Adam would satisfy me so well I wouldn't need to look for another man for weeks.

Or months.

I moved the base of my palm over my clit so I could slide two fingers inside, just like Adam had. I wondered how big his cock was. Would he fill me? Would his hips rock against mine so that his dick reached placed my fingers couldn't?

Normally I was quick to satisfy myself, but I let my fantasies take over. The more I thought about Adam, the more I wished it was him inside me. My hand was suddenly completely unsatisfying.

I gave up with a groan and rolled over to my nightstand, digging down beneath the notebooks and pulled out a bag. I knew where it was even in the dark. Unfortunately my lack of desire for relationships also meant I had to call in a bag of toys from time to time. One-night stands and the occasional fuck buddies were nice, but they were hard to come by and didn't last long.

I felt inside the bag and my fingers fell on the large, shockingly lifelike dildo almost immediately. I tossed the bag aside—lube wasn't going to be an issue. I was ridiculously wet.

It was large and took several strokes to get wet enough to move inside me. I liked them big—the bigger the better. A little pain with my pleasure always added to the fun. I pushed and stroked until it glided all the way inside to where I'd just fantasized about Adam reaching. Would he feel like this? Satisfy me so completely by stretching me until I thought I might scream?

I rocked my hips as if it were Adam on top of me, his weight pushing back against me. My body ached and contracted around the invasion and my arms quivered as my breath quickened. Yes, I knew Adam would feel this good. I knew he would because he'd been this good with just his mouth and fingers. If I had all of him...well, I was confident in his skills as a lover.

I slowly pulled the dildo out until I was empty and my body was aching for more before I slid it all the way back in. I loved the feeling of expanding until my body could accommodate the girth. I was so wet it was everywhere, on my fingers and palms, and dripping down onto the sheet beneath me.

It had been a long time since I'd been this turned on. I left it buried inside me and my body throbbed until it ached, the pressure of so much being inside me when all my body wanted to do was explode. What would it feel like when Adam's hands were massaging my breasts? I let my legs fall open, freeing up my hands to explore. Would he be gruff and grab? Or gentle and caress? I tried out both motions, deciding either one worked. Then I ran my thumb over my erect nipple. It took my breath away.

My entire body heated and trembled. I brushed my thumb again and again and called out when the pleasure became too much. My hips rocked automatically and the dildo moved just enough to drive me wild from the inside out.

I ran my other thumb over my other nipple and gasped. *Even better*. Having both of Adam's hands *and* his mouth at my disposal was going to be a fantasy come true. I teased both nipples at the same time, groaning and calling out incoherently until I *needed* more, rolling my nipples between my fingers, taking the pleasure up one more notch.

My core was painfully throbbing now. The large fake cock was on the edge of being too much for my body to handle. I released my right nipple and fumbled for the toy, yanking it out a split second before I slammed it back in. The bite of pleasure and pain overwhelmed. I did it again and again until I was panting and seeing stars. Then I buried it deep inside me, imagining Adam burying himself inside me just before coming hard and long, then rolled both my nipples one more time, throwing myself over the edge of insanity.

I yelled out, groaning and grunting, pinching my nipples, rocking my hips, and letting the dildo move inside me until I collapsed against the bed, completely incapable of doing anything but panting.

Chapter 4

Tuesday Morning

I actually slept pretty soundly after that. I was just about to walk across the street to the diner when my phone rang. It was Allison.

"Good morning!" She was far too chipper. She was on London time and probably on her third cup of coffee.

"Good morning," I replied as I searched for a hair tie.

"You have time to talk before work?"

I bit my lip. Allison was going to know something was up the minute I said no. "Actually I'm about to have breakfast with a client."

The line was silent for a moment. My position on the historic preservation board meant that I occasionally met with business owners about renovations and construction projects around town. But I never had breakfast meetings. I wasn't a morning person. Allison had lived with me for years and knew this all too well.

"Who with?" she finally asked.

I hesitated, and that was what did me in.

Allison gasped. "You met someone. You're having breakfast with someone!"

"I didn't meet *someone*. I met a guy I want to bang while I'm bored."

"And he's taking you to breakfast."

My chest ached. I didn't want Adam to be *someone*. "It's just breakfast."

"Liz, you can't hide for the rest of your life. I know you think you're doing yourself a favor keeping everyone at arm's length, but you're not. At some point you have to let people in."

"I let you in. That's enough."

"No it's not. I'm not there and I won't always be there for you, Lizzy. You need more than two people in your life."

A small part of me knew she was right, no matter how much I hated hearing it. "I don't think a vacation fuck is the place to start."

That got a giggle out of her. "Vacation fuck? So he's only in town for a few days? Score. He's perfect."

"How is he perfect?"

"No strings, sweetie. You can have fun, eat breakfast, and let yourself go for a change. He'll be gone soon enough. You couldn't find anyone more perfect for you."

She sounded just like Adam.

"Well, I'm supposed to be meeting him in two

minutes."

"Just live in the moment for a change. Seriously, you can't control everything. And what... what might happen? I promise it's not the end of the world to feel something."

That was where she was wrong. I liked being numb. Numb and alone were safe and I'd come to treasure my safety more than anything else.

"Have a good day at work Allie."

"You too."

I slid my phone into my messenger bag, slung it over my shoulder, and locked the door before heading across the street. I loved eating breakfast at the diner. The food was exceptional and fantastically greasy. It was perfect for hangovers.

At exactly six o'clock I was seated in my favorite booth next to the window. The morning news was playing on a television mounted on the wall and the waitress set a steaming cup of coffee in front of me without asking.

I was halfway through my cup when Adam ducked through the door. His hair was more tousled than I'd seen it and he didn't look like he'd slept particularly well, but he looked fantastic. His black t-shirt was tightly fitted and instead of pants he wore red basketball shorts and sneakers.

I stood up as he strode toward me. He lightly grabbed my fingertips with his again, the simple connection sending a jolt of electricity up my arm, before he gently tugged and planted a soft kiss on my lips, sending my head back into a tailspin. "Thanks for meeting me." His voice was still husky from sleep.

It was hot.

"Thanks for making me come." This time I meant it exactly how it sounded.

Adam grinned and bounced his eyebrows. "The pleasure was all mine."

He quickly looked over the menu and we both ordered. I got my usual: an omelet with hash browns and sausage. Adam grinned like a fool at the way I'd emphasized the sausage order.

"Did you get your problem taken care of?"

Adam grunted and took a sip of coffee. "Yes. It took several hours but it's handled."

"I guess that explains why you look so tired."

"Actually, it was this girl. I had her on my mind all night. It made sleeping difficult."

I looked at him over my mug as I tried to come up with something witty to say. Anything that would turn the banter back into something playful. "You should watch out for girls like that. I've heard they can be dangerous."

Truth and deflection all in one.

He stared me down, a frown pulling on the corners of his lips. "I'm not worried." His face hardened and I noticed he was making a tight fist around his coffee mug. And then all of a sudden he relaxed, a friendly smile washed away everything I'd just seen.

"So, what do your friends call you? Elizabeth sounds too formal for you."

I cleared my throat and adjusted on the bench seat. "Well, my family actually calls me Elizabeth, believe it or not. It's a family name." Allison told me to relax and go with the flow so...I was going to relax and go with the flow for a change. A few details here and there weren't going to kill me.

I could see the curiosity in his eyes. He wanted to ask for more, but didn't. He let me continue.

"My students call me Professor or Dr. Filler. My colleagues call me Dr. Filler or Elizabeth."

"Dr. Filler," he was trying it out. "I like that. I might have a few leftover fantasies from college I need to work out this week."

That sounded like fun. "I'll see what I can do."

Adam grinned.

"And my friends call me Liz or Lizzy."

The waitress returned with our food, interrupting the almost uncomfortable examination I was receiving from Adam. "What do your friends call you? Adam seems pretty straightforward."

"It is," he agreed as he began cutting up his omelet. "But a select few call me AC."

"AC," I repeated. I didn't like it. I could see guys calling him that, but not me. I liked Adam. It sounded seductive the way the vowel formed at the back of my throat and required the use of my diaphragm to power the word out.

"Don't like it?" he had one eye pulled down and a grimace on his face.

"Not in the least."

We ate in silence for a few minutes, letting the food and coffee wake us both up.

I'd told Adam a few things and it hadn't killed me. I was really starting to warm to the idea of this fling. Adam was safe.

"So," he said, setting his fork down and leaning back with a satisfied grin. "Let's talk schedules."

"Needy," I teased.

He shrugged his shoulders. "Hey, this is all your idea. I wanted to woo you, take you out and get to know you. You want specific terms and I've agreed to them. So let's talk schedules."

His tone was serious but his eyes were light, just like the smile on his face. "Ok. Well, today is my long day, unfortunately. I have classes and consults until seven. We could meet at my place after that."

"No," he shook his head. "I have a better idea. You like music?"

Music? "Uh, yeah."

"Great. My buddy is playing tonight. I can pick you up after your last class and we can grab dinner at the bar he's playing."

Wait. What? "I thought we were planning to go back to my place..."

"And we will," he agreed. "But we both have to eat. We might as well have fun." He must have seen my hesitation because he rushed on. "I promise, I want to be between your legs just as badly as you want me between your legs."

The waitress stopped at our table to refresh our

drinks. Her cheeks were red and she refused to meet my eyes. I grinned at Adam and he grinned back.

"Then why the delay? Meet me at my place, we can take care of business and then you can go see your buddy play."

"Nope." He shook his head and leaned forward with his elbows on the table. "I want to have some fun with you. Good *friendly* fun. It'll be loud so you don't have to worry about conversation. We'll eat, and then we'll head out. That way, once I get you in bed, neither of us has to leave."

My whole body groaned. I very much liked the sound of that. "Who says I was going to let you stay?"

"You didn't," he replied. "But I promise to make it worth your while."

Chapter 5

Tuesday Night

The bar was elegant, dark, and relaxed. It stretched the length of the building with a collection of round tables filling the floor. Three small semi-circular booths led up to the stage on either side. A male singer with a guitar was crooning into a microphone. His voice was clear and deep and he was singing about an island somewhere.

I followed Adam through the maze of tables to the first booth on the left of the stage. It had a *Reserved* card sitting on the table.

So much for casual. He stood to the side, allowing me to scoot into the booth first. As I sat, I saw Adam and the singer exchange a nod.

A nervous energy crackled between us. I wondered how he managed to keep such a cool façade when I was dangling sex right in front of him. He must have amazing control. Certainly more than I had.

The waitress was making rounds so I grabbed the little flip-top menu from the middle of the table and glanced at the drink list.

"They have fifty beers on tap... if you like beer." He was close enough that his breath danced across my skin.

We each order a local brew and I turned my attention to the singer on stage. He was engaging to watch, very charismatic, and his voice was deep, but crystal clear. He was one of those rare singers who had a truly gifted voice. He could probably sing anything. He wasn't just following along to memorized words. He understood how the music worked.

It was too loud to talk. We drank our beers, ordered some food to split, and listened to his friend on the stage.

Adam was fun. He was relaxed and laidback, hollering at the stage between songs and drawing snickers from the crowd on more than one occasion. He gave me a few flirty glances and ran his hand up my leg more than once, but otherwise, things were just...*easy*.

The singer finished his last song and announced a fifteen-minute break just as the waitress arrived with our food. Adam squeezed my thigh and smiled. "What did you think of Travis?"

Travis. "He's fantastic."

"You don't hate me for dragging you out?"

"Nope," I laughed as Travis plopped into the booth beside Adam, slamming a full pitcher of beer onto the table.

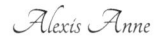

"Hey AC! Glad to see you made it! Hi, I'm Travis!" He stood halfway and offered his hand.

It was obvious Travis was an entertainer through and through. "Elizabeth." Now that he was closer I could tell he was handsome in a goofy way. Longer blonde hair, scruffy beard, and a gravely southern drawl.

"I asked the bartender what you were drinkin' little lady, and I brought us a pitcher to share." He refilled all our glasses. "To old friends."

"So, what's the story? How do you two know each other?" Travis seemed crazy and Adam was straight-laced. I was dying to know how such radically different guys became friends.

They both grinned and I could tell there were probably a hundred stories that went with those smiles. "Well," Adam replied, taking the lead. "When I moved to town I was the outsider. All the kids around here grew up together and even though my family was from here, I didn't have a history with these kids."

Travis picked up the story from there. "I moved to town a few weeks earlier. Same problem. But the minute Adam walked in the door I knew we'd be friends. He was the only other tall guy at school who could care less about all these idiots," he waved his hand around the bar at the oblivious locals.

I ate while the guys caught up. Adam talked about Germany; Travis brought him up to speed on his most recent tour of the East Coast. There was an indie record coming out, but a label was making a competitive offer.

"Well, I think you're fantastic," I assured him. "You have a great sound, a great voice, and a great look."

Travis stared at me, then dramatically stood, walked across to my side of the booth and sat down, slinging his arm around my shoulder. "I like her. Dump this loser and go out with me?"

I laughed, a chicken wing dangling from my fingers. "He's promised me sex that will blow my mind. What can you offer?"

Travis's mouth fell open and he pressed a hand to his chest. "Fame and fortune...as soon as I hit it big."

"No sex?"

He wiggled closer and dropped his head on my shoulder. "We can cuddle."

I laughed harder and pushed him away. "It's sex or no deal."

He pushed out his lower lip and then slid back out of the booth and moped back to Adam's side, sitting down and dropping his head onto Adam's shoulder instead. "Hold me. I've been rejected."

Adam pushed Travis off and shook his head. "You'll always have the stage, my friend."

"She's a lonely lover," he replied wistfully. Then became serious. "How did you two meet?"

Adam glanced over at me. "We bumped into each other at a bar the other night."

"Alone, eh. Sounds like you. Where at?"

"We were at Seychelles," I interjected.

Travis busted out laughing. "At your mom's joint? Did she set it up?"

Adam punched Travis in the arm. "I hadn't mentioned that yet. Thanks."

Travis rubbed his arm like Adam had really hurt him. "Sorry dude. Didn't mean to step on your toes...Well, I gotta get back up there anyway. It was very nice to meet you Elizabeth." He bowed somewhat dramatically before disappearing into a side door.

"Your mom's *joint*?" I asked with raised eyebrows.

Adam shrugged. "It's not a big deal. My mom owns a couple of restaurants around town. Seychelles was her first and it is still my favorite. I stop in every time I'm in town."

"Why didn't you tell me?"

He smiled, running his hand over my thigh. "Because we were keeping things simple."

It was definitely simpler when I didn't know that.

"And just so you know," he ran his hand up the inside of my thigh, "I wasn't there for dinner that night. I stopped in to see Mitch and have a quick drink. But when I saw you...I couldn't leave."

"Oh," I gasped as his hand began to massage. "Why?"

"I had an immediate hard-on."

And suddenly my mind was filled with my middle of the night fantasies. "Can we go back to my place now?"

Adam stopped massaging, grabbed my hand, and pulled me out of the bar.

We were only three blocks away and we ran most of it. "I can't believe you've held out this long," I gasped as we rushed up the stairs.

He yanked on my hand, pulling me around. I was two steps above him but only an inch taller. He kissed me, one hand around mine, the other tangled in the hair at the nape of my neck, holding my lips firmly against his. "I have wanted to be inside you from the moment you said hello, Elizabeth. But I needed to be sure."

That surprised me. "Sure?"

He swallowed. His hand was still holding my head and our noses were nearly touching. He was panting. "Once isn't going to be enough, Gorgeous. I needed to be sure this wasn't going to be a one-night stand." He stepped up onto the next step, bringing our bodies together. He kissed me lightly. "I've tasted you. I've made you come. And I needed to know I'd be around long enough to get my fill."

My body ached. The longer he stood there, holding me so close, the more I needed him, too. "Two weeks," I repeated. Two weeks of this...it made me dizzy just thinking about it.

"Two weeks."

"Then let's get started."

He let me go and I turned, finishing the walk up the stairs and to my door. I could feel Adam behind me. It was like a wall of desire. His need for me was almost as erotic as my need for him. I pushed open the door and locked it behind him. "I think we should just get right to some sex, get it out of the way so we can actually enjoy each other for the rest of the night—" I barely had the words out of my mouth when Adam grabbed me, lifting me up so I could wrap my legs around his waist.

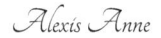

He pushed me up against the door. "Excellent idea. I like the way you think," he gasped as he kissed and suckled my neck, all while grinding me into the door.

His body pressing against mine was more overwhelming than I'd imagined while alone in my bed that morning. He was more intense, his body was more out of control, and his hands were more insistent.

He buried his face in the crook of my neck as his hips ground against me. I ran my hands over his sculpted shoulders and hooked my fingers in his hair, tugging. He growled and grinned up at me.

"Bedroom," I moaned and pointed over his shoulder.

He turned—without any effort at all—and stalked across my living room and into the open door. His strength and confidence were a turn-on all on their own. There was no hesitation or doubt in anything he was doing, or in the look in his dark eyes. This was a man who knew what he wanted…and he wanted me.

I grasped frantically at the cotton of his shirt. It needed to go. I needed everything preventing our bodies from melding together, gone.

He helped me, peeling the shirt over his head and then grabbing for mine. He was like candy. I wanted to touch him but knew it was borderline evil. Having a taste wouldn't be enough, I needed the whole display.

Sure enough, as I ran my fingers over his abs and chest, a shiver rippled over my skin. I wanted to know what those shoulders and abs looked like while he was thrusting inside me. I unhooked my own bra and shoved my jeans to the floor as Adam did the same, then pushed me back onto the bed and slid over the top of me.

Skin against skin.

The contact was so overwhelming I gasped and automatically wrapped my arms and legs around his body as an anchor. It was like freefalling, only I wasn't going anywhere. I was just getting lost in Adam.

All my fantasies came flooding back. He was finally mine for the taking. With a gentle push I directed Adam down towards my waiting breasts. They were heavy and achy after all my early morning dreaming. I *needed* to know, once and for all, what it felt like to have Adam's lips on my breasts.

He responded automatically, moving to my right breast first with a grin on his lips. They were fire against my skin. My nipples tingled and my sex throbbed with anticipation.

I wanted it. I wanted him. I couldn't take it anymore. I grabbed the base of his neck and thrust my nipple into his mouth as I squeezed my knees tighter around his waist.

I moaned as his warm tongue swirled against my erect nipple and his soft lips closed, sucking gently against my skin. *Ecstasy*. It felt exactly like pleasure and blissful nothingness: my favorite place to get lost and stay for as long as I could.

Adam didn't hesitate to capitalize on my enjoyment. He leaned into my body, giving me friction to work against, his cock sliding beneath me and against the bed. I hadn't gotten a very good look at his dick before he was on top of me, but I'd seen enough, and I could feel his erection. Adam was just about the size of the dildo I'd used that morning. He was perfect.

But for now, I was enjoying every second of finally having his mouth on my breasts. He groaned like he was in pain (good pain), thrusting his erection beneath me harder, and moved to my left breast. It tingled with anticipation just like my right breast had. I knew what it was going to feel like when his lips closed over the sensitive and waiting flesh, and yet I didn't. The one thing I did know was that it was going to blow my mind.

This time, instead of forcing his path, I let Adam choose. And instead of going straight from the fullness of my breasts to my nipple like I made him do the first time, he took a lazy route with the tip of his tongue, tracing a trail of burning electricity along the underside of my breast, where the skin was more sensitive to everything. His hot breath mixed with the cool wetness left behind by his tongue.

I reached my arms above my head with my palms flat on the mattress, and arched, throwing my head back and thrusting my breasts up, while pressing my clit up against his flat abs, and my wet core down toward his cock.

"Are you sure you want to jump straight to fucking?" he gasped and then wrapped his mouth around my nipple.

I yelled out, squeezing my legs around him and clutching at his head with a hand that had wildly reached forward to hold his head in place.

I was on fire. I never wanted to stop feeling exactly how I felt right then, and yet I wanted it all. I wanted him buried inside me. I wanted his mouth on my breasts with his hands everywhere. I wanted to come hard—over and over until I was senseless—and yet I wanted nothing to change.

But my sex throbbed and his cock kicked like it could feel the heat and wetness just out of its reach. "If you don't get that gorgeous cock inside me right now, all bets are off."

He grinned, a full megawatt smile, and raked his teeth over my nipple, pulling until it popped free. "This is going to be the best vacation I've ever had."

For both of us.

Then he hopped up and found his jeans, pulling out a condom. "I'm clean, by the way. I've been tested, always use a condom, the whole nine yards."

"Good little boy scout," I murmured as I pushed up on my elbows and spread my legs. The ache to have him inside me actually hurt.

Adam shuddered and rolled a little faster.

I grinned. "I'm clean, on birth control, and always

use a condom."

"Girl scout," he winked. "You ready for me?"

"I've been ready since you sat down at the bar." Which was true. I'd reacted to him strongly from the moment I'd first laid eyes on him. I wanted him so badly I was willing to risk complications. Hell, I was even willing to become his friend.

That was a pretty powerful reaction in my world.

Adam moved carefully over top of me, holding his body just barely over mine, positioning his erection against me. The moment his cock made contact against my sex he grunted. "Oh god, you feel as good as you taste."

I didn't know how Adam tasted yet, but he certainly felt as good as I'd fantasized with my toy. Actually, he felt better because this wasn't a fantasy—this was real. His body was pushing against mine, his arms were brushing along my skin, and his lips were *everywhere*. His cock was firmer, yet softer than what I'd used on myself. There wasn't any of that cold resistance of plastic or the uncontrollable flexibility of silicone. Adam was real.

He pushed inside, just a little. He was going slowly at first, probably from past experience with women who couldn't handle a man of his size. But I wasn't most women. I was needy and desperate. If I didn't get him inside me soon I was going to go insane.

"More," I whispered. My hands and arms were starting to shake from the desire to have him and my breathing was getting faster and shallower. He thrust a little deeper and I arched automatically to accommodate him. There was a bite of pain at the intrusion, but I liked it. "More," I whispered again. My breathing got deeper, but the shaking was just as intense.

Adam was watching me carefully, his shoulders straining and eyes locked intently on mine. He swallowed and pushed deeper. I groaned.

"Too much?"

"No." I had my eyes closed, savoring the feeling of his cock inside me. "It feels so damn good."

He sighed—probably with relief—and then grinned. "Where have you been all my life?" Then he slowly withdrew and thrust back inside me, moving even deeper. Two more thrusts and he'd be buried.

Two more. And then I'd finally have what I'd been craving for two solid days.

Out and in. Then Adam's eyes rolled back in his head and the muscle in his arm flexed a split second before he pushed all the way in. *Finally*. I hooked my arms under his and around to his shoulders, holding him still.

This was one of my favorite parts and I was going to enjoy every second of feeling my body expand to accommodate Adam. He was large and firm and hot. It almost hurt, but mostly my body was spasming with intense pleasure at having something so perfect buried inside its warmth.

My muscles contracted around his solid dick. There was nowhere else for my body to go and the tremors moved along his cock looking for somewhere to escape. They travelled from somewhere deep inside me—where the head of his cock was nestled—all the way down to the entrance to my sex, where his body was melded against mine.

A tiny pulse throbbed at the tip of my clit. The warmth of Adam's body pressed back and sent the pulse back inside. I almost came right then.

But I really wanted to know what it felt like to have Adam fuck me.

I *needed* to know if he was as intense and driven in bed as he was in real life. The idea alone, of Adam commanding me as he pushed into me over and over, was almost as fantastic as lying with him inside me, not moving.

"More," I whispered into his ear. His arms tightened and he turned his head to look me in the eye. He sucked in a quick breath and nodded, moving his cock slowly out and back in several times before we really got going. Things moved fast from there. Our first time was a blur of raw need. Thrusts and hands grasping for leverage. Adam took me harder and harder as he grew accustomed to my body. I guided him with my hips and my hands, letting him know when to change speed or pressure. He responded to my commands like he'd always known me.

I'd never felt anything as satisfying as Adam thrusting his cock inside me: his body slamming against mine and settling for a moment before pulling free and doing it all over again. It was intense and overwhelming going from nothing to such sharp, sweet pleasure. My core spiked with pain a split second before a wave of pleasure washed through me and out to the ends of my body.

Then he bent me over the edge of the mattress, his hands firmly wrapped around my hips, his cock moving in and out, and my clit slamming against the bed. I liked it when his fingers moved up into my hair for leverage. I liked it even more when he was so overwhelmed he whimpered and pulled out, rolling me over and pounding back into me from above.

I liked that Adam was so lost inside me he didn't seem to know what to do. He was wild but not out of control. He moved with the abandon of someone who was so turned on he didn't know whether he wanted to feel pleasure or ecstasy.

I hadn't expected him to last as long as he did. Not after nearly two days of teasing and foreplay. I was watching Adam much more than I ever watched anyone. I was fascinated by his sounds and the wild look in his eyes. He was intent but focused. He watched me almost as much as I watched him. I wanted to see him come. I wanted to see the strain of his muscles as he fought for control. I wanted to know what his eyes looked like when he was lost to pure pleasure.

Why? I had no idea, but the desire was so strong I couldn't stop myself. "I want to watch you come," I whispered.

His eyes shot to mine. I could see the loss of control. The combination of relief and relaxation in his eyes and shoulders. That was when I knew: I didn't want to see what he looked like when he came. I wanted to see what he looked like when he was out of control.

His hands shook slightly as he ran his hands over my body, around my breasts, and hooked under my shoulders. He thrust inside with a grunt and a shudder.

It was one of the most erotic things I'd ever seen. I was making him insane and he was losing all control while inside me. I knew it wasn't normal for Adam. He was the kind of man who knew what he wanted and wasn't afraid to go after it. That was why he met me for dinner last night and why he relented to my proposition. He was willing to negotiate to get what he wanted.

But neither of us had expected what was happening in my bed. There was no control once our bodies were locked together. Adam was barely able to focus and I wasn't acting like myself at all. I had a feeling I would do anything and everything Adam asked as long as it meant I could have this.

No one had ever erased the world and made me forget about my life, like this. Nothing else existed outside of the pleasure Adam was giving me. Each thrust of his cock was a shock of satisfaction I couldn't find anywhere else. His hands were a balm, and his tongue brought out levels of ecstasy I didn't know existed. When he was working my body, nothing else mattered.

I was dangerously addicted to the freedom he was giving me.

There was going to be a high price for giving in to all of this and I didn't care.

Adam leaned forward, dipping closer to my body, and kissing my lips. He thrust faster and harder, his jaw propped open and his eyes watching my body with fascination when it hit him. His neck muscles flexed, his shoulders bunched, and he buried his cock completely inside me.

It was a jolt shooting through my entire body, like being shocked by electricity. His cock was deep inside and the tremors rippled through my body, turning my vision white and taking all of the air from my lungs.

The heat and the spasm, combined with my total fascination at seeing Adam lose all control because of me, pushed me over the edge, too. The tremors reverberated back from the ends of my body, faster and harder than when they'd shot out, detonating at that place inside me where we were locked together. I cried out, grabbing his ass and using his cock to create the last bit of friction I needed.

I was too overwhelmed to do anything but scream and tremble until the white in my vision turned to black and my arms slid off his slick body. There wasn't an ounce of energy left inside me. I'd given it all to Adam.

He was just as drained as I was. His arms were shaking and he was breathing so hard the whole bed was shaking. I lay there, unable to move, with Adam on top of me. He was heavy and I liked the way his weight felt oddly comforting. I would have wrapped my arms around him or run my fingers through his hair if I could've moved, but I couldn't. He finally collapsed onto the bed beside me, groaning and panting.

It was the best sex of my life. I was already completely addicted to Adam. I was exhausted and drained, and craving my next fix. Pleasure like that wasn't easy to come by. This was just a little tease. I wanted everything he could give me for the rest of his vacation, the consequences be damned.

This was worth it.

Chapter 6

Wednesday night

I blindly unlocked my door, one hand turning the key, the other fisted in Adam's shirt, holding his body against mine as I kissed the hell out of him. It was an exceptionally long day at work and all I wanted was to get my hands back on Adam.

His tongue moved deep in my mouth and his leg was bent between mine. I was grinding against his thigh when the lock finally slid free. The door opened behind him and I pushed Adam through, throwing the keys carelessly at the table and dropping my bag on the floor. "Couch," I commanded.

Adam panted and his eyes were dark. He nodded as I pushed him backward. "Yes ma'am. Need some relief?"

"Shut up," I said with a shake of my head and pulled my shirt over my head. He did the same just as the couch came up behind him.

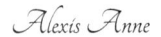

He grinned and popped his eyebrows as he dropped his jeans and then hopped effortlessly over the couch. "Come on, Gorgeous. I'm waiting."

I was naked and on top of him a moment later. He kissed a trail up from my breasts to my lips, when I sank my tongue into his mouth all over again. I was wet, but not incredibly wet the way I needed to be for Adam. So instead of lowering myself down onto his fully erect and waiting cock, I let him kiss me, massaging my ass and hips, as my hands roamed over his muscles.

I loved the feel of his shoulders and biceps, plus he had this scent. It wasn't cologne or body wash—at least I didn't think it was—but he always smelled like it. There was a hint of something spicy.

"Do I smell? I just showered." Adam's forehead was scrunched up and he was watching me with confusion.

"No," I replied quickly and stuck my tongue back in his mouth. There was one sure fire-way to shut down conversation with Adam and it involved my tongue and my body.

I pressed down on his cock, letting his large head slide inside enough to find some lubrication. Adam groaned. I sighed and finally began to relax. Somewhere over the course of the day I'd become crazy for exactly what we were doing: more sex with Adam. I would have thought after two intense rounds the night before I would be satisfied, but by lunchtime, my body was aching from the previous night's activities. It was that dull kind of ache that constantly reminded me how good the sex was and it made me crave more.

"Please tell me you aren't working late again this week," he gasped as I sank a little deeper.

"No. Today was the last day. Now shut up and let me fuck you."

Adam closed his eyes and leaned back against the couch. "Use me and abuse me any way you wish."

A relaxed Adam was a gorgeous sight to behold. I bit my lip and rocked my hips, grinding all the way down. I was finally full again. That peace I'd found the night before, it was back. My mind was quiet and my whole body was relaxed. I took a moment just to enjoy it.

His hand moved up the middle of my back and stopped to rest between my shoulder blades. When I opened my eyes, Adam was watching me with a lazy look in his eyes. "You are beautiful, Elizabeth."

"Because I like the way your cock feels?"

"Exactly."

I rolled my eyes and proceeded to fuck him until he was swearing like a sailor.

An hour later I was lying on the couch while I waited for Adam to return with our dinner from downstairs. So far our arrangement was working out well. Granted we were barely twenty-four hours into it, and Adam was still in town for another ten days, but the sex had been incredible and the complications had been minimal—that complication was my job and it keeping us from staying in bed every minute of the day.

So, not really a complication as much as a reality.

I'd managed to clear a few meetings until after Adam's vacation and handed off grading to my graduate assistant, leaving me more time to enjoy my sex-cation with Adam. Things were working out well, all in all.

I grabbed my phone and called Allison, even though it would be late for her in London.

"What is up?" she droned with a robotic voice. Something she only did when she was drunk or at least solidly buzzed.

"Just checking in. I haven't talked to you all day."

"Word. We had meetings all fucking day. By the time we got out, I went straight to the pub. How are you and hottie-pants?" *Definitely buzzed.*

"Hottie-pants? Is that the best nickname you can come up with?"

She snorted. "I see your challenge and raise you 'details'. Whatcha got for me?"

Details. Allison wanted me to be friends with Adam. According to her, his vacation timeframe and job on the other side of the world made him a perfect test case for my new life in Calhoun Beach. "He is nice, has a giant cock, an amazing tongue, and likes it a little rough."

"Not what I meant."

"His last name is Callaway?"

"Still not what I meant," her voice dropped an octave with frustration.

"He likes steak, scallops, his coffee with way too much sugar, and thinks bacon is a food group."

The line was silent for a moment. "Better. Not

great, but better."

I lay there staring at my bookcases. They lined one wall of our living room from my bedroom door to the windows that looked out over the beach. "And he likes to read."

"Bingo!" She yelled. "Now *that* is something you can work with."

"What?"

"Books! Something that isn't too personal. You can both talk about books and find a connection without it crossing all your safety lines."

I glanced over the spines and titles sitting on the shelves. "You do have a point. If I get stuck, I will go with books for getting to know Adam Callaway. Happy?"

"Very," she slurred.

"Perhaps you should go get some sleep…"

"Excellent idea!" she agreed. "Have sweet sex tonight!"

"Good night Allison," I said just as my door opened.

"Your friend in London?" Adam called as he slammed the door shut.

"Yep."

"How is she? I love London."

"She had a long day at work," I replied as I took the food from him and started laying it out on the coffee table. "How was Mitch?"

Adam grinned and sat down on the floor across from me. "He warned me that you only order the burger and fries when you are running marathons or getting your period. He says he made sure the fries were loaded and both sauces were in the box."

The amount of sex Adam and I were having was pretty much equivalent to running, so I was craving carbs and protein. There was no doubt in my mind that I was going to devour every bite. "Mitch knows too much about me."

"I think it's cute. I'd be jealous if I didn't know how much he loves his wife."

I shook my head and rolled my eyes. "Did you go to high school with her, too?"

Adam nodded, sticking a fry in his mouth. "Yeah. She was sweet and Mitch always adored her. I couldn't imagine either of them with anyone else. So which is it?"

"Which is what?" I asked, confused. My burger was perfect. I poured ketchup, the strange orange sauce Mitch always gave me, and mustard over the beef before carefully arranging the onions and lettuce and replacing the bun.

"Marathon or period?"

I stopped just before taking my first bite and glared at Adam. "I'm carbo loading for more sex. *Obviously.*" And then I sank my teeth into the first delicious bite of meat. "Oh god. It's so good."

Adam swallowed and his eyes zeroed in on my mouth. "You should be careful moaning like that around me."

I popped my eyebrows and talked with my mouth

full of food just to ruin the effect. "Why? Want some of this?"

He shook his head, but his eyes travelled up and locked with mine. "I don't think you realize how fucking hot it is when you moan. And now that I know how much you do it, all I can think about is fucking you when I hear it. So watch it, Filler. I may get turned on by your burger fetish."

I took another giant bite and moaned while chewing like a cow. "Hot for me now, baby?"

Adam laughed just I like I wanted him to, and went back to his own food. I noticed how he was examining my apartment as he ate. "I guess I should give you the grand tour. We kinda skipped that the first time."

"I think I've got it figured out." He pointed at my door. "Your room, this is the living room, the kitchen is over there, and I'm guessing that door is Allison's."

"Bingo. You're like an architectural genius."

He shrugged his shoulders. "I have heard the term 'genius' tossed around with my name before."

I choked on my food.

"What?" he asked, mocking offense.

I shook my head. "You should really look into finding some self-confidence. Your ego isn't enormous or anything, *Mr. Genius*."

"Just sayin' it like it is." He bounced his eyebrows and grinned. "Besides, you seem to enjoy my ego, confidence, *and* my intelligence."

I cocked an eyebrow and shrugged my shoulders.

"They certainly have their uses."

He ate a few more bites then stopped and frowned. "Where is your television?"

I shrugged. "We don't have one out here."

He stared at me like I'd just said the craziest thing he'd ever heard. "You don't have a television out here?"

"No," I said slowly.

"Why?"

"Why do I need one?"

"How else do you watch football?"

I snorted and set the last few bites of my burger down. "That is what the bar is for. Football, wings, beer. No mess, no cooking."

Adam's eyes lit up. "You don't cook, do you?"

Oh geeze. It was like Twenty Questions all of a sudden. At least they were all easy questions. "Not really. I have about three meals I can manage and all three involve cheese."

"Cheese?" He coughed like I was choking him.

"Grilled cheese, mac and cheese, and cheesy scrambled eggs. Oh! And I can heat up soup from a can. Most of the time." I cringed thinking about being sick last month and burning chicken noodle soup on the stove top. Mitch and Allison both vowed to never let me forget that one.

"Wow," Adam looked truly shocked as he took another bite, finishing off his burger. "It really is good you moved in here. You might starve otherwise."

I rolled my eyes. "Like you can cook."

"Of course I can. My mother is a world-renowned

chef. I grew up in a kitchen."

I was an idiot. Of course Adam could cook. It was just that in my world, no one cooked. It hadn't even occurred to me he would know what to do in a kitchen. "Well maybe you should dazzle me with your skills one night instead of getting takeout."

"I think I will," he agreed, and then eyed me suspiciously. "What did you eat growing up?"

Alarm bells started clanging in my head. Just mentioning my childhood was enough to make me panic. "Takeout. Sometimes we had a cook. I lived in a lot of hotels and we ate at a lot of restaurants."

"Right," he murmured. "You moved around a lot."

I nodded and shoved the last few bites of burger in my mouth and Adam let the subject drop without any more questions. "So, Mitch mentioned you might need a tour guide."

"Mitch talks too much," I swore, closing my box and stacking it on top of Adam's. I was going to have a special talk with my favorite bartender.

"Well do you?"

"Need a tour guide? No." I did not want Adam taking our friendship that far outside of the bedroom. Books I could talk about. Food was fairly safe. But going around town? Too much.

"Really? He said you were just complaining about not getting to all the places you monitor for the board."

Damnit all. Mitch really didn't know when to shut up. "Well that's for work. I will get around to it." I needed to know as much about local history as I did anything else, but I was so busy I hadn't had a chance to move outside the city limits.

Adam crossed his arms and glared at me. "I'll have you know I'm a perfect tour guide for that. Passing up on my expertise and local knowledge is just plain dumb—especially if you are only saying no because we're fucking and you don't want to cross your 'boundaries'." He actually air-quoted the word and rolled his eyes like my desire to keep our relationship in the bedroom was a problem.

"You know the country roads, fish camps, and outer plantations?" I asked incredulously. I could see Adam knowing the local restaurants and bars. Maybe even the stores and markets. But the historical stuff?

"As a matter of fact, I do. Very well." His voice hardened on the last two words.

"Fine. If we find time, you can show me around a little."

"How about tomorrow? When do you get off from work?"

Pushy. Why was Adam so hell-bent on showing me around? "I get off at one tomorrow."

"Perfect. Wear a sundress."

"What?" Just...*what?*

He grinned and popped his eyebrows. "Remember when I said I might have an unfulfilled college fantasy or two? Can I pick you up at your office?"

I stared at him for a long minute trying to decide if it sounded like a helluva lot of fun or insane. Considering my week with Adam was supposed to be all about fun, I decided to ignore the fact he'd just told me what to wear. "Fine. I'll wear a dress tomorrow. Make it count."

"Excellent. Now, I need to fuck you again."

"Perfect," I agreed, standing up and stripping off the t-shirt. "Here?"

"No," he shook his head. "I really want you in the bed again."

With a nod, I stalked off toward my room.

Adam was a bit worked up. He was quieter than he had been the night before, more aggressive with his motions, and his mood seemed darker somehow.

I liked it. Something in my own mood had shifted. When Adam and I talked, things always got too personal. No, actually, it wasn't even that. I just felt too out of control. I never knew what Adam was going to ask next, what secret I might accidentally divulge, or if he would hear something that ended our relationship before I was ready to end it.

But in the bedroom, my control was back. Whether Adam was taking the lead or not, this was a scenario I could understand. I knew what to expect and, more importantly, I knew I had all the power. Sex was my safe place.

Just to prove it, I perched on the edge of the bed and started touching myself. "Want to watch me turn myself on?"

Adam tossed his shirt onto the floor and started kicking off his shorts. "You're the boss."

A shiver coursed down my spine. *Control.*

Then I opened my legs a little further and grabbed my breast with my free hand. "You want to see what I like?"

Adam stood naked in front of me, his cock quickly growing as he watched me swirl two fingers over my clit. He swallowed. "I think I already know what you like. Want me to show you how much I know?"

My hand faltered. His words alone made me hotter and wetter. The way we bantered and challenged each other was such a turn-on. "Not today. I want you to watch."

He nodded slowly, his right hand coming up to stroke his shaft. "Then by all means, show me whatever you want."

I arched back on the bed, my legs spread open and my breasts thrust up in the air, as I stimulated myself and slid two fingers inside. I heard a faint intake of breath from Adam, but nothing else. I worked my fingers in and out several times, fantasizing about Adam in the foyer all over again. His fingers were so much larger than mine, so I added a third.

Another faint gasp of air from Adam, along with a slight groan.

I massaged my breast and worked my hand. It was all fantastic, but not nearly as good as what I wanted. And unlike the other morning when I found my hand so incredibly unsatisfying, I didn't need a toy to play with. This time I had the real thing.

"I think you're gonna need to put on a condom," I gasped.

"Yes ma'am." I heard the sound of my nightstand drawer opening and then a moment later, the bed dipped as Adam climbed up.

His eyes were intent and very serious as he pulled my hand away and pinned it down on the bed. With his free hand he grabbed his cock and pushed it against my sex. I was so wet his head slipped right in, but stopped when it hit the resistance of my much smaller body. He withdrew slightly, the tip of his cock now soaked, and slid it back in harder, faster, and deeper.

I moaned as his body invaded mine. He pulled out again and pushed back inside with purpose. This time he wasn't leaving. This time...he was going to force his cock all the way inside. He slid slowly, his shaft gliding into me, forcing my body to expand around his. It was exquisite torture to feel, but I wanted to see it, too.

I cocked my hips up and watched as Adam's body moved closer and closer to mine. The sight was beautiful. His dick was a work of art. And my body loved the feel of taking in all of him. He was panting, but it was controlled. "Now you have me. What do you want me to do?"

"Don't move a muscle," I whispered and started rocking my hips upward. His cock twitched a little at first, but then it stopped. I moved back and forth against the bed like Adam's dick was my very own personal dildo. Then I took a breast in each hand and ran my nails over the tips of my nipples.

Adam lost his breath and his arms shook a little as he held himself over me, but he stayed exactly where I asked him to.

The more I worked my nipples, the hotter I got, increasing the speed of my hips moving up and down his cock.

Adam's eyes rolled back in his head and his mouth hung open. It was all so hot: the look of Adam's barely restrained lust, his perfect dick, my body quivering for release. I wanted more.

"Your mouth. I need it here," I held up my right breast.

He swore under his breath and sucked my nipple into his mouth hard, his tongue swirling and his lips moving over my skin as he adjusted.

My body pulsed from deep inside. My muscles were bunching tight and my hips were rocking out of rhythm as I started to lose control. "Fuck me now, Adam," I gasped and braced for the impact.

He grabbed my wrists and pinned them down beside my head. Restraining me.

Then his cock slammed into me, our bodies making contact, and mine lighting up from the inside. The sudden change in pressure and speed was perfect. I was alive everywhere. I started moaning uncontrollably, screaming out each time his body crashed against mine, filling me to the brim.

Adam was using me just like I'd used him.

He was in charge now, but only because I'd given it to him.

I liked how it felt to have my hands restrained. I liked knowing I couldn't touch him. And the thing I loved most was watching him use me. He was so focused but not quite holding it all together. I think I found his abandon the hottest thing about him.

My body started to shake as my orgasm built, my arms pushing against Adam's hands. He pushed back and looked me in the eye for confirmation that I was fine.

I smiled and moaned, breaking the eye contact. It was just too much. I only wanted his cock. *Just his cock*. The one that was filling me over and over again.

He slammed into me and swirled his hips, pushing against my body. That was what did it. The world went white as my orgasm rocked through me. My feet flexed, my arms fought against Adam's hold, and every muscle in my body tensed and relaxed all at once.

I'm not even sure when Adam came. It didn't matter. This was about me getting what I needed out of a man I didn't care about.

Chapter 7

Thursday Afternoon

At precisely one o'clock, Adam knocked on my office door.

"Come in," I called while shutting down my email and browser.

Adam whistled low and shut my office door. I didn't miss the faint click of the lock, either. "Nice place you have here."

"Thank you," I replied as I watched him glance around. My office was small, like almost every other professor's office on campus, but mine had a window. It looked out over the main green where students laid out, had picnics, and played Frisbee. Bookcases lined two walls, mostly stuffed with textbooks and research, and the other wall held my display of diplomas, work pictures, and awards.

"I feel like I should call you Doctor Filler instead of Elizabeth," he said quietly. "I had no idea you were so accomplished."

"Thanks?" I asked. It didn't exactly sound like a compliment.

"Sorry," he replied and fell into one of my two brown office chairs. "I didn't mean that the way it sounded at all. You are fairly young and while you are obviously a professor at a great college, I had no idea you'd already done so much. This is very impressive."

"Thanks," I replied again, but this time with less question and more genuine thanks.

"It looks like you've been everywhere..." he started reciting the places he saw in the pictures.

What Adam probably didn't notice was that I was only pictured with colleagues, or Lilly and Allison. There was a lot more of me on that wall than I'd ever realized. For a split second I let myself dwell on all the reasons I took this job: to get away from my family and start a new life.

"I've been travelling since I was very young. It was when I was touring old cathedrals and ruins that I decided I wanted to study historic architecture and preservation."

"Sounds like a natural fit," he agreed. "Are you ready for your tour?"

I turned off my monitor. "Am I fulfilling an old college fantasy first?"

He grinned. "If you're up for it, Dr. Filler."

There was something about the way he was saying my name. It was like a student, but not. It was borderline creepy, yet dirty and hot. I liked the way it walked the line. I'd never once considered doing anything with a student, but that didn't mean the fantasy of off-limits sex hadn't crossed my mind. To be able to fulfill it without getting in trouble, well that was kind of fun.

I stood up and closed my blinds before walking around my desk, stopping in front of Adam. "How can I help you, Mr. Callaway?"

He grinned. "I don't seem to understand what you were teaching in class today," he moved to the edge of the chair, looking up at me. "Perhaps you could tutor me one-on-one?"

"I might be able to arrange it, but I'm very busy, Mr. Callaway. My time is valuable." It was fun playing a role.

"Perhaps," Adam played back, "I could make it worth your while. Pay you in advance?"

I leaned back on the desk, my sundress flittering around my thighs and settling against my skin. "How would you pay me?"

Adam swallowed and kneeled down in front of me. "I was thinking of something like this." He slid his hands up my thighs, under my skirt, and hooked inside my panties. "Would that be enough?"

He pulled my panties down my legs and I stepped out, the fresh air against my newly exposed sex felt cold and light. It turned me on nearly as much as Adam's hands on my skin.

"I don't know...this isn't right," I whispered, moving my thighs further apart.

"But I *want* to do this for you."

"Well," I gasped as Adam's fingers lightly ran over the entrance to my sex. "If you really want to."

He dove between my legs. Unlike the foyer, Adam was able to take his time and explore. His tongue moved up and down my folds, teasing me until I was panting.

Then he began to explore with his fingers, tracing the same path his tongue had just taken, but with more pressure and purpose.

It was crazy how well Adam knew how to turn me on. It was like he'd instinctively known the first time, but since then, he'd carefully studied me. Like he was committing my likes and dislikes to memory. He knew how sensitive my nipples were but that going too far was a turn off. He learned how much I liked it hard, but he also knew how to change things up and tease me with slow. He knew where that bundle of nerves was that made me gasp every time his cock stroked past it, and he knew exactly how much pressure I liked on my clit right after I started to come.

In a way I felt bad, almost selfish. I wasn't a terribly giving lover. I tended to get what I needed and move on before things got complicated. It was an advantage of being a woman who wanted sex. If I offered it, I got it—even when I had to do most of the work. I very rarely needed (or wanted) to do anything more. It had never occurred to me, before Adam, to make an effort to remember how he liked his balls cupped or whether he liked his nipples touched.

I muffled a groan as Adam slid his fingers inside,

curling and stroking until he found the spot that made me convulse and writhe. "Quiet," he whispered, "we're at school..." I felt his grin as he kissed along my inner thigh and back to my clit, working me with his tongue and finger until I was red and hot from the heat I was generating. I was panting and sweaty, desperate to come, and loving knowing that I was on top of my desk, my hands braced on the smooth wood where I would grade student papers and go over blueprints with local business owners. Tomorrow morning someone else would be sitting in the chair my heel was braced against, but they wouldn't be licking and sucking me into a mind-blowing orgasm.

I heard voices in the hallway outside my door—Dr. Prescott, the department chair, and Dr. Mueller whose office was next to mine. They were just on the other side of my door talking about a new class we were offering next semester on student preservation initiatives in public schools. I was so turned on knowing my colleagues were steps away while Adam was buried between my thighs. I came around his fingers, shuddering as I desperately fought to keep quiet and Adam pushed me further into climax. He didn't let up. He sucked and pushed, teasing out my pleasure as far as it would go, not giving me a single inch.

When I was done, I relaxed and collapsed back on the cool surface of my desk. I was panting and managing to keep my moans to myself. How, I had no idea because that orgasm had been every bit as fantastic as the rest. I usually yelled as loud as I could when I felt that good.

A moment later, Adam slid my panties most of the way up my thighs and then reached out his hand. I took it and stood, pulling my lacey panties into place and letting out a deep breath. "Well, I don't think you need any other tutoring, Mr. Callaway. You get an 'A' for effort this semester."

He grinned and took the bottle of water I offered him. "Well thank you, Dr. Filler. I sure do appreciate that." Then he winked and we unofficially ended our role playing.

"So, how about that tour?"

"See?" He grinned and handed me back the bottle. "I like it so much better when you are agreeable to my suggestions."

I grabbed my bag, locked my office door behind us, and followed Adam out to his car. Only it wasn't just *any* car waiting for us in the guest parking lot. It was *his* car. Why it never occurred to me that Adam, super car designer extraordinaire, would have the hottest sports car on the market, I have no idea.

I huffed, but it was really more of an exasperated laugh. "A Merccdes SLS AMG. Are you fucking kidding me?" The AMG was sleek, fast, and expensive as hell, even for a Mercedes designer.

Adam bounced his eyebrows and snatched my hand, pulling me around to face him. "What did you expect me to be driving? A Dodge?"

"This isn't just any Mercedes, Adam. This is a *two hundred thousand dollar* Mercedes."

He walked me backward, a devilish look in his eyes, until I was pressed up against the gull-wing door of the car. "How do you know so much about cars? You holdin' out on me, Filler?"

I shrugged and looked up at Adam sheepishly. "I know a thing or two about foreign sports cars."

"Just the foreign ones?"

I nodded.

"And here I thought all this time you didn't know anything about cars at all. We could have been talking about so much more..."

I groaned. "No, that's the problem. No talking. *Fucking.*"

He looked thoroughly exasperated by me. It was kind of adorable how frustrated I made him. "You don't want to hear about the formulas we use to calculate weight versus thrust?" He flexed his hips into mine and I laughed.

"Alright, so some car lingo is a bit dirty..."

"A lot dirty. Men love to make love to their cars."

I kissed him lightly on the lips. "How much do car designers make anyway? This is a really expensive car."

For once it was Adam who looked like he wanted to avoid conversation. "They pay me well to be the best at what I do."

"And are you?" I asked, even though I had a very good idea Adam was a natural at that, too.

"Yes I am."

His eyes were burning a hole through me and the energy coursing between us was almost unbearable. I either needed to take him in the rather tiny cabin space of his fancy sports car, or drive it. Otherwise I was going to short circuit from the lust surging through me.

"Give me the keys," I whispered and held up my hand.

He cocked an eyebrow and chuckled low in his chest, pulling out the key and letting it drop. "Show me what you got, Filler. I expect to be impressed with an attitude like that."

Impressed? I had to imagine impressing a man who built the world's most exotic cars would be hard to surprise, but I could certainly give him a show.

Like many of my father's fastest cars, the AMG was hard and uncomfortable. It wasn't a car designed for comfort, it was designed for speed: to hug the curves of the road in the lightest frame possible. I pulled the gull-wing door closed and adjusted the seat while Adam moved around to the passenger seat.

"Fun fact, we decided to keep the doors manual instead of the much cooler automatic doors in order to shed ninety extra pounds."

"I know," I replied without looking at him. "It was a good choice."

I turned the key and closed my eyes as the engine rumbled to life. It was a lot like foreplay. The way the throaty engine purred and sent a vibration through the car always made me feel alive and I liked to enjoy it for a moment.

"You need a minute?" Adam laughed, but the look in his eyes was serious.

"I'm fine. Just haven't sat behind the wheel of something this fast in a little while."

"How much experience do you have driving cars like this?"

I fastened my seatbelt and backed the car out of the parking space. "Enough."

I drove carefully while we were in town. The tourist heavy streets were filled with pedestrians and tiny lanes. It also gave me an opportunity to get used to the car, from the way it shifted to how sensitive the pedals were. By the time we reached the outskirts of town, I knew the car pretty well.

"Which way?"

"Turn left. You can really open her up out here, by the way."

I glanced over at Adam while I waited for the light to change. "Oh really?"

"Yeah, the cops don't watch this road, it's long and pretty straight, and because of the plantations there aren't many other cars."

"You sound like you have experience running cars out here."

"Might have raced a few down this road..." The light turned green and I gunned it, the car shooting forward at a ridiculous speed, like a bullet out of a gun or, as I liked to think of it, a jet taking off from the deck of an aircraft carrier.

This was why I loved driving and it was probably the one and only trait I shared wholly with my father. The adrenaline rush of being flung from resting to over sixty miles an hour in less than six seconds…well, exhilarating wasn't the right word. It was more like the feeling of an orgasm that sneaks up and knocks you on your ass, leaving you breathless and immediately ready for round two.

The car was a work of art. Designed for precisely what I was doing: going fast. I was in love and wet as a river from the lust I felt toward the machine. It was smooth, powerful, and, for the moment, all mine. If it was possible to love a car, I was madly in love with Adam's AMG.

"You may want to slow down a tad. There is a crossroad in about a thousand meters."

I backed off the gas pedal, but the car didn't slow down, it was too finely tuned and maintained its speed almost entirely, so I lightly tapped the brake. "Thanks for the heads up."

I fingered the paddle shifter, ready for more. My father claimed they ruined the experience of driving a 'real' car, but for me, the convenience and ease of shifting gears far outweighed the ego-boosting fun of mashing a clutch and palming a stick.

Although that was fun, too.

Chapter 8

"We're coming up on Mossy Oaks, you'll see the brown signs," Adam pointed at a sign that was fast approaching on the side of the road.

A chain of plantations ran along Long Branch River. Mossy Oaks was the closest.

I noticed Adam was quietly watching me from the passenger seat. I wasn't sure if he was silent because he was enjoying the ride or because he was studying me, but I had a feeling it was the latter. His eyes were on me but they were focused somewhere else, like he was deep in thought.

Oak trees lined the road as we approached the heavy wrought iron gates at the entrance to the property. The driveway was smoothly paved and wound down through large green fields before the towering white house came into view. Beautiful gardens, a massive fountain, and a cobbled circle drive sat in front of the columned porch.

I parked in the designated guest parking lot and

turned off the engine. "Fucking fantastic car, Adam. Thanks for letting me drive it."

"You are most welcome. Not too many people can handle a car with this much power." He let his unasked question hang as he looked at me intently.

The reaction I had to that was strange. Instead of feeling like I was being forced to answer questions, or being exposed, I was strangely comfortable. For the first time in a long, long time, I felt like I wanted to talk.

"My father collects foreign sports cars. I learned to drive in a Ferrari F50."

Adam's eyebrows shot up and he nodded slowly. "Helluva car to learn to drive on."

I turned slightly in the seat so I could face him. "No shit. He said if I could drive that, I could drive anything."

"That's not what I meant, but that's true, too."

We were quiet for a moment and I waited to see if Adam was going to explain. The silence stretched and I realized, finally, that Adam wasn't going to ask questions unless I wanted him to. For once, someone was actually respecting my wishes.

"You meant that the car was expensive?"

Adam nodded, but still didn't ask anything else.

"It's the only thing we have in common. Me and my father. Outside of sports cars we have absolutely nothing to talk about."

Adam chuckled and shifted in his seat. "That's actually kind of funny. My grandfather, the one I told you about, the one who taught me how to build cars? That's all we had in common. He was a racist, closed-minded asshole, but damn did he know his cars. At least when we were under the hood he kept conversation about the engine."

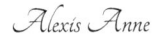

"You don't get to pick your family," I sighed.

"But you do get to pick your friends," Adam smiled and squeezed my hand. "Let's go get a tour."

For the next hour a docent gave us a private tour of the house and grounds that were still a working plantation and museum. The owners of the property no longer lived on-sight, preferring instead to keep the house open to the public. I learned a lot and was happy to finally be able to say I'd been to the plantation instead of just reading about it.

"Ready for the next one?"

I nodded and slid into the passenger seat this time. Unlike me, Adam apparently didn't feel the need to impress, driving very reasonably down the road to the next plantation. "This is the Green Hills Plantation." His voice was unusually even.

I enjoyed the view of another long, winding drive lined with oaks. Beyond the trees were large lawns and, in the distance, I could see the river off to the right of the house. To the left were rolling hills covered in crops. I tried to recall what I knew about Green Hills. It was another working plantation and, I was pretty sure, the food grown here was used for local restaurants. The house and grounds could also be rented out. It wasn't a museum like Mossy Oaks. But that was where my knowledge ended.

Instead of parking in the parking lot or the driveway, Adam veered off toward the barn. It was completely renovated and enclosed except for a covered area with parking slips. Each one was filled except the one Adam slid the car into.

"You seem to know your way around here," I murmured.

He turned off the engine and set his hands on his lap like he was nervous, which on Adam looked incredibly strange. "I should, this is where I live."

"What?" I gasped before I could stop myself.

He cringed a little. "This is my family's plantation. I have a little apartment inside here, along with the workshop I told you about."

He finally turned and looked at me out of the corner of his eye.

I let out a slow breath. "This is yours?"

He nodded slowly. "We can leave if this is too personal, but both my parents are out of town for the night and I thought it would be fun to show you around."

Too personal? My sex-cation friend had just brought me home. Granted his parents weren't there, but still...this was where he'd spent summer vacations and high school. This wasn't just another plantation on a tour.

Taking me to Green Hills was the very definition of personal.

And while my muscles were locked in place and

my heart was beating hard inside my chest, I wasn't panicking. Nervous? Yes. Uncomfortable? Very much. But not freaking out.

Adam was working some serious voodoo on me. "Just a tour?"

"Just a tour," he repeated and his eyes lit up. "Of the plantation, my workshop, and a special surprise."

Surprise? The way he said it made a surprise sound like a good thing. "Ok," I agreed. "Show me around." Adam grinned and I realized I was beginning to really enjoy putting that smile on his face. It was oddly (for me) rewarding to know I was making someone happy.

Had I ever done that before? Freely and without planning, gone out of my way to please someone with the intention of seeing them smile? I didn't think I had.

Adam locked the car and took my hand, threading his fingers between mine. I let him, even though it felt strange. The gesture was intimate, but not forced. I wasn't being commanded to hold his hand or even be his friend. We just were. He was sweet, an incredibly good fuck, and open to everything I suggested. He wasn't my enemy. I didn't need to fight him or protect myself from him. Adam was safe.

He led me inside the side door of the barn and flicked on the overhead lights. "These are my babies," Adam murmured, throwing out his hand.

The space was very large and long with three bays for cars. In the first bay was a car that had seen far better years. It was rusty, in several pieces, and on jacks.

In the second bay was a beautiful red and white car that looked like it has been completely restored. The paint job was immaculate and the tires looked like they were brand new. The little chrome name plate on the side said *Duster*.

In the third bay was a motorcycle up on some sort of stand. It was also pretty sad looking, but it had beautiful lines and a lot of potential. I wasn't a big fan of motorcycles, there was something about being completely exposed that scared the crap out of me, but I did appreciate them.

Along the back wall was a stainless steel work table with shelves above, and in the back corner a gorgeous black motorcycle was parked next to a door.

"Your babies are beautiful."

"Thanks." His chest actually puffed up a little. "This first one is a mess. I started it the last time I was home and honestly, I don't think I'll ever finish it. But this one," he moved to the red and white car in the middle, "she's my favorite. I've fixed up about a dozen cars over the years—sold them when I was done for a nice profit—but this one…I'll never sell her."

"Why?"

He was running his hand along the paint job on the hood and up the roof as he spoke. "I'm not totally sure. She's special. I keep finding new things to change and different ways to upgrade her. I guess she's a project I'll never finish because I don't want to."

I wasn't sure if I thought Adam's attitude toward the car was adorable or disturbing. "So fast cars *and* fast motorcycles?" I pointed at the two bikes.

He shrugged, barely turning his eyes away from the Duster. "I really don't ride that much. I like working on them more than anything. My heart is with my cars."

I liked him even more.

"Want to see my apartment?"

At the end of the garage was a door one step up from the garage floor. Adam fished in his pocket for a key, unlocked the door, and pushed it open, stepping to the side. I walked in ahead of him and waited while he flicked on the lights. It was a very simple, clean, modern studio apartment. The walls were grey and the furniture was black and stainless steel. A bank of sliding glass doors lined the wall to our right with simple gauzy white curtains. A tiny kitchenette with a bar was tucked into the corner opposite of us. Immediately to my right was a large king-sized bed with a white comforter and large pillows. A black couch and coffee table completed the room.

"Nice place. It looks like you."

Adam closed the door and frowned. "I'm not sure what that means, but thanks?"

"It means you're clean and simple."

"Again, I'm not entirely sure that is a compliment."

"I'll just stop talking then," I laughed, moving around the room. I wanted to get a feel for Adam. He had car magazines on his coffee table and nothing more than tissues on his nightstand. The bar to the kitchen was a little more informative. Beside a cup stuffed with pens and pencils was a notepad covered in drawings, a bowl of change, and a candy bar. "Snickers lover?"

"Don't touch my candy." He was joking. Sort of.

"And here?" I asked as I walked to a door beside the kitchen.

"Bathroom."

"I like it." I could imagine all kinds of fun new places to have sex with Adam. Keeping the back windows open was definitely near the top of my list.

He smiled and wrapped an arm around my waist. "We could sleep here tonight. Change things up?"

He took the thought right out of my head. "I like the idea, but I didn't bring anything. Are you kicking me out of your bed after you have your way with me?" I held my breath as he dropped a very slow, very soft kiss on my lips.

"Never. We can get up early and I'll take you home to change before work. I can even drop you off at your office."

I automatically started to protest, saying Adam didn't need to take me to work, but then I stopped myself. He was being nice and it would help make the morning move faster. "That would be great. Thank you for offering."

"No problem. By the way," he replied as he threaded his fingers back through mine and started for the door. "We're having sex in the shower."

"The shower?"

"Yep. I've always wanted to have sex in that shower."

"Oh, do I get to be your first?"

"You do."

"Wow...*your first*..."

"Smartass." He closed and locked the door behind us and started across the driveway toward the main house.

"There are worse things to be called."

Adam sighed and squeezed my hand. "True. So, let me give you a quick rundown on the business side of Green Hills. The plantation is from my father's side of the family, but it is my mom who transformed it into the operation it is today. She used to be a big name chef in New York, but when my grandfather died, Mom and Dad saw taking over the plantation as an opportunity to change things up. She opened Seychelle's and transformed the fields. We are a farm-to-table operation now. She owns and runs three restaurants in Calhoun Beach and every bit of food is grown and raised here except for the seafood which is handled by our partner."

"Three restaurants?"

Adam nodded slowly and I could see he was holding back. "Seychelle's, Green Tavern, and Rivard Bistro."

"Impressive, those are all top of the line. I've eaten at all three."

He nodded again and led me up the stairs to the massive wood front doors. "Dad is an accountant and has taken over managing my mother's empire."

"And where are they today?" I asked knowing full well I wasn't getting the full story out of Adam.

"They had meetings in New York. They'll be back late tomorrow."

I nodded, but didn't press. He opened the door and we stepped into a tall, open foyer. Above us hung a massive chandelier and below us were dark wood floors covered in rugs. The walls were stark white and covered in paintings. It was a beautiful home that managed to straddle both the beauty of its past and the necessity of the present.

"The back of the house was converted into a massive commercial kitchen. We can serve guests upwards of five hundred without batting an eye."

I glanced around the kitchen. Three employees were working on cakes and desserts. The ovens, sinks, and countertops all looked high-end. "Very impressive," I murmured. "How often do you have such large events out here?"

Adam shrugged. "I honestly don't pay that much attention, but it seems like they are always booked for something. Weddings, retreats, big corporate affairs...you name it."

He bypassed the rest of the first floor and led me upstairs. "This floor is available for overnight guests. All the rooms on this floor are bedrooms except for a sitting room at the end of the hallway."

We walked up and down the floor, glancing in the rooms that were all decorated in frilly designs and dark woods. "And the third floor?"

"My parent's apartment. They had the third floor completely redesigned. There are two bedrooms, a living room, a dining room, and a full kitchen up there. It actually looks a lot like our apartment in Manhattan."

I was glad Adam didn't offer to show me upstairs and I didn't ask to see it. We wandered down a different flight of stairs that led us back to the front of the house. "The last thing I want to show you is in here."

He pushed open a heavy door just off the foyer and stepped inside.

"A library?"

He nodded. "This wall," he waved his hands at the wall on our right, covered in dark wood built-in bookcases, "is all for use by the guests. It's mostly popular fiction. But the rest," he waved his hands at the other three walls, "are all records, family history, blue prints, photographs, the whole nine yards of Callaway family history."

"Impressive," I murmured, walking up for a closer look. "I'm sure this has all been digitized and copies offered to the University?"

"It's an ongoing process, but yes."

I ran my hands along the shelves as I walked around the room. It was an impressive collection of documents. I could easily spend a week going through the records. For a split second, the image of Adam reading on the massive leather couch in the middle of the room, hit me. I could see him lazily combing through his latest book while I sat at the desk in the corner studying his family documents.

I shook my head and worked my way around to the popular fiction. "How much of this wall have you read?"

He folded his arms over his chest and looked lovingly over the shelves. "Probably a good, oh, two-thirds."

It was quite possible Adam had out-read me by a significant amount. I quickly counted a group of books and multiplied it across the shelves on the wall. This didn't include the ebooks he undoubtedly had as well.

"You may have a reading problem, Adam."

He was at my ear, catching me by surprise as he whispered. "I'm pretty sure I admitted to that on the first night we met."

A shiver raced down my spine. His warm breath against my skin was electric. "That you did."

He kissed my cheek and wrapped his arm around my waist, turning my back to the shelves and lightly pressing me against the wood. "I just had a vision of us on that couch behind me. It involved books and a distinct lack of clothing. And sex."

I laughed lightly at the way he managed to combine images in my head all while throwing in sex. "I wouldn't be opposed to it if you found a way to arrange it one day."

He groaned and flexed his hips into mine as he kissed me. "I'll remember that. Now, how about I show you your surprise?"

"This wasn't it?"

He shook his head, eyes locked on mine. "Not even

close."

I clenched my legs together as an ache began to throb between my thighs. There was something about the way Adam looked at me when he said 'surprise' that made me want to jump in his lap and ride him all afternoon. Whatever his surprise was, it had him excited and me hot. "Lead the way."

Chapter 9

*A*dam snagged a key ring from a nail on a wood post inside a second, smaller barn where a very old red Ford pickup truck was parked.

He drove out onto a dirt path that led to the fence line, hopping out to unlock the gate and swing it open for us to enter. We did this three more times, passing rolling fields along the way.

"The lower fields are mostly berries. Did I tell you we make our own wine, too? It's still a small operation and we're not sure it's going to take off, but Dad is really having fun with it. He's looking at whiskey or bourbon next."

"No, you didn't mention," I replied quietly while looking out the window. I was suffering from information overload.

Adam was talking away at this point, lost in childhood memories and the simple joy of sharing something he loved. I let him go, not really listening to everything he was saying. Instead I was watching him talk. His face was so animated, his smile so genuine—Adam was incredibly handsome. Not just sexy. But *beautiful*.

I was overcome by an urge I couldn't quite wrap my brain around, to kiss his lips and straddle his lap. Not just to fuck him, but to *be with him*.

That couldn't possibly be right. I must be confused. *I had to be confused.* Those feelings weren't *feelings*...they must be some sort of new desire I'd never felt before. I didn't usually spend this much time with men, so I was probably feeling something new but normal. It was desire, not feelings.

Adam stopped the truck under a tree and turned the engine off. "We're going to walk from here."

I blinked a few times and took a deep breath. "Where are we going exactly?"

"It's a surprise," he repeated.

In the middle of nowhere? I was starting to wonder about Adam. Maybe he was actually taking me out into the woods to kill me. But by the deep look to his eyes and the gorgeous smile on his face there was no possible way this man could ever want to hurt me on purpose. We walked through the trees and a lot of brush before we got to a clearing. "I'm not sure your dress suggestion was such a great idea."

"Really?" He swept me off my feet and into his arms. "I'll carry you if you prefer. But I refuse to say this dress was a mistake. I can still taste you."

And just like that, I was hot again. Weird emotions were pushed back in my mind, unanswered questions placed back in their cabinet, and my raw need for Adam's body was brought out to center stage. "You have a very talented mouth," I replied, dragging my finger across his cheek and over his soft lips.

He stepped over a branch that was sticking out of the brush and set me down, turning me so that his front was pressed to my back. "Welcome to the original Green Hills."

In front of me were the eerie remains of stone foundations and crumbling chimneys. I looked over my shoulder and into Adam's eyes. "This is beautiful."

He squeezed my arms and pulled me flush against him. "Only you would think this was beautiful. But I knew you would—that's why I wanted to bring you out here."

"Thank you," I replied genuinely. The confusing feelings started to creep back up inside me. Adam knew I'd like seeing the ruins on his family property because he knew my job was more than work. He already knew how much I loved things like this.

"This was where my ancestors first settled," he explained. "They lived out here for about fifty years—we think—before the main house was built."

I stepped away from Adam and all his thoughtfulness to examine the foundations closer up. Grass was growing between the stones, and moss covered most of the surfaces. "It is fairly large for the time period. I'm guessing late eighteenth century? Wood floors over the stone and a cistern below?"

He shrugged his shoulders and followed me inside what now looked like a low stonewall instead of the base of a home. "You're the expert, not me. I just know it was awesome to play army out here."

"The archaeology department would probably love to study that chimney fall over there," I pointed to a pile of stones that extended from the base of the foundation out toward the trees.

"They are more than welcome to come study anything they like." He stepped into me, his lips grazing my ear and cheek. "Especially if it brings you out here." He kissed down my neck as his arms came around me, holding me close. "You are different today, you know."

"So are you," I replied with more force than I meant. It sounded more like an accusation than an observation.

Maybe it was.

He nodded and kissed my lips. "I'm sorry. Do you want me to stop? I knew bringing you out here was a risk."

I shook my head. I didn't want him to stop. I didn't know what I wanted, but I knew I wanted his kisses. I returned them and ran my hands over his shoulders, down his arms, and to his buckle. "I would like to keep us on track. We may be friends, but we're also sex friends."

He laughed, deep in his chest, the sound warm and inviting, as I slid his belt free and unbuttoned his pants. "You were so kind as to give me a present earlier. Maybe I should return the favor?"

"Out here?" He didn't stop me from sliding his zipper down and hooking my thumbs in his waistband.

"Are you expecting any company out this way?"

He shook his head and smiled.

"Then yes. Out here." I slid his pants down and knelt on the grass growing inside the walls of the old foundation. I wrapped my hand around the base of his large cock and ran my thumb up his length. I'd done my fair share of licking and playing with his dick during sex, but I hadn't yet taken my time and focused exclusively on only pleasuring Adam.

As confident as I usually was in the bedroom, this was the one area I rarely got to practice, and for once, I felt my nerves tick up. Adam had set the bar on oral sex very, very high... I needed to step up my game. Big time.

"You don't have to do this...it wasn't my idea."

I looked up and found Adam watching me with the strangest expression on his face. "It's just..."

"Just what?"

I ran my hand up and down his length feeling ridiculous. "Um... well, I actually don't do this very often. I was going over a plan of action in my head before I got started."

He cocked an eyebrow. "You sucked my dick yesterday."

I rolled my eyes. "I sucked it, yes. But I didn't give you a blowjob. That is entirely different."

"Not really."

"Do you want me to suck you off or not?" I asked, running my tongue around his head.

He shuddered. "Oh I want your mouth wrapped around me, trust me. I just wasn't sure what that look was in your eyes."

I shrugged and ran my hand up and down a few more times. "I'm a selfish lover. I take far more often than I give. I was just taking a moment to make sure I remembered what I was doing." And then before he could say anything else, I shut him up by wrapping my lips around his cock, swirling my tongue and taking him in deep.

Adam groaned and stopped talking. He did however, run his fingertips across my scalp and through my hair. Lightly, not forcefully. He didn't grab my head and hold me in place the way some guys did. He let me do all the work and simply enjoyed what I was giving him: a good time out in the middle of nowhere surrounded by trees and blue skies.

I realized there were quite a few things I knew about Adam. He liked it when his balls were cupped lightly—not firmly—and he really, really liked it when I massaged the space between his balls and dick. So as his breathing quickened and his fingers moved from my hair to my shoulders, I massaged the spot with increasing pressure.

His cock was large and firm, but also soft and smooth as my lips and tongue moved against it. The wind blew my hair and Adam brushed it out of my face, pulling it around his hand to keep it out of the way. I liked hearing his grunts of pleasure and the twitch of his muscles as he started to lose control. I got more pleasure out of driving Adam wild than I ever got out of pleasing a man before. In the past it had either been a risky bit of fun, or a dirty means to an end. Both were fun, but it was something I did because it added to the moment.

I was doing *this* for an entirely different reason. Making Adam lose control was incredibly pleasurable to me. I got an insane and inflated sense of pride out of watching him find satisfaction because of me.

I didn't understand it and I wasn't sure I wanted to.

He grunted deep in his chest and his fingers tightened around my hair that was still wrapped around his hand, the added pressure sent a prickle across my scalp. I sucked harder, taking him deeper until his cock was gliding against the soft spot near the back of my throat. I felt the pressure all the way down to my sex each time the tip of his cock made contact, and I moaned with my own pleasure.

"Fuck," Adam swore. "Do that again..."

I moaned again and Adam gasped, his other hand tightening on my shoulder and his thighs shaking, and then, as his cock slid against my tongue and the back of my throat, I felt the warm spray of his climax. He grunted and groaned, fingers flexing and legs jerking, until he was done.

When he relaxed and let out a deep sigh, I sucked lightly up his length, kissed the glistening tip of his cock, and then met his eyes as I swallowed.

"Oh shit that's hot," he groaned.

I grinned. Mission accomplished. I may not be as practiced as some, but I sure as hell knew what I was doing.

Chapter 10

Thursday Night

"So," Adam had on his serious face as he filled both our glasses from the pitcher of beer. "Tell me more about your love of cars."

I groaned. "I should've just pretended I didn't know anything."

"No, this is awesome. I had no idea I could talk to you about this."

I rolled my eyes. "See, this is the problem. I like to drive them, not talk about them. If you go too far, I'm just going to fall asleep. You'll go from my fun and mysterious fuck buddy to boring engine nerd. Don't be the boring engine nerd. You're too much fun to have sex with and I'm not ready to be done with you yet."

He put his hand to his chest and winced like he was hurt. "You sure know how to kill a guy."

I drank my beer and looked out over the river. We were eating dinner at the fish camp a few miles down the road from the plantations we'd visited over the afternoon. Oysters and fish sandwiches were on their way and, in the meantime, we were splitting drinks and an appetizer of shrimp and hushpuppies.

"You know what's interesting? I almost never drive. Part of the reason I loved this job at CBU was because it would let me walk to work. I have a car, but I almost never use it."

"If you like to drive fast cars why don't you own one?"

I shrugged my shoulders wondering the same thing. "I'm guessing it has something to do with some deep-seated fucked-up childhood shit. I'm probably projecting. If I spend money on a fast car and drive it the way it was designed to be driven then I will somehow magically become my father."

"You should let yourself buy a fast car. That's my humble opinion."

I laughed and took another sip. "You going to get me a deal on an AMG? How good is the employee discount anyway?"

He looked down at the beer in his hands. "I do get a pretty nice discount, but that car still cost a pretty penny."

Should I ask the question I really wanted to ask? I didn't think I could avoid it. My curiosity was driving me absolutely insane. "How *did* you afford that car?"

He sighed. "You really want to know? It will change things. You'll know more about me and," he gasped, putting his hands to his mouth in mock horror, "you might actually become my friend."

I sat forward, putting my elbows on the table as I leaned in. "I've got a secret... I have accepted the fact we're going to be friends. As much as I avoid this whole relationship-building crap normal people do, you seem like a nice guy and I could use some nice people in my life."

Adam grinned and leaned forward too, meeting my gaze. "Well then, *friend*, on top of my very generous salary from Mercedes, I happen to have a ridiculous trust fund sitting in a bank account somewhere."

"Somewhere?" I coughed. Did he not know where his money was?

He shrugged and looked a little sheepish. "I live off of my salary except for the AMG. I kind of bought it to piss off my parents when we had a fight last year."

"That's an expensive way to piss off your parents," I murmured, searching his face for some sign of this rich, spoiled brat who bought expensive cars as a kiss-off.

"Indeed. It worked though. I made my point." He was looking at his beer, not me, obviously ashamed.

"I'd be pissed if my kid bought a car that expensive but kept it in a garage because he was only home a few weeks a year to drive it. Seems like a shame."

"That was exactly why I bought it. I don't think I could have made my point any clearer."

"What was the fight about?" Adam always spoke about his parents with respect. This was the first sign he had any issues with them.

"My trust fund. It originally came from my grandfather. Old family money that gets passed down generation to generation. I always knew I'd inherit part of the money and eventually, one day, the plantation. I've accepted my legacy," he frowned and took a sip of beer. "On top of that, I'm an owner in my parent's company. Between my salary and my share of the profits from Green Hills, I have more money than I know what to do with."

I stared at the top of Adam's head. He still wasn't looking up at me and he seemed to have hit a stumbling block in his explanation.

"So what's the problem?" I prompted. "Too much money?"

He shook his head and finally looked up. His face looked so different. Regret and unhappiness looked all wrong on Adam.

"I've always been happy to leave all that money sitting there for a day when I knew what to do with it—but my parents started giving me a hard time."

"About having money?" I was attempting to make him laugh, but it wasn't working. Adam was really upset.

"They think I'm not happy. They said a man approaching thirty should be out having more fun. Dating, buying stupid things for the hell of it—shit like that."

Now I was really confused. "You had a fight with your parents because they wanted you to spend your money and have fun? I'm not really following you…"

He caught my eye and crooked an eyebrow. "Says the mysterious woman who learned to drive in a Ferrari."

I blushed from head to toe but stayed silent, entirely too embarrassed to say anything.

He touched my hand lightly. "Hey, I didn't mean to drag you into this. I... hell," he swore some more under his breath and ran his long fingers through his hair, letting out a long breath. "For someone who clearly comes from some sort of money, you don't live like it. You're kind, generous, your apartment doesn't even have a football television in it. I just figured maybe we had more in common—"

"We do. You're right." I cut him off.

He locked his eyes back on mine. There was a hunger in them this time. Something ravenous that came out every time I offered up a morsel of information. "I do know what it's like to have money and I don't like to live that way. I can honestly say I understand your desire to live simply."

I held his gaze and felt all those walls I kept around me start to crumble. Keeping Adam out was impossible.

He licked his lower lip and sighed, taking my hand back. "What was it I said that night at the bar? Kindred spirits?" I nodded and my heart thumped against the walls of my chest. "I think we were destined to be friends, Elizabeth."

I was pretty sure too. "You always call me Elizabeth or Filler. You can call me Liz, you know?"

He shook his head and lowered his eyes. "No. I thought about it. I tossed it around in my head, but no. I don't think you'll ever be Liz to me."

It was either getting hotter out, or I was. Suddenly my skin felt like it was on fire and the blood in my veins was pumping so hard I could feel each beat. "Why?"

He shook his head, "I don't know. You just *aren't*."

Never in my life had I ever felt so much all at once. There was energy coursing between us and my entire body craved more of Adam. I wanted to make him laugh and lose control but I also liked how he made *me* feel. I liked that I wasn't Liz with him. I was someone else. Someone new.

"So tell me about the fight," I whispered.

He nodded, as if he could read my thoughts, and continued his story. "I told them spending money for the sake of spending money was the stupidest thing they ever asked me to do," he laughed and wrapped his other hand around mine. My hand was inside both of his and for all intents and purposes, it felt like the most intimate thing I'd ever experienced in my life. "They told me wasting my youth was a mistake. I just got so mad...I can't explain it. I just...hated that they didn't seem to understand me. The next thing I knew I was driving home in a new car."

"Dumped a bunch of money into something you'd barely use. The very definition of wastefulness."

He hung his head. "I love the car, really I do. She's amazing. But it was a dumb move. I regret it almost every day."

And that was what drew me to Adam—his genuine heart. I squeezed his hand. "Trust me when I say this, there are far worse things to spend your money on and you shouldn't waste time on regret over a single act of defiance."

He smiled and squeezed my hand back. "I hate that I believe the conviction in your voice right now. I don't know who's done what to you, but it makes me mad to hear that sadness."

I suddenly wished I could go back and reintroduce myself to Adam with my real name, start over fresh without any secrets between us. I wanted to tell him everything, even the crazy things. I wondered if he'd always doubt me because of the lies I told him in the beginning. "There's a lot about me you don't know."

"Only because you won't tell me."

"You do understand that once I tell you these things…there's no going back. How you're looking at me right now, this will all change. I won't ever be the same person to you. Don't you want to keep things simple? Just enjoy this time we have together?"

"Did you murder someone?"

My eyebrows shot up. "Um, no."

Adam shrugged, "Then I highly doubt you will ever tell me anything that will change how I feel about you."

"And how do you feel about me?"

He looked me directly in the eye and spoke with absolute conviction. "Like I finally found someone who understands me."

Not love. Not need. *Understanding*.

There was no pressure here and no obligations. Simply a declaration of acceptance. It was the most beautiful thing I'd ever heard. It made me want to tell him everything.

"I've had a crazy life. Learning to drive in a sports car is just kind of icing on the cake." I paused, wondering where to start. "Beginning at the beginning isn't even worth it. And I've never really done this before."

Adam released my hand and sat back lazily in his chair, grabbing his drink. I had a feeling he was trying to make me believe this wasn't a big deal. "Not even with Allison?"

I took a deep breath and blew it up into my hair, sending it flying. "No. She met me before things changed and, well... she kind of found out about my parents the hard way. It was a traumatizing enough experience that I've never done it again."

"Changed?" Adam was trying very hard to look casual, but the hunger in his eyes was as obvious as ever.

I nodded and swallowed, rubbing my face and fidgeting in my chair. Mercifully dinner arrived and put me temporarily out of my misery. "Maybe we should eat first." Instead of attempting to fill Adam in on every detail all at once, I picked and chose as we ate, giving myself time to acclimate to each new thing I shared.

"Filler isn't my real last name."

Adam stopped mid-chew and raised his eyebrows.

"Ok..."

"I changed it just before I graduated from college to my grandmother's maiden name. My real last name is Lawrence."

He chewed slowly, looking like I'd just knocked the wind out of him.

"I told you there was a lot..."

"Keep going," he replied with his fork, and stuck another bite in his mouth.

"My name is *Elizabeth Lawrence*," I repeated.

He nodded and chewed, waiting for me to keep going, except that was it. I needed him to understand my name before I could explain anything else.

And then it hit him. His eyes widened and he swallowed the bite of fish in his mouth. "*The* Elizabeth Lawrence. As in the daughter of Cybil Hope the reality star and Roger Lawrence the American hero."

I nodded and waited.

"As in the granddaughter of Vivian Hope, *The* Vivian Hope. The Oscar winning, crazy famous, super talented, Vivian Hope."

I nodded again. It was weird how people always added *'the'* to our names, as if no one else on the planet were allowed to have it.

Adam set his fork down and rubbed his chin, sitting back in his chair. I wished I could see inside his brain. I had no idea what he was thinking and since I'd never done this before, I was freaking out inside.

"You sued your parents for child exploitation. *And won*."

I nodded. I hadn't been in front of a camera in over twelve years. And twelve years ago it had only been long enough to get in and out of the courtroom.

"I take it everything they say about you is true then." He didn't look upset or disgusted, just sad.

And that made me sad.

I hadn't expected that.

"To say the least." I confirmed. Unfortunately in my case, most of the crap in the tabloids was true—and it wasn't even the good stuff.

Adam paled, then nodded. "I think I understand now. All of it."

I nodded and picked up my drink. My heart was racing in my chest. It was beating so hard I couldn't hear anything else. I downed the rest of the drink and realized my hands were shaking when I clunked the mug against the table.

Adam stared at my hands and then stood up, fishing out his wallet and dropping money on the table. "Let's get out of here," he commanded, holding out his hand and cocking his head. "You look like you could use a good distraction."

I swallowed and grabbed his hand. "Please."

Chapter 11

Adam's shower was amazing. If there was a bell or whistle for a bathroom, he had it. Waterfall from the ceiling? Check. Long bench? Check. Removable shower heads? Check and check.

My clothes started falling off before we made it fully into the apartment and there was a trail of garments leading through the apartment to the bathroom. You know, in case we got lost or something. Not that I was ever planning on leaving the safety and comfort of the bathroom. It was like a cocoon, and we were hiding from the world.

"It's a good thing I didn't see this earlier. We might've starved by now. I'm never leaving."

"Why do you think I kept you from looking in here?"

I shrugged. "I just assumed it was because there was nothing special to see."

He laughed, pressing me up against the damp wall with his large body. He dropped down and kissed my neck before nuzzling the spot behind my ear. "You were wrong." His voice was very close to a deep growl.

I grinned as his large cock pressed into my belly. "Yes, yes I was."

"How am I going to teach you to stop making assumptions? It's a terrible habit."

"I don't know," I replied. "It's not all bad. For instance, I assumed you'd be a fantastic fuck and well... you are."

That earned me an actual growl as well as a hike up the wall. I wrapped my arms around his neck, and legs around his waist, letting him press his weight against me, pinning me in place. The room was filled with steam and the light scent of soap. It was as close to paradise as a small room could get.

He'd made a special effort to leave my revelations outside the bathroom and only bring fun, distracting pleasure into the shower.

He nipped my bottom lip with his teeth. "Has anyone ever told you that you have bitable lips?"

"I'm absolutely positive no one has ever said that to me before."

He made a noise that sounded like confusion mixed with wonder. "Well they are."

"Well thank you. You know," I ground against his waist and squeezed my knees against his sides. It was enough to make him smile. "I am actually enjoying being friends."

He sucked my lip gently between his and groaned, flexing his hips up. His cock pressed up against my sex, asking for permission to enter. "Not to totally freak you out, but I'm already hoping you don't shut me down at the end of vacation. I really like being your friend...and not just the sexual kind."

I ground back against him, giving him permission to enter.

"You know, I was thinking it would be fun to get random text messages with stupid pictures of you at pubs or eating weird German food."

"Really? I was thinking more along the lines of really dirty video sex."

Now that was an interesting idea. "Definitely video sex. I have toys..."

"Really?" He pushed inside and I sank my nails into his shoulder. It was still amazing to me how insane it felt to have Adam inside me.

"Yep. Lots of them."

"Why are you holding out on me?" He looked genuinely disappointed, mixed with insanely turned-on. "I love to play with toys. I'd love to play with *your* toys even more. I'd love to play with your toys on *you* best of all..." He was a kid in a candy store. His eyes were wild and there was a goofy grin on his lips. Oh yes, I was letting Adam into my toy box. If he was this much fun without toys I could only imagine what he'd do with props and tools to assist him.

I moaned and wrapped my arms tighter around his neck, pushing his face into the crook of my neck. He was almost buried inside me and the feeling was somewhere between overwhelming and mind-blowing. "*Sweet Jesus*, you feel so good."

His moan vibrated against my skin. "You have no idea what you're talking about."

That made me laugh. "I think I know what we'll be doing this weekend."

He slowly moved in and out of me several times, testing his balance and mine. "Not that I wasn't already excited to spend the weekend in bed with you but now...holy shit I can't wait."

My eyes rolled back in my head as Adam teased me. He was carefully building up my pleasure, moving from light foreplay to slow sex. I was reaching that plane I loved so much. I could stay wrapped around Adam all night as long as he kept moving like that. I opened my eyes and realized he was watching me again. He was clearly turned on. His cock was hard as a rock inside me and his jaw was set. "Travis is playing a special set at a club this weekend. All old school rock and blues...want to go?"

Dancing with Adam? Sweaty and grinding to good music and lots of booze? That sounded like an amazing way to break up hours and hours of sex. "Oh yes," I moaned. It made Adam lose control for a moment. He pumped into me harder for several strokes, but then backed off his rhythm again. Back to teasing.

"And Elizabeth?" he whispered. God how I loved the sound of my name when Adam whispered it like that.

"Yes?"

"You can't scare me off that easy. You're stuck with me." He thrust into me, taking away my ability to reply for a moment.

"Don't make promises you can't keep," I replied between thrusts. Adam had no idea what he was talking about. If he thought a foggy recollection of decade-old tabloids was enough to know me, he was sorely mistaken. There were so many secrets and lies even I had trouble keeping them straight.

"And don't you go assuming you know what I can handle." He stopped, looking me straight in the eye while buried inside me.

"We haven't even known each other a week…" I reminded him. And yet I knew my warning was a lie as soon as it was out of my mouth. It was as if I'd always known Adam. It was like there had been this hole in my life that he'd suddenly filled. I didn't know Adam was missing until he stepped into it, and now that he was there, I finally understood that weird, empty feeling I'd always had when I was alone.

"Don't," his voice was a low growl. "Just don't do that. You and I both know this isn't some bullshit vacation fling. I swear if you lie to me…you know me better than almost anyone. Five days, Elizabeth. You know me better than almost anyone in *five days*. And I know you. I know I do. Do I know everything? No. I don't have to…I know *you*. The rest is just details."

He didn't give me a moment to respond, not that I could have. I was so overwhelmed by his words—by their truth—I didn't know what to say. So instead I did what I knew, I threw myself into sex with Adam. He lifted me off his cock and I pushed him backward onto the bench seat. I turned my back to him and he grabbed his cock, angling it so that it slid inside me as I moved in front of him and down onto his lap.

He was almost too much from this angle. He was so deep and large it overwhelmed me and took my breath away, but it was also glorious. And I was in control. He always did that. Adam always found a way to step back and give me room to work when I was lost.

I found my footing against the slick tile and braced my hands on his thighs, moving up and down his shaft until I found my rhythm and angle. My back was arched, my hips were back, and my head was resting on his shoulder. The position allowed me to vary the depth of his dick, and my hands on his thighs ensured his hips wouldn't rock up to meet mine.

I closed my eyes, letting the sound of the waterfall drown out the world. It allowed me to concentrate on what I needed. I brought myself right up to the edge of orgasm. It was exquisite and overwhelming. Somewhere in the back of my mind I knew those crazy sounds were me, moaning and yelling out.

And then Adam shifted slightly beneath me. At first I ignored it—it wasn't enough to disturb me, but then warm water washed over my breasts and stomach. Adam had grabbed one of the showerheads and was working his way down.

When the warm water reached my clit, it took my breath away. I faltered at first, my mind going blank, my body desperately trying to decide whether to focus on the cock inside me or the stream of water outside.

That was when Adam stilled my hips with his free hand and concentrated the water with the other. Instead of my hips setting the pace and depth, it was Adam doing the work. He didn't do much, and I had a feeling it was more raw instinct than actual concentrated planning. His cock rocked into me and the water pounded until I was digging my hands into his thighs, arching my body up as far as it would go, and yelling out his name over and over.

At least I thought it was his name. It was mixed with a lot of swearing and completely unintelligible words, but in the middle somewhere, I gave credit where credit was due.

When I was done coming, Adam let the showerhead fall away, grabbed my hips, and jerked into me fast several times before pulling out and coming all over the back of my thigh. The wet, warm spray was just about the only thing I noticed in my fog of ecstasy.

He pulled up the showerhead, washing me clean, before gently pulling me back into his lap, wrapping his arms around my waist and resting his head on my shoulder. If felt so good to lazily rest in his lap. I let my head fall onto his and waited for my body to calm.

"Thank you for christening my shower," he whispered. He almost sounded drunk.

I felt drunk. Drunk on Adam and good sex. "Thanks for another amazing orgasm."

He made an approving noise. "We're gonna have a good weekend."

I replied with the same noise. "A good weekend."

Chapter 12

Saturday, 1 a.m.

The bed was cold. That was my first thought as I stirred from a deep sleep. That, and how damn empty it made me feel.

Odd.

And then I realized what had woken me up—Adam's voice in the next room.

"Naw man. I can't yet. I told you, not until I know for sure. I'm glad the stuff I sent you the other night worked out so well, but until I see the results I'm not taking a chance like that. This needs to be a sure thing or I'm out."

Out?

"If the temperature readings you sent hold true tomorrow, then everything should work as planned and you'll get the extra speed you were looking for."

Adam was probably trying to be nice by going into the next room for his middle of the night phone call, but unfortunately it wasn't doing any good. My apartment had shockingly good acoustics and he happened to be standing in the exact spot—just in front of my bookshelves—where sound bounced off the back wall, right under the closed door, and into my room. He may as well have been lying in bed beside me. At least then I'd still be warm and not experiencing this weird feeling in the pit of my stomach.

"See how things go today, talk with the team, and then if everyone is on the same page I'll let Dave know. I get back a week from Sunday." There was a brief pause followed by Adam letting out an exasperated breath of air. "No Raif, I'm not doing this over the phone. I owe Dave a face-to-face conversation about this. End of story."

The hair on the back of my neck stood on end as they said their goodbyes. Did this have something to do with Adam rushing off the other night after dinner? Mysterious late night calls seemed to be a thing with Adam.

I had no idea what this phone call was about and I hated how curious I felt. It made me want to sit up in bed and demand answers to my millions of questions. It was an instinctive response I seemed to have absolutely no control over.

I didn't want to be that girl. I didn't want to ask him to explain his phone call or the details of his life. Sure, if he wanted to *voluntarily* share I was probably at a place to listen, but asking questions of my own volition...I didn't know how to be that person yet and I wasn't ready to act purely on gut reactions to feelings I didn't fully understand.

So as I heard Adam moving back toward my room I pretended to be asleep. I relaxed all my muscles, took a deep breath, and tried to keep my breathing as even as I could. Adam quietly opened my door and closed it behind him. No wonder I didn't hear him leave—he was like a ninja. I barely felt the bed dip as he slid underneath the comforter and slowly moved right up beside me.

His skin was hot against mine and my heart rate immediately skyrocketed, making my act even harder to maintain. *Stupid lust-filled body*. Perhaps I could pretend I was having a wet dream and he could 'wake me up' from it with some real fun.

But before I could decide whether to roll my hips against his, or moan seductively in my 'sleep', Adam brushed the hair back from my face and sighed. *What in the hell was that?* It was tender and intimate. His sigh sounded confused and frustrated.

When had I gotten to know his sounds so well?

I knew he was watching me. His eyes had this intensity I could feel even when I wasn't looking at him. Then he wiggled down a little further on the bed, pressing even closer, and pulled my arm across his broad chest, placing his hand over mine as it rested against his beating heart. He sighed again and within moments his breathing fell into a rhythm and he was asleep.

I lay awake, frozen and completely afraid to breathe or move in case I accidentally woke him back up. I needed time to process everything that had just happened. That and the fact he was holding my hand and brushing my hair when he thought I was sleeping and, and...I *liked* it. So much. I liked Adam. I liked every damn thing about him.

It had finally happened.

I *liked* a guy.

A guy who was leaving in just over a week.

Chapter 13

Saturday Morning

My bed was empty and cold again, but this time the sun was streaming in through the open windows and the smell of bacon was wafting in from the kitchen. Adam was a naturally early riser, plus he usually lived in a radically different time zone. Needless to say he was up early and accomplishing more before Calhoun Beach woke up than normal people completed all day. Certainly more than me. I got up early during the week for work because I had to. Otherwise I'd sleep until noon.

But he didn't mind. According to Adam, my desire to sleep-in was actually a good thing. It gave him time to do his thing before I got up—that way he didn't feel the need to go back to his place just to work on a few things since he was still working remotely on his laptop in the mornings. Nothing big, but stuff that needed his touch each day.

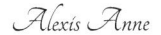

Our opposite schedules worked for me, too. While Adam was already passed out beside me, I was reading late into the night in peace and quiet. It gave us each the space we needed while also maximizing our time together.

The clock was ticking, at least that's how it felt. A week had already flown by and next Saturday would be our last day together. That weird feeling was back in the pit of my stomach—the one I knew was attached to my growing connection with Adam. It was stronger when he was gone. I missed him...like, seriously, deeply missed him when we weren't together. Fuck, even when he was up taking that call he was too far away. This was bad. So, so bad.

When I rolled over to get up, I found a steaming cup of coffee on the nightstand with a note, "*Good morning. I told you I could fuck you and bring you coffee without ruining your life. Mission accomplished.*"

For some stupid reason, that little hand-written card made heat pool between my legs so hard and fast I had to squeeze my thighs together to stem the sudden flow of desire.

Coffee. I needed coffee before I jumped Adam's bones.

I kept adjusting while I drank in an attempt to find a position that didn't turn me on even more, but the damage was already done. I was horny and every move only made me hornier. So I sucked down what I could and swung my legs out of bed on a mission to seduce my breakfast chef.

"Good morning, Gorgeous," he murmured without looking up from the sink. He was dressed in boxers and nothing else. They hung low on his hips revealing the very top of his short happy trail.

I bit my lip as I tried to pry my eyes away from my prize. "Good morning. Thanks for the coffee."

He looked up and grinned. "I keep my promises. Bacon is ready. Would you prefer waffles or omelets?"

I slid behind him and pressed my t-shirt covered breasts to his bare back as I reached around to the bacon on the counter. "Or you could just eat me." Let's face it—I was never going to be subtle. Not where Adam was concerned.

He froze with a wet strawberry in one hand and his other on the faucet. He shuddered ever so slightly before setting the strawberry down and turning to face me. His eyes were dark and intense as he put his hands on my hips and picked me up, placing me on the countertop. "You make very dangerous suggestions early in the morning."

"We're on sex-cation. Danger is my middle name."

That got a grin and an eyebrow pop. "I'll compromise. I'll give you a little of what you want while I make you breakfast. Deal?" He slid his hand over my hip and down between my legs, massaging lightly in a slow circle.

"Deal," I gasped as my hips bucked forward, looking for more friction.

But his other hand came down and held me in

place. "Oh no you don't. My kitchen, my rules. You want what I got?"

I nodded quickly as I began to throb for more. I hated when he made me wait...but only because of how much I loved it.

"Good. Now, waffles or omelets?"

His question brought me temporarily back to reality. "Wait, what? I don't have a waffle iron-thingy." I paused while I actually gave it some serious thought. Did Allison have one? No, I definitely didn't remember her ever making me waffles.

Adam grinned and stepped over to the large storage container he'd brought with him last night. "I came armed to cook for you this weekend. I assumed, rightly so, that you wouldn't have anything useful. Seriously, how do you survive?"

I shrugged and inched a little closer to the edge of the counter while I waited patiently for Adam to arrange his ingredients and tools. Kitchen things weren't called tools, were they? Instruments? What the hell were they called?

"What are you thinking so hard about over there?" Adam asked as he mixed the batter.

"You'll laugh." I tried to wave him off but, dang it, I really couldn't think of the word. Tools just sounded so appropriate.

He cocked his head with curiosity and walked over to me with the bowl. "Tell me and I'll reward you."

He was training me to respond to incentives. The moment he said 'reward' my whole body lit up in anticipation. "I'm not sure it's worth it." Admitting I didn't know the proper name for kitchen tools in exchange for foreplay was a close call.

He paused, eyes fixed on me, as he attempted to assess my latest vague reply. Then his eyes lit up and he grinned, pulling one side of his lips up in a drop-dead sexy way. I wanted to kiss the corner of those lips but he was too far away. Adam set the bowl down and dipped a finger in the batter as his other arm wrapped around my waist, pulling my hips against his and tipping me back so that I had no control. "I need a taste tester," his voice was deep and husky, the way it always sounded when he was very, very turned-on. "Open."

I immediately complied, like a puppet on a string. He slid the battered finger into my mouth while pressing his erection between by legs. It felt so good and I groaned as I closed my lips around his finger and licked the batter.

It was sweet and Adam's finger was warm. The combination of sensations made me want more. I sucked harder and closed my eyes as we ground against each other. I slid my palms up the ripples of his muscles and wrapped my arms around his neck, but he shook his head and pulled back, waggling his damp finger at me. "No more until you tell me what you were thinking about."

He immediately turned back to his batter and checked the temperature on the waffle iron, ignoring me completely.

How did he do that? How did he simply walk away

from me when I was so ready to have him inside me? It was like a super power. One I most certainly did *not* possess.

I grabbed another piece of bacon, crossed my legs on the countertop, and sighed. "I was trying to think of a word."

"A word? You probably just need more coffee."

Oh, if only it were that easy. But I knew coffee wasn't my problem, it was a distinct lack of experience where the kitchen was concerned. "No, it's a simple word. That's why I didn't want to tell you."

He poured the batter and closed the iron before leaning against the counter and crossing his arms over his chest. "Just ask me. I won't laugh and you shouldn't feel silly. Everyone forgets simple words sometimes. It is not that big of a deal. Especially before breakfast."

He was sexy and adorable cooking for me with barely a lick of clothing on his gorgeous body. God, I wanted him inside me. I grabbed the tool on the counter beside me. If asking got me fantastic breakfast sex, then so be it. "This. What are these things called?"

Adam shrugged. "They have a lot of names. Spatula, flipper—"

"—no. *All of them*. What are kitchen tools called?"

He paused with the most confused look on his handsome face and then realization dawned on him. "Oh... *utensils*. They're called utensils."

I squeezed my eyes shut. Of course that's what they were called. Now that he said it, the word sounded so completely ordinary. Well, for normal people, anyway. Sometimes being around Adam reminded me how totally not-normal I was. It left me feeling unsure of myself. My normal safety nets were gone and the things I usually did (like keeping people out of my life) didn't work. He wasn't doing it on purpose. It was quite the opposite—Adam was simply being himself.

He walked back across the kitchen to stand in front of me with a weird look in his eyes. I wasn't sure what the look was, but I had a feeling it landed somewhere in the neighborhood of pity and wonder. Adam had acted differently around me ever since my little admission about my past. Not bad, but a little more cautious. He hadn't asked any more questions or necessarily treated me any differently, but in little things like this, there was a different tone to his reactions. They were softer and deeper. It made me feel vulnerable and safe all at the same time.

Adam reached down into the sink and pulled another strawberry out of the strainer. He dipped it into a bowl of sugar and smiled as he moved my legs back down from their crossed position. "You seemed to like the batter, how about the strawberries?"

I'd never understood the attraction behind feeding someone else as a form of foreplay, but the way Adam was holding food out for me to take, with that dark glint in his eyes and rasp to his voice, I realized there were ways it could be very, very sexy.

I opened my lips, but he held it just out of my reach while he moved his hands up my thighs and under my panties. By the stupid grin on his face, I could tell Adam was very happy with my state of arousal.

He dipped his finger inside me and I moaned. The invasion was so very welcome. It was good to finally have something inside me, pushing back against all the need swelling between my legs. He pressed a second finger inside and I tilted my head back and gasped, unable to catch my breath. That was when I finally tasted the sugar on my tongue. Adam delicately rested the strawberry against my lips. His fingers pressed inside as I ate, sucking the juice and licking the sugar. His palm pressed against my clit and rubbed a slow, inconsistent circle, not that I could pay attention to any of it. My mind was torn between the strawberry and the way his fingers were making me feel: hot and bothered and ready to rip those boxers off his body and screw breakfast. The waffles could burn for all I cared.

I bucked against his palm and thrust my breasts up against the soft cotton of my t-shirt. There was just enough resistance to make my nipples feel good. I was ready to grab for Adam and pull his cock inside me, more than happy to have sex on my counter or in my sink—however we ended up, I didn't care—when the buzzer on the waffle iron went off.

Adam withdrew his fingers and the strawberry with a wicked grin. "Breakfast."

I wasn't sure if I was going to reward him or punish him for teasing me like that. Either way, I was going to get my orgasm.

Chapter 14

"Are you sure you're ready for this?" I asked. It was my turn to be evil. I was holding my box...well, my main box anyway. My *favorite* toys.

"I've been ready since you mentioned them." He reached out and I pulled it away.

"Oh no. I need to hear promises first."

"Promises?"

"Promises. Opening a woman's box is like opening her diary. I need to know you can handle the knowledge you are about to get."

"Oh, I can handle it. Trust me."

I rolled my eyes. I had no doubt he could 'handle' whatever wild things he imagined I had hidden in my box of fun. The question wasn't whether I was going to shock him—it was whether I could trust him to keep his shit together. "Sometimes men get a little too excited when they see toys to play with, Adam."

He arched an eyebrow and folded his arms over his chest. "And what have I ever done that would make you think I would lose it now? I think I've done an excellent job of demonstrating how much restraint I have in me." He took the box out of my hands and set it on the bed, all without taking his gorgeous eyes off of me. "I just want to have some fun. With you."

"It's all fun and games until someone gets hurt."

"Elizabeth."

I kissed him lightly on the lips. It was fun to play back. "Yes?"

"Open the box."

"You know I have more than one, right?"

He stopped breathing. The shadow of control was wavering. "Is that right?"

"Mmmm," I nodded. "I *might* show you the other one. We'll see how this goes."

He shook his head. "And why would you keep some of them from me?"

This was where I knew I had the advantage. The other night at dinner I'd offered to continue our friendly arrangement via video. "For the future. I've gotta keep some tricks up my sleeve for the video sex we're gonna have."

He perked up at that. "Oh, you don't need any tricks for that, I'm still excited you agreed to it at all." He pulled me against him and kissed me. "Toys are fun, but I don't need something new every night to keep my interest."

"Just the same," I kissed him back, "I like keeping some things to myself. One step at a time...isn't that what you keep telling me?"

He groaned and stepped back. "Using my own words against me. Evil."

I shrugged and flipped the top off my little black box of toys. "Evil or smart. It's a fine line. Now, are you ready?"

He made a noise in the back of his throat as he peered inside. He ran his fingers over the assortment I considered my 'go-to' toys for normal play. The other box I still had hidden was for more uninhibited adventures. "This is so hot and kinky..." he whispered it as if saying it any louder would cause him pain.

"Kinky?" I sputtered. For some reason I was surprised by his choice of words. "This isn't kinky. It's totally normal stuff."

He raised an eyebrow.

"It is! You're looking at vibrators and dildos, not whips and spreader bars...Jeez."

He pushed the box aside and sat down on the bed with his legs on either side of me as I stood in front of him. He was doing it again, putting me in control when I acted uncertain. It was subtle, but I noticed the way he tended to move into non-threatening positions—like having me stand above him. It was simple but effective body language: *you're in control and I'm just here to please you.*

"You misunderstand me. I find it kinky and very sexy that you know what you like and aren't afraid of it. Having a box of toys that are precisely what turns you on? That is so fucking hot, Elizabeth."

Ok, so maybe we were pulling vocabulary from two

different dictionaries, but I understood what he meant. "I'm glad you like it."

He groaned in the back of his throat and tugged on my arm. I turned and sat on one of his legs, leaning into his shoulder. Adam fished inside the box and pulled out a vibrator. "Which one is your favorite?"

"I should give you the full tour."

"Unlike your apartment."

I laughed, "Hey, *Mr. Genius*, you figured that out. I'm sure you could figure this out, too." I leaned forward and opened my nightstand drawer, pulling out my trusty bag. "My favorites are in here. There are three stages to the Elizabeth sex toy system."

"Three?" he wrapped his arm around my waist a little tighter.

"Mmm... Stage One is the bag in my drawer." I pulled out my favorite dildo—the one I'd fantasized with before Adam and I actually had sex—a small bottle of lube, and a small vibrator. "These are the basics I prefer for day-to-day needs."

Adam waggled the dildo in the air before squeezing it. "Very lifelike."

My body ached just at the thought of having either the fake cock, or Adam's real one, inside me. "It's actually a lot like you."

His eyebrows shot up and his lips turned down. Then he held the toy down between his legs and grunted. "You're right." He studied it for another moment before setting it on top of the bag and picking up the white vibrator. "This is your favorite?"

"Yes and no. It's my favorite battery operated one. My favorite is under the bed."

A slow smile played on his lips and Adam reached under my bed, searching for a moment before he held up my 'back massager'. "The Hitachi. Nice choice, Filler."

"It does the job well. There's a reason it's the preferred vibrator of women everywhere."

He carefully set it on the nightstand—not back under the bed—then arranged the other vibrator, lube, and dildo beside it.

I turned back to my box. "But sometimes I'm in the mood for fun." While my bag usually did the trick, I occasionally wanted a lot more than a few basic toys could give me. I started laying out the items one by one, explaining a little as I went. "The glass dildo is especially nice for playing with temperature. This little one vibrates so it can be fun to turn on and just leave in there while I play with other things. I like—"

Adam reached into the box and pulled out two silver balls on a black string. "You have a set of *the balls*?"

I shrugged. A whim purchase to see what the fuss was all about. "They don't exactly work as advertised, so to speak. I'm not going to be walking around with those inside me. But I have been known to write a paper or two with them in."

Adam's eyes widened and he swallowed hard as he lowered them back into the box. "I am going to picture you with those every time you mention working from now on."

I rolled my eyes.

He picked up another toy. "You like this?" His voice notched up with excited curiosity. For some reason I'd never understand, the ass was like holy territory to guys.

I took the rather small butt plug from his hands and shook my head. "Occasionally I like a little extra. That's all." Seriously, not that big of a deal.

He grinned. "I like that you like a little extra. *That's all.*"

I raised an eyebrow and looked him sternly in the eye. "*That* is one area where you better watch yourself buddy. I'm very moody when it comes to the back door. You make the wrong move and you'll wind up with your balls in a vice."

He wiped the grin off his face and nodded. "Got it."

Good.

Then his eyes lit up all over again. "What is this?"

Ah, one of my favorite expensive purchases. A rare and unusual beauty. It was essentially two suction cups attached to an LED control. A shiver ran over my skin just thinking about using it. "It is a 'spinning nipple stimulator'." I made air quotes as I recited the official title from memory.

"It feels good?" his voice dropped an octave into the deep, seductive territory.

I closed my eyes and nodded slowly. It was the next best thing to having Adam's mouth on my breasts.

Adam groaned.

When I opened my eyes he was staring me down like he was going to fuck me senseless. "You want to try them out?"

He nodded quickly, running his fingers under my t-shirt. I held up my arms and let him pull it over my head. "You want a go at them first?" Adam liked teasing me so damn much that I was planning on giving him a taste of his own medicine. A little bit of nipple in his mouth and then nothing more for him.

His tongue was warm and wet as it swirled over my nipples and I arched back, letting my head fall and chest rise further into his mouth. I let him play until I felt his erection rising and his hips starting to move. Then I pushed his head away and licked the edges of the silicone suction cups before placing them where his mouth had just been. It was time for him to watch but not touch.

"Can I control it?" He asked, picking up the control panel.

"Nope." I swatted his hand away. He frowned but didn't say anything else as I adjusted the cups and flipped them on. Even though I knew what to expect, it still took my breath away when the tiny little fingers started swirling around my erect nipples.

Adam's hands tightened on my waist and thigh. My sex began to throb and my hips began to flex automatically as my arousal kicked up several notches. I was already very wet and imagining all the fun things I could do to draw the pleasure out for as long as possible.

Today seemed like a good day for a nice, *long* round of play.

"You like to tease yourself, don't you?"

I nodded, my eyes mostly closed. "Sometimes."

"It's fun, isn't it?"

I nodded again.

"That's why *I* like to tease you. You become someone else when I distract you with sex." His breathing was very deep. His voice was a rasp. "You let go of everything you carry on your shoulders and just relax. You become *you*."

I shuddered as his whispered words washed over me. Adam saw a side of me no one else had ever seen before—even me. That was why I liked the way Adam made me feel. When we were together, everything disappeared except the two of us. I craved that feeling of freedom I couldn't seem to find anywhere else.

"Want to see how much that dildo is like you?"

He swallowed hard and kissed the side of my neck. His eyelids were low and his eyes were dark with lust. "Yes," he breathed against my skin as he fumbled on the nightstand. He inched backward on the bed until I could sit sideways between his thighs. I leaned back so that the small of my back rested against his thigh and my shoulders rested on the bed. Adam slid my panties down my legs and flung them across the room. I let my knees fall open, giving him full access to my body. "You are so wet," he groaned. Then he placed the tip of the toy at the entrance to my sex.

"What are you waiting for?" I whispered. I was

more than ready.

He shook his head. "Just taking my time." Then he pressed it inside me. I was so wet it slid in several inches before it stopped. My core throbbed and I adjusted my hips. The swirling on my nipples was driving me higher and higher into my cloud of pleasure and the fake cock between my legs anchored me to Adam. I closed my eyes and got lost in the pleasure.

Adam worked me. Slow and hard. Fast and soft. I moaned and arched, his erection digging into my side. The toy filled me so completely, just like Adam's cock, that with each stroke my body quaked, as if it were looking for somewhere else to go.

His breathing was heavy. It was erotic to hear Adam struggle with me in his arms. It made me wilder and gave me more freedom to enjoy myself. As the fake cock slid inside me, my hips rocked, my breath caught. The pleasure shooting through me in little sharp spikes. The spinning on my nipples driving me higher and wetter with every passing second. I'd never had this much fun with my box before. Sure I'd tried this combination of toys before, but it was completely different with Adam in control.

And Adam was clearly enjoying himself as well. His erection was hot against my skin as it pressed into my side. I reached out and wrapped my hand around his cock, running up his hard length and my thumb lightly over his head. There was a pool of liquid arousal sitting on the tip. Adam was just as turned-on as I was and judging by the twitch of his cock in my hand, he was fighting the urge to be inside me.

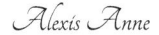

"Fucking hell," he groaned and shuddered as I ran my palm up and down his shaft. "I'm gonna come if you keep doing that."

Good. That was precisely what I wanted to hear. "I know. Let's come together." I was riding a line between enjoying the pleasure I was receiving and needing the climax rumbling just underneath my surface.

"Alright then." A moment later the air filled with the sound of vibrations from the Hitachi as he pressed it to the flat end of the fake cock.

I moaned at the change in sensations as the vibrations ran up the silicone deep inside me. Somehow I got wetter and spots filled my darkened vision. The pleasure was downright irresistible and I opened myself up to all of it. The quicker I pumped my fist over the head of Adam's cock, the more he grunted and flexed his hips.

My climax began to climb and I started calling out in anticipation. There was so much happening to my body there was no way I could hold my noises in—not that I wanted to. Adam's cock pulsed in my hand and a moment later there was a warm spray of liquid over my arm and stomach as Adam came. He faltered, but only for a moment, letting the Hitachi drop away before catching himself.

Adam's orgasm spurred on my own. I came hard, reaching up to release the suction cups on my nipples so I could enjoy the feeling of my body contracting around the large toy buried and vibrating inside me without distraction. My inner muscles clenched over and over, riding a seemingly endless wave of cock, when Adam ran his palm lightly over my clit.

"Oh fuck..." I gasped as a second, just as powerful orgasm came out of nowhere. I rode the extended wave of pulsing, convulsing pleasure, rolling my hips and shouting anything and everything that popped into my wonderfully blank mind until there wasn't a drop of energy left in me. Every cell in my body had been replaced with a newer, brighter, lighter one—I was sure of it.

"Was that a two-fer?" Adam asked. He was still panting as he snapped off the Hitachi and threw it onto the bed.

I nodded because there was no way I could possibly speak. Two glorious orgasms, one right on top of the other. I hadn't had one of those in a few months. I didn't think it was possible, but adding toys to sex with Adam actually made things better.

Chapter 15

Saturday Night

"Right this way," I said, swinging the door open for the cable guy. "The television is in front of the window and the outlet is on that wall beside it."

He looked dubiously at my hack-job of a setup. "This is going to look terrible. There will be cables everywhere."

"It isn't supposed to look pretty. It's only for a couple of weeks."

The cable guy shrugged his shoulders and dropped his little tool bag on the coffee table. "Whatever you want. Name's Jim, by the way." He was my height, a little soft around the middle and scruffy on the chin, but he had nice eyes and a crooked smile that seemed to match his personality: a little quirky.

"Do you need anything else from me?"

Jim looked around the TV I'd pulled out of Allison's bedroom. "Nope, I've got it from here. I'll be in and out a couple of times and then you should be good to go."

"Perfect!" I said just before I slid back into the bedroom. Adam and I were about to head out to dinner and then a blues club where Travis was playing. I was already dressed in my favorite jeans and a skimpy black tank top. All I needed was to finish touching up my makeup and pick my jewelry.

"Hey Gorgeous, I was wondering where you wandered off to." Adam stepped out of the shower. His skin was glistening and I had to stop to take in the view. No red-blooded woman could possibly keep themselves from staring at the sight of Adam naked and damp. It was just too good to pass up.

He shook his head. "You know I have a face, right?"

"And it is just as handsome, but your body will be covered in a few minutes and I really want to enjoy what I can, when I can." I tilted my head to the side.

"It's like I'm just a piece of meat..."

A delicious piece of meat. "Are you unhappy with the way I use you?"

"Not in the slightest."

"Good. I have a surprise for you. Finish getting dressed."

He froze, watching me in the mirror as I applied my mascara. I think the very fact I had a surprise for him at all was the biggest surprise. "Well, I better get dressed then." He quietly tucked his towel around his hips and disappeared into the bedroom.

In a way I was nervous. It wasn't much of a surprise, at least it didn't feel that way, but I'd never given a guy something. So to me, this was a pretty big damn deal. I just felt like a weekend with Adam during football season, which was so obviously important to him, would be a lot more pleasant with cable.

I ran some stain over my lips, tucked my favorite gloss into my back pocket next to my ID and credit card, pinned some of my hair back, and took stock of myself in the mirror.

It was a simple ensemble—comfortable and sexy at the same time. It would seduce Adam in all the right ways while giving me the freedom to get good and sweaty while we danced in a packed and smoky club. For good measure I grabbed a black hair tie and slid it over my wrist just before I left the bathroom.

Adam was sitting on the bed waiting for me. His damp hair was casually brushed back—just the right amount of messy to look good without crossing the line into ridiculous. I wanted to run my fingers through it.

"So what is this surprise?" He was also dressed in jeans with a sexy navy blue tee-shirt that hugged him in all the right places.

"Come with me," I said, crooking my finger.

Jim was standing in front of the TV flipping through the channels. "You're all set, ma'am. I just need your signature and I'll be out of your hair."

Adam stood there with his jaw open.

"Close your mouth," I chuckled as I scrawled my

signature.

"Is this what I think it is?"

Jim smiled and grabbed his bag. "Enjoy the game."

"Did you—" he sputtered as he moved around the couch and picked up the remote. "Oh my god, you did!"

I closed the door. "You said every home needs a football TV."

He whooped and fist pumped. "I get to watch the game *and* see you naked. This is the best present I've ever gotten. Ever."

Well, that was a little bit more impressive than I was going for... "It's temporary."

He shrugged his shoulders and flipped on ESPN before tossing the remote. "Don't fucking care! I can't believe you did this. Did you buy a TV just for me? Because you really didn't need to get a TV this big."

"It's Allison's."

"Holy shit. What is this fifty, sixty inches? She must have a bigger room."

I shook my head. "Nope, she just really loves movies. The more action the better."

"I like her." His voice was obviously joking, but something inside me hated that tiny, little, innocent statement.

"C'mon Romeo, you can seduce my roommate on your next vacation. I need dinner."

Before I knew what was happening my back was to the wall and Adam was kissing me. His body braced mine against the wall and one hand cupped my cheek, holding my lips to his. "I will not be seducing anyone but you." His sincerity was shocking. "Thank you for the surprise. That was..." his voice trailed off and he blinked several times, like he was forcing himself to stop talking, before he kissed me again.

There was something about his confidence that always affected me. It was like I fed off of it. Adam's decisive nature somehow made me feel stronger. My apprehension about the 'gift' melted away along with my worries about the future. I liked Adam and I was damn well going to enjoy my time with him. Because I could, damnit.

"Dinner. Let's go to dinner," he murmured against my lips.

I nodded quickly. He nodded back and took my hand in his as nervous little butterflies took flight in my belly. It happened every time he took my hand. I stared at my fingers entwined in his as I trailed behind him to the door. I loved the way he held onto my hand every chance he got. But it terrified me how much I loved it.

"Mitch is on tonight. Want to sit at the bar?"

"Sounds good," I replied, turning the key.

He didn't move when I turned around. Instead he stood there, looking down at me with the most peculiar expression on his face. "Thanks for the cable and television," he repeated before kissing me very, very softly. "And thanks for trusting me to play with your toys."

I grinned against his lips. "Who knew so many of them were even better in the shower?"

"You're welcome."

"I'm starving."

"Then let's eat."

Dinner was quick and Mitch was delighted to serve us, making all sorts of comments about how a week earlier we didn't even know each other. He was right. It was amazing how fast Adam had woven himself so firmly into my life. A week ago seemed like a lifetime ago.

And in another week he'd be getting ready to leave. A blip on the timeline of my life. It was funny how someone could make such a significant impact in such a short time, but it was true. When I thought back on my life I realized all the most important people had done the same thing, whether they stayed in my life or disappeared, they made an immediate and life-altering impact.

Adam was no different. I didn't know what it was going to mean down the road, but my life would never be the same now that he'd stepped into it.

"So Travis sings the blues as well as rock?"

Adam shrugged. "I guess so. He sings everything as far as I know. His records have all been pretty much straight rock, but when he plays live he's all over the place."

I could still remember the raspy vibration of his voice. It stuck with me, which was saying a lot for his sound. "I can't wait to hear him again. It should be a fun night...plus I get to see you dance." I was grinning from the inside out. Even if Adam was a terrible dancer (which I simply could not imagine) it would be fun to grind against him.

He let out an exasperated sound. "Seeing you dance is the whole reason we're going out. Talk about foreplay."

A light bulb went off in my head. I finally understood Adam and all his super-human restraint. I had it all wrong. It wasn't self-control, it was self-torture. Foreplay. *Teasing* he was doing to himself. It was no wonder he was so fantastic at drawing out my pleasure, he was a master at his own game. Adam craved the exquisite torture of foreplay and the drawn-out reward of climax.

I finally had his number.

And just like that, I had a whole new level of control.

Chapter 16

"Knob Creek on the rocks with a splash of tonic, please." I leaned against the heavily lacquered bar at the Midnight Blues Club on 7th Street. It was everything I expected from the dark woodwork to the plush black leather seating and the vintage bar (with bartenders dressed to match).

Jazz music was pumping through the speakers as people started to trickle into the club. A seating area toward the front was already filled with cigar smokers, but the dance floor was nearly empty. Only one other couple was slowly warming up as they lazily swirled around the floor.

"And some water," Adam added as he tapped his credit card.

The bartender added two bottles to the drinks he'd just placed in front of us. While Adam paid, I wandered closer to the dance floor on a mission to find us a quiet spot to claim. Booths were setup all around the dance floor, rising up two levels, so you could watch the band

and dancers without obstruction. I picked a table on the second level and flicked the sign around to let others know it was taken.

"Nice spot."

"I like it," I agreed as I ran my hands over the seat.

Adam held up his drink, "To a fun day and an equally fun night."

I clinked his glass and took a drink. Oh, yes. Tonight was going to be fun. I liked the vibe of the club and couldn't wait for Travis to take the stage. "So...how's work? They don't miss you when you're gone on these trips?"

Adam smiled. "Wow. Talk about progress. You actually asked a question."

I punched him in the arm. "Stop it or I'll take my question back."

"Oh no you don't." He slid over and tucked me into his side.

I relaxed against his shoulder and drank in his spicy scent. The one that made him wonder why I was smelling him all the time.

"I usually take my trips between big project stages, so there isn't much going on while I'm gone."

I thought about his mysterious phone call. "You like what you do?"

He chuckled low in his chest like I'd just asked the craziest thing in the world. "I get to play with, and make, the most wicked cool shit in the world. Uh, yeah...I like what I do."

Well now I was more confused than ever. I should

just ask him about the call... But no matter how I formed the question in my head, it came out sounding like I was asking him to stay in Calhoun Beach with me. *Is there any reason you'd leave your job?* Yeah, he wasn't going to hear it the way I meant it.

"I guess playing with cars for a living is a dream come true." I tried instead.

"Pretty much. Sometimes the length between conception and production is so long it hurts. Some things will never be practical enough to see in the real world. Every once in a while I feel like I live in a fantasy world instead of the real one."

"Now *that* I understand."

He kissed my temple. "Can I ask you a question?"

I shrugged, "Sure." There really wasn't a point to fighting Adam's questions.

"You like what you do?"

I laughed. He was so unexpected sometimes. "Yeah. I love it. I never fit in anywhere until I walked onto campus in college. All of a sudden I felt like I'd found home."

"Home is an important place to find."

Yes it was. "You said New York used to be home but it wasn't anymore. Have you found another?"

My question seemed to throw him. His muscles stiffened just a little and his breathing sped up. "I'm not sure." He adjusted, sitting up straighter. "I've had a lot of things change recently. It's made me rethink things."

"What kind of things?"

He cleared his throat. "Before I answer, can I ask you something else?"

I nodded even though I knew I was going to hate whatever he was about to ask. "How did you handle it all?"

"All of what?" There were several ways I could take his question and I wasn't about to start talking about anything I didn't need to.

Adam studied his glass. "During the stuff with the courts and afterward...who did you turn to? How did you handle all that chaos?"

Oh. All of that. Part of me seized up, wanting to hide and defend myself from the invasion of my privacy. But part of me desperately wanted to open up to Adam. I'd been holding so much in, dealing with it all on my own. It was relieving to have someone who honestly seemed to care. I knew how rare this was. In ten years the only other person I had let completely into my life was Allison. If I'd finally found someone else I thought I could trust then I needed to trust him.

I ran my fingers over his. "I'd already spent most of my life alone, Adam. Cybil and Roger were absentee parents at best. I always had Lily, but she was a kid. It was my Uncle Oliver that stepped in. I lived with him until I started college. He's who I still call when I need an adult in my life."

Adam nodded slowly and squeezed my fingers. "I'm glad you have someone."

I realized Adam hadn't gone and dug up all the old articles on me. He could have easily found most of this out on his own if he'd wanted to. But he hadn't. He'd come to me with his questions. I ran my hand along the stubble on his jaw and kissed him.

It surprised him. His eyes widened at first, but then closed as he returned my kiss, threading his fingers up into my hair and running his tongue along my lips. Whatever preconceived notions I had about people, I had to throw out that book when it came to Adam. He was different in every possible way. Every way that mattered to me.

The microphone popped and a guitar was strummed. Travis's gravelly voice filled the room with a quiet chord. "Let's dance," Adam murmured against my lips.

I nodded. I didn't care about my past or his future. Questions didn't matter. All I cared about right then was being with Adam. I wanted to feel his body moving against mine as we got lost in the music.

Adam, as expected, was a natural dancer. He held me firmly against him so that all I had to do was follow his lead. I rested my head against his chest and my hand on his shoulder, feeling the movement of his muscles. His breathing was steady and it kept me grounded. I loved the sound of the air in his lungs. It was soothing.

Travis and his band made the sexiest music. It was almost impossible to avoid swaying my hips, mimicking the seductive moves of the other couples on the floor. We were sweaty and hot after more songs than I could count. "I need a drink," I sighed, turning from the floor with Adam's fingers intertwined with mine.

He sidled up behind me with his arm around my waist and his lips on my bare shoulder as we walked back up to our booth, pressed together. "Fantastic foreplay," he murmured.

"Mmmm..." I agreed. Dancing with Adam was like one long night of fantastic fucking. I slid into the booth and had my bottle of water at my lips before I settled into my spot.

That was when a man I didn't recognize came running up to our table. "Oh my god. Are you Elizabeth Lawrence?"

Every hair on my body stood on end. I didn't get recognized very often, but it did happen from time to time. Usually I could shake it off, convince them that I merely *looked* like the actress from the famous Hope-Lawrence family. But if he could recognize me, sweaty and glued to Adam on a dance floor, my guess was that this man was no passing fan.

Adam put his arm around my shoulder. His jaw flexed and his position was clearly protective as he settled closer to me. I placed a hand on his thigh, connecting us, and took a deep breath. "How can I help you?" I didn't think I could play off the mistaken identity card tonight. This fan seemed too sure.

"Oh my god. You are. Aren't you? Can I take a picture with you? My sister is never going to believe this. Or my wife. We loved *One More to Love*. I can't believe there wasn't a second season."

I dug my nails into Adam's leg. "Thank you." I did

not want to take a picture with this fan, but I also didn't want to cause a scene.

One More to Love had been the final straw before I sued my parents. I didn't want to do the show and I didn't want to be an actress, but they'd forced me. The official story was that the show was canned for low ratings, despite a rather intense cult following of teens and pre-teens.

The *real* story was, of course, that I had quietly quit the show and was getting ready to sue my parents. But all of that had always stayed nicely under-wrap. Funny how certain things never made their way into the spotlight while others were dragged out and presented.

And by funny, I meant ridiculous.

"We're trying to have a date here..." Adam spoke up and I realized I had two problems on my hands. A fan I didn't want rehashing a life I hated, and a lover who wanted to protect me at any cost, despite not having all the details.

The man looked stunned to realize there was anyone else at the table. Apparently he only had eyes for me. "Dude. I'm just asking for a picture."

"And I'm just asking you to let us have a nice night alone."

The fan turned his eyes back to me, dismissing Adam. "Please? Just a quick pic?"

It was never a quick picture. Tomorrow morning it would be on the internet. If I was lucky it would pass around a few social media accounts and die as old news. But I wasn't much for luck. "I'm sorry but I'm no longer an actress and I don't pose for pictures anymore. But," I held up my finger when his face fell, "I would be happy to give you an autograph."

A tentative smile spread across his face along with a slight nod. "Alright. That would be fantastic. Thank you."

I'd found that if I offered something it usually appeased people. My old signature scrawled across a cocktail napkin wasn't nearly as interesting to the internet as my photograph. A sighting of the missing and estranged Lawrence daughter? Now that was news. But my autograph? Not so much.

I flagged down the cocktail waitress and asked for a pen. The girl was so young she probably had no idea who I was as long as my crazed fan didn't mention my mother. Everyone between the ages of fourteen and forty knew Cybil. "What's your name?"

"Kevin." He leaned on the table, a little too close for my comfort, or for Adam's. He tightened his arm around my shoulder and I could practically hear him growling.

"Are you visiting Calhoun Beach?" I asked politely as I wrote his name at the top of the napkin.

"Yeah. Guys golfing weekend."

I paused at the end of 'Elizabeth' and repeated *Lawrence* to myself three times before I put the tip of the pen against the white of the napkin. It had been so long since I'd signed that name...

"Calhoun Beach has some great courses. I'm sure

you'll have fun." Adam's voice was a strange combination of blunt and polite. I had a feeling Kevin was about thirty seconds away from meeting Adam's fist.

"Here you go, Kevin. Enjoy your trip. Now if you don't mind, I really am on a date."

Kevin took the napkin and beamed a smile at me. "I'm so sorry for interrupting. Thank you so much."

The moment he was out of earshot Adam grumbled, "I'm so sorry I didn't kick your stupid ass."

The waitress giggled as she took back her pen. "I guess that means I shouldn't ask for your autograph, too?"

I cocked an eyebrow. "Are you a fan of washed-up pseudo-celebrities?"

She shook her head and shrugged her shoulders. "I'd answer if I knew what that meant. Can I get you two anything else while I'm here?"

"No," Adam answered so abruptly it surprised me. "We're leaving now."

"But—"

"What? You want to hang out and see if the entire bar wanders over for an autograph?" His eyes were dark and hooded. Protective. That was when I realized every muscle in his body was tensed. His shoulders were bunched and there was a twitch in his forearm that was equal parts frightening and sexy. While I was annoyed and feeling more than a little vulnerable, Adam had become downright pissed off. Or maybe it was worried.

"We're leaving." Adam slid out of the booth and

held out his hand. He wrapped his much larger fingers around mine like they might somehow slip away. He seemed more than a little bit worried one enthusiastic fan was about to become many. Like we were moments away from being mobbed.

Even stranger, this didn't seem unusual to Adam. I got the sense he knew exactly what to do in situations like this. He was making the same defensive moves and taking the same preventative steps my bodyguard would have in the same situation. *Odd.*

As I stood up, Adam nodded at Travis who saluted him with a pic between his fingers. Then he started muscling his way through the crowd toward the door as fast as he could. Normally Adam was quiet and polite, but there was a passion that vibrated under his skin—and it was backed up by a powerful body. Adam was most definitely not the kind of guy I ever wanted to piss off. The quiet guys were often the most dangerous when they were provoked.

And the most mysterious. As I tucked myself into the safety of his back I wondered about all the things I'd been avoiding. I'd purposely sidestepped as much information as possible about his past. I was starting to regret that. He deserved more from me.

Unfortunately, Adam's instinct to get me out of there had been dead on. As we were about to step down from the bank of booths surrounding the dance floor, Kevin stumbled into me with his phone up in the air, the flash flickering over and over as he took an endless string of pictures. "C'mon! Just one…" he said as he leaned into me and grinned.

Adam was in front of me in a heartbeat. Kevin shrieked in pain as Adam wrestled the phone out of his hands, twisted his wrist, and pushed him to the floor. "The lady said no."

I didn't see where the phone slid off to. It was buried somewhere in the gathering crowd of onlookers. I crossed my fingers that none of his shots came out clear and ducked my head so that no other eager onlookers could get a full shot of my face.

I wanted to disappear into the shadows or melt into the floor and vanish. The old life I wanted to forget was colliding with the fantasy I had for my future. And they were obliterating each other.

The entire club came to a standstill, some watching us, others just unsure of what was happening. The music stopped and Travis leapt off the stage when he realized it was Adam causing the commotion.

"Adam?" I tried to reach for him but Travis got there first.

"Let's take this outside, ok?"

Adam ignored us both. Kevin was howling in pain and Adam wasn't letting up. His face was set and his pupils were dilated to the point his eyes nearly looked black.

"Adam? Let the man's hand go." Travis said slowly and clearly.

I stepped forward, my hair over one shoulder and my hand cupping my mouth, and touched Adam's arm. "Let's go."

His eyes locked onto mine and it took several heartbeats, but the fog of anger in his eyes began to clear. He finally released Kevin's wrist and to my relief, stalked silently outside, the crowd parting to let him through. I knew what possession and envy looked like. The look in Adam's eyes was neither of those things. I'd never seen a man defend someone he cared about in real life, but I knew instinctively that was what Adam had just done for me.

My ears rang with a high-pitched buzz as we stepped out into the quiet streets of Calhoun Beach. Adam didn't stop when we stepped outside. He kept moving down the sidewalk.

"What in the hell was that?" Travis barked at Adam.

He stopped and paced back up the sidewalk with his hands in his hair before letting out a frustrated growl.

This was all my fault. Somehow, this was all my fault. If I'd left Adam alone that night at the bar at Seychelles, or if I'd kept to my plan, we wouldn't have been in the club and none of this would have happened.

"What is going on?" Travis asked me after he gave up on Adam.

I started and stopped several times trying to figure out what Travis actually needed to know, if he needed to know anything. He stepped closer to me and lowered his voice. "I'm only asking because this isn't like him. Adam only gets physical when he has to. I've seen him punch, like, one guy ever."

What the hell was I turning Adam into? I was making this otherwise happy, mild-mannered, easy-going guy into someone else. This was what happened when I let people in. I infected them with the poison of my family. "He was just defending me," I finally answered.

"Well, then I'll go back in there and finish the job. If this was about you, I'll kick the dude's damn teeth in myself."

I reached out in a panic and stopped him. "No. *Please*. All this started because I'm trying to *avoid* a scene. I *can't* have a scene. *Legally*."

Travis looked at my hand on his arm and then back up at me with a raised eyebrow. "Ex-boyfriend?"

I shook my head and for some weird reason, I couldn't stop. I just kept shaking my head over and over. That was when I realized my hands were shaking and I didn't feel quite right.

"Oh shit. Sit. Sit right now or you're gonna pass out." Travis forcefully pushed down on my shoulder and then guided my head between my knees. "Adam, I'm gonna need you to pull it together, man."

The world was a little black along the edges of my vision and bright spots flashed all over the place. My vision twisted and tilted even though I knew full well I was sitting firmly on the edge of the sidewalk. I couldn't have a scene. As long as this stayed contained everything would be fine. The photos on Kevin's camera wouldn't come out and everyone would simply remember tonight for the brief moment one guy got mad at another guy.

"Fuck," Adam swore and I heard his heavy footfalls as he came back to my side, replacing Travis's hands on my back. "I'm sorry. I'm so fucking sorry, Elizabeth." Even though everything was fucked up and Adam was apologizing, I loved hearing my name on his lips. It made me feel a little bit better.

"You want a water?" Travis asked as he shuffled a few feet away.

I shook my head, my hair swaying back and forth in front of my face. Adam sighed and wrapped his arm around me, putting his head down on mine and holding me close. "You ok?" he whispered.

This time I nodded. "Just give me another second, ok?"

"Ok," he whispered back, then sat up. "I'm sorry we interrupted your set."

I heard Travis pacing and could imagine him and Adam having a silent conversation of facial expressions, probably the kind that looked like "what the fuck was that?" and "leave me the fuck alone".

"Feel better Elizabeth," Travis finally grumbled and left us on the sidewalk.

Adam rubbed my back for several seconds before brushing my hair back and leaning down to look me in the eye. "I just crossed a helluva lot of lines, didn't I?"

Were there any more lines when it came to Adam? I didn't think there were. I wasn't sure what happened in that club or what the consequences would actually be, but I knew I didn't want any more lines keeping

Adam and me apart.

"Take me home and make it up to me?"

His whole face softened like I'd just given him the perfect present on Christmas morning. "Can you walk or shall I carry you?"

Chapter 17

His hand caressed my shoulder, worshipping every inch of skin from my collarbone to my navel. My clothes were gone—I wasn't sure when or how or where. I was lost in a fog and had absolutely no sense of anything but Adam.

His tongue was soft and his lips were like fire as they traveled over my neck. Somewhere between my ear and my shoulder was a patch of sensitive skin that made me shiver in the most erotic way each time Adam's lips touched it. I felt it everywhere, from the hair on my head to the curl of my toes.

Adam made my toes curl.

That got me every time. My grandmother always told me to watch out for the man whose kisses made my toes curl. I thought it was ridiculous. Clearly she was spinning another of her yarns, an actress who could never quite let the fantasy world go. But she was right...Adam made my toes curl.

He was possessed and for once, I wasn't quite sure

what to do. Adam took the lead and I didn't want to interrupt whatever it was that was driving him. It felt important. "Lie back for me and *do not move.*"

He was only gone for a moment while he rolled on a condom, then he was back on top of me, his arms on either side of me and his lips kissing the tops of my breasts. His cock was nudging against me and my hips rocked.

"Are you ok?" he whispered against my skin.

"Yes."

He paused, his mouth near my ear, his body heavy on top of mine, and his cock throbbing between my thighs. He kept his head down but I could see that his eyes were closed. "I can't tell you enough how sorry I am that I went off like that." His voice was deep and rough.

It surprised me, the depth of his regret. Adam was visibly upset. "Adam," I murmured as I ran my hands up into his hair and turned his face to mine. "Don't you understand?"

He opened his beautiful eyes and stared at me. "No, I don't."

"No one's ever done that for me before." Adam had no idea what his overreaction to a ridiculous fan meant to me.

"Done what? Blatantly ignore your wishes?"

I shook my head slowly and angled my hips so that his cock slid into the wet entrance to my sex. I wanted him more than I'd ever wanted him before...but slowly. "You didn't ignore my wishes, you acted on instinct—

there's a difference. And that's not what I meant."

He sucked in a surprised breath as his cock slid deeper inside me. He wasn't moving, it was all me. My hips. My body. My arched back. I kissed the corner of his lips. "I've always had to take care of myself. I could have managed Kevin on my own...just like I have every other time, but I didn't have to."

My eyes rolled back in my head and a shudder rolled through me as Adam finally pushed back, his cock moving deeper, to the place where we met so perfectly. "No one's ever stepped in for you before?"

I shook my head slowly. "Not anyone who wasn't being paid." That was the raw truth. Whether it was sad or ridiculous was for someone else to figure out. All I knew was that it was my reality. To my family, paparazzi and scenes with overzealous fans were a good thing. To a lot of bystanders it was what I deserved. To a large number of people it was considered downright normal for a woman—especially a famous woman—to be accosted like that. After all, I probably asked for it.

Adam didn't reply, but the way his jaw flexed and his hand caressed my hair I could tell that he was overwhelmed by that piece of information.

It made me feel a lot more things I wasn't prepared to feel but enjoyed anyway. I'd picked up this man for a fling because of the way I responded to his body—and I loved every minute of the pleasure he'd given me since that first night. But what I was really enjoying was the way he made me *feel*—like I didn't have to keep compromising in order to be happy. There were more possibilities out there. There was more life to live. I didn't have to keep hiding or looking over my shoulder every time I found a little piece of happiness.

I realized that was what I'd been doing ever since I moved to Calhoun Beach. I was happy but was damn near terrified it was all about to be taken away from me. I was constantly looking over my shoulder, waiting for the dark clouds to appear on the horizon. Waiting for the pain that would overwhelm me when my taste of freedom was taken away.

I didn't know what was going to happen tomorrow or next week. I didn't know where I'd be in a year. But I finally understood that I had to stop living in fear. I was missing out on too much by letting the past rule my present.

And I was going to be in control of all of it. I pushed on Adam's shoulder and he grinned, rolling onto his back and sighing as I straddled him, sinking slowly back down onto his fantastically large dick. It was so deep from this angle that it almost hurt, but I didn't care. I wanted that amazing feeling I only got when I was completely full—and only Adam could give me that feeling.

I rode him slowly, enjoying each stroke of pleasure. Rising up until his head was just barely still inside me and waiting for the ache of emptiness to throb from deep inside, before I tilted my hips at just the right angle to ride straight down his cock with all the pressure on the underside of his shaft. When my body finally locked with his I stopped, savoring the feeling of my body expanding around his—of his body throbbing inside mine.

It may have driven some guys wild to have a woman stop moving with their cock buried inside, but not Adam. No, I knew how much he liked the slow torture. I knew he was groaning, but it was with pleasure, not frustration. He loved the tease. The heat of my body fed off of his. I was slick and wet the way only Adam could make me. The more I moved the louder our sounds became. The suck and smack of wet cock moving in and out of my drenched core.

I arched up, getting lost in the pleasure I was giving myself, thrusting my breasts up into the air and running my hands wildly through my own hair.

Adam groaned. "You are so fucking gorgeous." His hands gripped my hips, massaging my ass with his long fingers, before sliding up my stomach and around my breasts. Even for his long arms it was a stretch, so I fell forward, shoving my breasts in his face and waiting for the feel of his tongue on my nipples.

He took his sweet damn time, massaging my breasts and then kissing the sides. "More," I gasped.

I felt his smile against my skin a split second before his mouth closed over my nipple and the world went white as an orgasm roared through me from out of nowhere. I'd been feeling good but I hadn't expected to come that fast.

I shivered as the waves of pleasure moved from my core to my toes, curling them and forcing my thighs together. I gripped his hair and tugged as he ran his teeth over my nipple before letting it spring free. He grabbed my hips and pumped into me several times, grunting and groaning before I felt the telltale kick of his cock as he was overwhelmed by his own orgasm.

I rode him until I was sure we were both thoroughly satisfied, then collapsed against the safety of his broad, sweaty chest, and simply enjoyed the way it felt to be happy.

Genuinely happy.

Chapter 18

Sunday, early morning

Adam was glued to the Formula 1 race on the Football TV. He'd been planted on the couch with his coffee since before I was awake. At some point I stumbled out of the bedroom and onto the couch with a giant blanket and had been happily sitting there, sipping my coffee, while Adam absentmindedly rubbed my feet ever since. I'd decided sometime between my orgasm and falling asleep on Adam's chest, I was going to forget the incident at the club ever happened. Maybe if I pretended it didn't exist, it would go away.

"I guess you're really into racing?" I finally asked after he yelled at Lewis Hamilton for holding back in a tight turn.

He glanced over at me with surprise. "Team Mercedes, Gorgeous."

Apparently work and play were all combined when it came to Adam, but it seemed clear to me the race was unusually important to him. "My only problem with Formula 1 is how early they race." I rubbed my eyes and finally gave the course a good long look. "Where are they? Japan?"

Adam grunted. "Singapore Grand Prix. Just be glad it isn't next month. When they race in Japan the engines start at two in the morning over here."

I groaned and shuddered. Though I had to admit it was kind of fun to have a lazy morning on the couch with fast cars driving in the background.

"You know," he replied, turning toward me, "I'm going to be at the Russian Grand Prix in three weeks. You could come meet me for the weekend...have another mini sex-cation."

Three weeks? That sounded awfully soon to be meeting up again. I was thinking more along the lines of December, when he came home for Christmas. It would give us a both a good, long stretch apart to clear our heads. I wanted Adam in my life, but slowly so I could process it. "I don't know if I'm up for a long plane flight just to watch cars."

"Race day isn't just about the cars on the road," he protested. "It's a giant party."

Oh, how I knew that all too well. "I've been to my share of races, Adam."

His eyebrows shot up. "I should have realized that. I take it you didn't enjoy them?" He looked absolutely devastated that I might not like races.

I shrugged and took a long sip of coffee. "I like the races, I just didn't necessarily like the company I was forced to keep."

He nodded tightly and his lips formed a thin line. Was that frustration directed at me, or my past? It was probably a leftover from the night before. "New company may make a difference. After all, there's me," he waved his hand at himself and grinned. "Plus I have a ridiculous hotel room booked. There will be lots of expensive champagne and fast cars on and off the course."

Suddenly my bad memories of trailing behind my parents and stopping for hundreds of pictures, of sitting quietly in a corner while they got drunk and high, of requesting our bodyguard remove the overly friendly gentlemen from my proximity, were replaced by fantasies of talking about cars with Adam, of rolling naked in thick, soft sheets, room service, and laughing.

Laughing. That one struck me particularly hard. As I sifted through my past I very rarely had memories of laughing. Definitely not at races. But with Adam, I almost always pictured us laughing, and I suddenly, very urgently, wanted to see him in Russia. "Let me think about it, ok?"

His eyes lit up. "Think away. But personally, I think you should say yes. We'll have a lot of fun." Then he turned and yelled at the TV again.

Hamilton was having a great year, but so was his teammate, Nico Rosberg, a fairly intense rivalry considering they were both Team Mercedes. "Do you have anything to do with the race cars?" I had absolutely no idea how these things worked.

Adam sucked in a breath and cracked his neck. It was a sudden shift from the relaxed and animated Adam from a moment before. "Uh, not really. I'm pretty friendly with the engineers on the team, though."

Pretty friendly my ass. My question threw him for a loop. Adam's jaw was flexing and he started bouncing his knee up and down like he was nervous. "Must be nice considering how much you love racing. You can be a groupie."

He chuckled, but it was more forced than anything else. "Pretty much. That's part of what will make it fun in Russia. I can get us passes to anything."

I let the conversation drop, but I kept studying Adam when he wasn't looking. The nervous energy around him didn't fade. If anything, he seemed to be getting more nervous and agitated the closer it got to the end of the race. He stopped rubbing my foot and drinking his coffee, like he'd gone off into his head and forgotten where he was.

And then when the race ended with Rosberg and Hamilton finishing first and second, locking up another dominating race by Team Mercedes, Adam turned completely white. He watched the post-race interviews with the drivers and crews with intense focus. I felt like I was watching something important but for the life of me I couldn't figure out what it was, and Adam didn't seem to be up for sharing.

Maybe I should ask. "Hey."

Adam turned and looked at me. "What's up?"

"Good race. Makes your company look badass."

He grunted. "Thanks."

"So what's the deal?"

"Deal?" His voice deepened and he didn't meet my eyes.

"What's going on? You're acting really strange."

He opened his mouth, but nothing came out at first. He took a couple of breaths and I started to wonder if Adam was ok. I'd never seen him speechless. "Well, uh, I guess..." his phone lit up and started ringing on the coffee table. His eyes darted to the phone. "I have to take this."

But before he could grab it, I saw the name emblazoned across the screen. *Raif.* The guy he was talking to in the middle of the night.

"Hey man. Just give me a second." He pressed the phone to his chest and looked at me like I was a stranger. I didn't like that look one little bit. "I'm gonna step outside if that's ok."

I held up my hands. "If you need privacy let me be the one to leave. I'll be in bed." It came out a little bitchier than I wanted, but I got my point across. Adam put out a hand to stop me, but I batted it away, giving him a look that would have stopped anyone in their tracks. He moved out of my way and waited for me to slam the bedroom door.

After another few beats of silence he began to talk to Raif, all while standing in the exact same spot as before, the spot that bounced all of that private conversation right under my bedroom door. I was such a miserable liar.

"Congrats. That was a fantastic race. You can't beat a one-two finish."

Raif. *Raif*...why did that name sound so damn familiar? And not from the other night. It was from somewhere else. It was an unusual name and I knew I'd seen it somewhere else recently.

"If everyone is on the same page then send over the paperwork. I'll talk to Dave as soon as I land on Sunday...No, I'm really excited I just—" Adam's voice dropped away and I could picture him ruffling his hair and pacing in a circle. "I just can't believe I'm doing this. It's a huge change."

I sat on the edge of the bed staring at the door. I was a big, fat eavesdropper. Even worse—I cared a whole helluva lot about that conversation I wasn't supposed to be hearing. There was something huge and important happening in Adam's life and he didn't want me to know about it.

I deserved the silent treatment. It was what I'd been giving him about so much of my life. Feeding him scraps of information only when I absolutely had to.

I was such a hypocrite.

"Thanks, I'll let you know a time frame as soon as I can. Go and celebrate."

An image of a man with dark hair and eyes flashed through my mind. I knew exactly who Raif was. He was the crew chief for Team Mercedes. They'd interviewed him twice during the race and once afterward.

What in the hell was Adam doing?

The door creaked open and Adam stuck his head

in. "Are you mad? You seem mad."

I shook my head. I wasn't mad at him. I was kinda mad at myself but that was for a whole host of reasons that began with eavesdropping and ended with wanting to know everything there ever was to know about Adam.

He stepped inside and leaned against the door. "I'm sorry. That was kind of a big phone call and I just didn't know what to do…where the line was with us."

That was fair. "I understand."

"No," he shook his head and came to kneel on the floor in front of me. "I don't think you do. My gut instinct was to take that call with my arm around you. I wanted you there. I wanted you to already know that I was expecting the call. I don't want to keep things from you, but I totally and completely respect the boundaries you've laid out. It was a split second decision and I erred on the side of caution."

"Tell me what's going on!" I blurted out and grabbed his t-shirt by the collar, pulling him so that we were nose to nose. "I can't take it! I heard your phone call the other night and I just eavesdropped on this one, too. Apparently, when it comes to you, all bets are off and I want to know everything."

Adam grinned like an idiot. "Really? Because I'm pretty sure if I don't tell someone I'm going to lose my shit."

"Really. *Tell me.*"

He carefully sat down on the bed beside me, taking entirely too much time to settle onto the mattress. "I just verbally accepted a job on Team Mercedes. I'm leaving the concept team."

That sounded kind of huge. "So you'll be designing race cars instead of the cars of the future?"

"Sort of," he was giddy. "It's not entirely different and a lot of the race cars incorporate the stuff we design anyway, ahead of production cars. That call I took the other night? They were having a hard time getting the cars to adjust to the track in Singapore. The handling was way off on one and the speed wasn't there on the other. The team couldn't get the cars right, so Raif called me. He already had the job offer on the table and damn did I want to take it, but I love my job. I wasn't going to leave it unless it was the right fit."

"I'm guessing you helped? They ran great today."

Adam looked like a proud parent. "I did."

"Is that what you'll be doing? Problem solving?"

He shrugged. "Mostly. I have a unique set of skills I can bring to the team from all different sides of the car and the engine."

We were both quiet for a few beats. Adam had just dropped a bomb full of information that was hard to process. "So what does this mean for you? Will you be travelling with the team or based out of Germany still?"

He shook his head and let out a slow breath. "That's the thing. I'm moving. Crap...*I'm moving.*"

I laughed at the perplexed look on his face. "And where are you moving to, exactly?"

He smiled. "The UK. The team is based out of Brackley."

Was everyone in my life moving to England? "Travel?" Why did this feel so important to know?

"I'm not sure of all the details, but I imagine I'll be with the team a lot."

Adam was going to be travelling the world. Formula 1 raced everywhere. "Congrats." Why did my heart hurt? That feeling of lead was back in my belly and my words sounded desperate, not happy, the way they should be.

Adam locked eyes with me. Whatever it was that I was feeling—he could see it, far more clearly than I could. He was studying me, processing what he saw and deciding what to do with it. I held my breath. Why couldn't I understand these feelings? Surely I was smart enough to figure out how I felt about Adam. Or maybe I was too emotionally stunted to ever be normal.

Adam blinked and his eyes lit up. A smile pulled at the corners of his lips. I completely lost my train of thought as my heart skipped a beat.

That was when Adam tackled me backward onto the bed. "Thanks. We should celebrate."

Chapter 19

Sunday Night

"Let me see the other box. Please?" Adam was begging. It was beautiful. We'd celebrated his new job and then spent the rest of the afternoon watching football and eating pizza, keeping things light and super simple. But now, it was time for some exercise.

I shrugged my shoulders. Damn it was fun to tease him now that I knew he liked the torture so much. "I don't think I will. I'd rather you use the rest of the toys in my first box."

His eyebrows shot up and I got a little rise of satisfaction out of knowing he was already hard. "All of them?" His voice dropped two octaves.

I pulled off my shirt and slid belly-down across the sheet. "Start with one and work your way up from there. Let's take it *one step at a time* and see how far we get. There's always tomorrow."

I'd never seen a man move so fast. He was naked

and holding the box beside me in about three seconds flat. He massaged my bare ass with one hand as he laid out one toy after another. There may have even been a giggle of glee. I rolled my eyes.

But I was getting off on the anticipation. I had no idea what Adam was going to do to me. I liked the idea that it was a mystery. I trusted him completely when it came to my pleasure. Although that was a little bit of a lie. I trusted him *completely,* not just in bed. Seven days was all I needed to know who Adam was as a person, and he was a really good person.

"Do you want me to tell you what I'm doing or keep it a mystery?"

A shiver raced over my skin and I had to close my eyes against the excitement that was running through me just at the *idea* of Adam doing things to me. "Start mysterious?"

He took a deep breath. A really long, deep breath, and let it out slowly. "Oh fuck, I'm so hard right now."

Now I had to giggle. We were like kids in a really, really dirty toy store.

"Could you possibly get up on your knees for me?"

I grabbed a pillow and moved up onto my knees, elbows down and ass up in the air. My mind raced with possibilities. This was so much more fun than doing it all to myself.

A cool steel ball pressed at the entrance to my wet sex. I sucked in a breath but I loved the way the cold was shocking against the heat of my body. He slowly pushed it inside before surprising me with the cold from the second ball. The first ball moved deeper inside me as Adam pushed the second one in, both moving over sensitive, wonderful, arousing parts of my body.

"How's that?" he whispered hoarsely. I'd made him speechless.

Fantastic. "Feels good."

He tugged on the silver flange tied to the end of the strings, drawing the balls back to my entrance, before letting go. They slid slowly deep back inside. This time the ache inside me was for totally understandable, sexual reasons.

"So, so hot to watch them disappear," he whispered. I liked how barely controlled he sounded.

"Not too bad to feel, either."

He groaned. *What was next?*

Cool silicone hit my breasts as Adam affixed the nipple ticklers to my skin and then turned them on low. This time I was the one groaning at the rough, wonderful sensation of the tiny fingers circling my nipples.

Then he tugged on the balls again and my whole body pulsed. And ached for more.

Sweet Jesus I wanted more. Anything that would push all the confusing thoughts and feelings from my brain and leave my mind deliciously blank.

Adam massaged my ass and hips with both his hands for several seconds before he asked the question I knew was coming next. "You said it was only a sometimes kinda toy...how would you feel if I put this in your ass?" He wiggled the butt plug in front of my face.

I wiggled my ass. "Yes, please." God I wanted it all. I wanted to be full. I wanted to feel the throbbing everywhere.

Adam poured some lubricant on the toy and then me before gently beginning the process of pushing it inside. It was a very small toy in the grand scheme of things. Something I'd ordered on a whim one night when I was bored with everything in my box and more than a little curious what the big deal was. It had sat in my box for several weeks before I even pulled it out. But when I finally did, I was shocked to realize how much I enjoyed the little extra it added to my play.

I sucked in a breath as it slid all the way inside, coming to an abrupt stop. Adam massaged my hips and cheeks all over again. His breathing was getting deeper and faster with occasional little groans of pleasure.

He was such a considerate lover. Seriously, how had I accidentally wound up sitting next to him at the bar? It had to be a gift from the sex gods.

"How's that?"

Since this wasn't a toy I played with very often, it bit a little on the way in, but now that it was in position, held in place by the large flange at its base, I felt fuller. And like something was slowly cranking up the volume on my level of arousal. My skin heated and my arms started shaking a little as I held myself up. "Fantastic. Now give me more." I could still think straight so it wasn't enough.

He chuckled low in his chest. "Like this?" He

pulled on the balls again. They massaged me from the inside out as they moved back and forth, creating a pocket of warmth low in my belly. I was getting wetter by the minute. The blood was pooling and throbbing. The balls weren't nearly enough.

"No. I want *more.*"

I heard Adam's breath catch and his hands faltered for a moment. Then he tugged on the balls and there were two soft pops as they were pulled free of my body. I felt achingly empty without them and ready for something else.

Adam disappeared for a moment and returned with a small stack of washcloths, placing the balls on one and setting the stack beside the box. A moment later something cool pressed into me and I knew it had to be the glass dildo. Adam slid it inside very slowly, the smooth, cool surface like liquid as it glided against my skin.

Adam's breathing was erratic now. It matched mine. We were both barely contained by the overwhelming sexuality of the experience. Every sensitive inch that could be stimulated on me was humming. I was vibrating with electricity. It tingled over my skin and powered through my veins, infecting Adam who, as usual, was torturing himself with watching.

"This is the most gorgeous sex toy I've ever seen. It's perfect for you," Adam murmured.

I bought it more for the visual than anything else. It was just *beautiful.* Clear, polished, phallic beauty. It could be heated or cooled for an added effect which was quite fun to play with from time to time... but today it was just regular, cool glass. He slid it in and out several times before leaving it deep inside me and massaging my backside again. The action was just enough to move everything at once—the plug, the dildo, and every liquid covered inch of skin—kicking my arousal up another notch.

I sighed. It was a glorious feeling to be so full. But it still wasn't quite what I wanted. I needed more. "Try something else." I quaked from the inside out, craving something to push back against the throbbing below and obliterate the last of my thoughts.

Adam murmured something that sounded like, "Oh, hell yeah." I was glad he was having fun. That was the point of all of this, but it almost felt like there was something missing. Or even a barrier separating us. I didn't like that.

I was empty for a moment and the room was incredibly quiet before Adam came back to me. "How about this?" he asked as he licked at my core with his tongue.

I gasped at the sudden soft warmth between my legs and shuddered with relief. *Better*. Adam's tongue was damn near the best thing I'd ever had inside me. His cock was obviously the best, but his tongue? A very close second. I almost came right then, especially when he massaged my clit with his palm, but I wasn't ready. I wanted to draw this out longer now that I had a connection with Adam back.

"I take it you liked that? That was a pretty impressive groan, Gorgeous."

His voice was like a soft, calming wave over my skin. "Yes. More please." More of *that*.

"Well, I certainly can't say no to a woman who's letting me play with her toys."

I rolled my eyes, but forgot everything the moment his tongue slid back inside me, obliterating everything but him in my world.

He worked me right up to the brink of orgasm and then stopped. And I knew what was coming next. I craved it. The bed shifted as Adam changed position, kneeling behind me. My sex pulsed in anticipation. It was hot and needy. So empty without anything inside. The plug was a strange throbbing my brain couldn't quite place. This was going to be just about all I could handle, so before Adam entered me, I disengaged the ticklers and tossed them aside just as his hands softly gripped my hips.

The sound of his heavy breaths was the only thing I could hear. My body was tuned to Adam's, heated and waiting for his cock. It was as if all of that play had been a lead-up to the moment we would physically connect. As if the separation I felt earlier was its own kind of twisted foreplay. All in order to make this, the moment he slid into me, even more earth shattering.

Adam pushed into me slowly, knowing that the combination of his size and the plug might be too much for me to handle. And sure enough, it was a lot to process. My mind went blank as it tried to understand the feelings washing through me. Good and tight. Painful, but not too painful. I was hyper sensitized and even the air seemed to be too much for me to feel.

I'd played like this before with my dildo, but it was very different to have a real cock inside—moving, warm and insistent. I felt like I was coming apart at the seams. I was sweating and panting and shaking.

"Oh fuck," Adam swore, wrapping one of his arms firmly around my waist as he shuddered. "I'm not going to last long like this."

It didn't matter. He'd already gotten me close enough that the added fullness was more than I could handle. As his cock slid all the way into me, locking us together, my orgasm hit. I'd never felt anything quite like it. It was fast and exciting. A powerful little orgasm. I yelled out and Adam came right along with me. My inner muscles squeezing him tight, his arm holding me in place. It was overwhelming in the best way possible. I ached. I finally felt free again. My mind was gloriously empty. And when my body was done wringing out every ounce of pleasure, I finally felt satisfied.

Adam pulled out slowly. Then I leaned down on my elbows as he pulled out my handy little toy. "Well, I'd say that calls for a nice hot shower," I mumbled through the haze as I collapsed onto the bed.

"Let me get it started," Adam was still panting pretty hard. He looked a little dazed.

"Hey," I called him back to me as I rolled to the edge of the bed. "You alright?"

He nodded and let out a slow breath before kissing me quickly. "I'm amazing. That was...well I don't think *fun* is an appropriate word."

"Good. I had fun, too."

"Good. Now let me get the shower going. If I sit down, I'm not getting back up for at least an hour."

I quickly cleaned up and let Adam have the shower. The poor guy was having trouble standing. I was just toweling off my hair when my phone rang.

Maybe it was the timing—late on a Sunday evening after I'd already talked to both Lily and Allison—but I knew before I looked at my phone that it wasn't good news. The hair on my arm stood on end and dread swelled low in my belly as I pulled a fresh t-shirt over my head and grabbed my phone off the dresser.

Edita was flashing across the screen. I held the ringing phone to my forehead and took a long, deep breath before mashing the answer button. "Hey."

"Hey," her soft voice replied. "So, this isn't a social call."

When did lawyers ever call on Sunday nights for fun? Obviously this was bad news. "Fuck."

"I'll give you three guesses why I'm calling and the first two don't count."

Apparently wishing my old life away wasn't going to work. "It was nothing."

"There's video. It's not nothing. Why didn't you call me? You know I hate hearing about this shit from your parent's lawyer. I play offense, not defense."

Edita had always been my lawyer. She'd been with me through everything. She was good people. "I really didn't think it was that big of a deal."

"Unfortunately that isn't the case. Your picture and the video of Adam Callaway holding Kevin Lindt down have both gone viral."

"I'm guessing I have Cybil to thank for that."

Edita grumbled on the other end of the line. "I have no proof of how they went from circulating the social media sites to the entertainment networks, but it was Smitty, so my money is on Cybil." Smitty was my mother's go-to sleezeball for 'leaking' pictures and rumors to the press. Most likely Kevin sent my mother the pictures and video and Cybil, seeing a prime opportunity for publicity in the thick of her fall season, had leaked it to Smitty. *Fuck.*

"It is clear that this wasn't planned or on purpose, but it does trigger the clause in your agreement with your parents. They have requested a meeting for information."

There weren't enough swear words for what I was feeling. I could barely breathe. A meeting with my parents. I'd successfully avoided being in the same room with them for two straight, glorious years. "I'll book a flight."

"See that's the thing. You don't need to."

"What?"

"I know. I'm worried, too. They are being very flexible and agreeable. It's freaking me out."

Typically meetings took place in Edita's office in New York. "Where? When?"

"Roger has requested a sit-down in a public restaurant in Fayetteville. He's giving a lecture there tomorrow. He's agreed to wear a hat and eat at an off time in order to avoid being recognized. He's even given you the choice of time."

"So weird." My parents were never accommodating.

"I've already put Andres on a plane." Andres was my favorite bodyguard. He accompanied me on every trip and every meeting with my parents. "He'll be at the bar watching in case you need him. Can Allison go with you?"

"No, she's in London," I replied quietly, wishing she were here.

"Crap. What about Adam?" Then her voice dropped to a near whisper. "Are you two dating?"

"No," I said it so fast it surprised me. "No. He's...no. And he's not going with me either."

Edita chuckled. "You sure aren't convincing. And by the look of his face in that video, he's dating *you*, whether you know it or not."

What in the hell was that supposed to mean? The look on his face in a dim, grainy video? "You know full well how I feel about that."

"He's a catch, Elizabeth. And he's a fucking Callaway. I know you're living in Calhoun Beach and all, but he lives in Germany now. How the hell did you meet him?"

A Callaway. The way she said that struck me. She said it the same way people said *my* name. "He's on vacation visiting his family."

"Well, you may want to reconsider your relationship. I don't know that you'll ever meet anyone else like him. And he is someone who can actually understand your two lives—"

"I've gotta go." I cut her off. The shower turned off and Adam would be able to hear my conversation.

"What time should I tell Roger?"

I had a meeting scheduled in Fayetteville on Wednesday that I could probably move to tomorrow. Squeeze in work and hell all at once. "Two o'clock. Email me the information."

"You got it."

"How do you know so much about Adam?" I let my curiosity get the better of me.

The line was eerily quiet for several moments so I slid out of the bedroom and across to Allison's room while I waited for her response. "How do you *not* know about Adam Callaway?" she finally said.

"What is that supposed to mean?" He was Adam. His family was local, owned a plantation and a few restaurants, and he designed cars for a living. What else was there to know?

"Lizzy, you may want to look into the man you're seeing. I don't care what you call your relationship, but you should know more about who you're spending your time with."

"That's all you're gonna say?" I was exasperated. And it was very unlike Edita.

"I don't think it's my place to say any more. Good luck tomorrow and let me know how it goes." The line went silent and I stared into the darkness of Allison's room.

"Babe? Where are you?"

I curled my fingers around the phone and slipped quietly out of Allison's room. "Sorry," I held up my phone. "Allison had a quick question about something she thought she left here." *Liar.* I was a lying liar.

He leaned up against my bedroom door frame, wearing a pair of navy boxers and a wicked grin. His perfect body on display for me to enjoy. I stopped and took it all in. *How do you not know about Adam Callaway?* Maybe I hadn't looked into him more because I didn't want to know anything else. I knew he was sweet and sexy. I knew he was kind and fun. I didn't need to know anything else. Not for a two-week affair. But Edita was right—I needed to know who I was spending my time with.

But not tonight. I'd worry about that after I knew if my life was crumbling down around me. A meeting with Roger had never once ended well. There was a very good possibility I'd be looking for a new name and a new home in twenty-four hours. God, I didn't want to leave Calhoun Beach. I was just starting to settle in here.

"What's that look on your face?"

I realized I was frowning. "Nothing," I murmured and walked up to him. His skin was cool as I wrapped myself around him and rested my head against his strong chest. "I'm just tired."

"Then let's get in bed," he said, kissing the top of my head.

Two minutes later I was wrapped around him again, but this time under the covers. His head was propped up on a pillow and I was draped across his chest as he read to me. It was a very old and worn paperback copy of *The Firm*. The front cover was missing and the pages were slightly curled. It was Adam's favorite and one I enjoyed as well.

He was reading quietly, but his voice was loud in my ear against his chest. I could hear the different sounds and levels that made up his beautiful voice. His heart was soft, slow, and steady. His skin was soft against mine and his free hand was running lazily up and down my back between turning pages.

I listened as he read about Mitch realizing he was being watched by the firm—that his job wasn't what he thought it was—that his company was in some deep, dark shit. I related to Mitch and Abby. Their desperation to escape. They just wanted to be happy and in love.

I just wanted to be happy and in love. *With Adam.*

That was what I was thinking as I drifted off to sleep in his arms, oblivious to the hell that was coming.

Chapter 20

Monday morning

My feet pounded the pavement on the trail that ran along the beach. I had a 10K in two weeks and I hadn't run a single mile in almost three weeks. If I didn't get my ass in gear I wasn't going to cross the finish line, let alone finish with a good time.

Of course I was also running because after my morning class I was making the long drive into Fayetteville to meet with my father for the first time in two years. I felt like I was preparing for battle, and battle preparations included purging unnecessary baggage like a weekend's worth of booze and good food, no thanks to Adam and his amazing cooking skills.

Dawn was breaking as I rounded the final corner and onto the street that led back to my apartment. The streets were empty except for a few other early morning runners. It was eerie and beautiful to see Calhoun Beach at this time of day. I always wondered if this was how residents saw it two hundred years ago with the brick roads so close to the beach.

When I pushed open my apartment door I was greeted by music and the smell of bacon. Adam, as usual, had woken up before me this morning and was damned determined to make me eat breakfast before work. "Hello Gorgeous. How was your run?"

"I'm out of shape," I mumbled as I stuffed bacon into my mouth and stuck a fresh glass under the water dispenser in the fridge.

"I highly doubt that." Adam looked me up and down with a very dubious glint in his eyes. "I seem to recall you have an amazing body and an unprecedented ability to keep up."

I grunted my agreement. "Sex is a little different from running, though."

Adam flipped an egg in the pan and grinned. "You got that right. Sex is a helluva lot more fun."

I kissed him on the cheek and took the plate of food he offered into the bathroom as I started the shower. I was in a mood with my mind stuck on an endless loop about my meeting with Roger, and I didn't want Adam to start asking questions. He followed me in a moment later. "I figured I'd watch while I ate."

Running certainly hadn't given me the release from my stress that I needed and if there was one sure fire way to keep Adam from noticing that something was up, it was to give him a show. "If you're going to watch, could you be a dear and go retrieve my toy bag?"

Adam stopped mid-chew and stared at me for a second before he grinned and scampered (yes, scampered) out of the bathroom. My shower wasn't as amazing as Adam's but it had some fun little tricks of its own.

He set the bag down just outside the shower door and backed up to the counter. He very slowly finished his breakfast as he watched me with razor sharp focus. I took my sweet time shampooing and shaving, letting the massaging showerhead beat over my breasts as I washed. I'd learned over the course of five showerheads that the right one was worth its weight in gold. Not all showerheads were created equal. Some were great for massaging sore neck and back muscles, for instance.

But others were excellent at massaging clits.

While others were better at nipples.

For a while I had one that was excellent at getting me off while between my legs, but not much else. Then it broke and I accidentally bought the one I had now. The difference was surprising. The pressure and spread of the spray was just right. When I stood at the back of my shower it hit both of my nipples at the same time, and with just the right amount of pressure, so that it was arousing, but not painful.

Now that I was clean and shaven it was time for some relief. I positioned the showerhead and relaxed against the cool shower wall, simply enjoying the pleasure I got from my nipples being stimulated by the steady stream of hot water. My core began to throb for more.

Once I knew I was aroused enough to be wet, I opened the shower door and dug through my bag. By that point Adam was done eating. "You are so hot when you are enjoying yourself. I just thought you should know that."

I grinned and looked up at him as I grabbed the blue silicone dildo and zipped the bag shut. "I can tell. You are as hard as a rock."

Adam's boxers were doing a terrible job of covering his cock. "Guess I should just lose these, huh?"

"Do whatever you want," I shrugged with a mischievous grin. "I certainly am."

Adam swallowed and groaned. Then he dropped his boxers.

I left the shower door open and returned to my spot on the back wall. After a moment back under the spray, I spread my legs out and began inching the giant fake cock inside me. The water was washing down my torso and between my legs, making it harder to keep the dildo lubricated, but that was also part of the fun. It was a challenge and required all of my focus. My stress and worries faded into the background and all things Hollywood related disappeared, replaced by a cock, my pleasure, and a desire to make the man standing ten feet away lose his mind for a few minutes.

I didn't look at Adam and I didn't particularly care what he was doing. I knew he was enjoying every single thing he saw. It was driving him crazy—and that was all that mattered.

The cock finally slid all the way inside and I moaned as it filled me, obliterating every last bit of tension that remained locked inside my muscles. I stayed like that for a minute, letting all the sensations wash over me, reveling in the release of my troubles.

Then I did what I knew was going to make Adam go a little mad. I leaned forward and suction cupped the dildo to the shower wall behind me, riding it back and forth like a real cock. That was when I finally turned my head to get a good look at Adam.

He had his erection in his hand, stroking up and down slowly as his eyes burned into mine. He shook his head slowly and mouthed the word '*hot*' as I shuddered, the water drenching me from above, my hands braced on the opposite wall, my feet on each side of the shower, and the fake cock sliding in and out of me as I moved.

It was like getting fucked from behind in the shower by Adam, but this way I got to watch him. I gave him a good show, pulling the showerhead down and massaging my nipples as I worked the cock, then down between my legs to my very swollen clit. I gasped when the warm water hit me there. It was almost too much to handle—too harsh against something so raw.

I stood up so I could control the showerhead between my legs easier, the dildo bending upward with my body, pressing against the front of me where I liked it so much. Up on tiptoes I moved up and down the silicone shaft slowly. I didn't need much, just a little movement to keep things going. The fake balls served as a slide for the water from the showerhead, flushing the water upward along my clit in a wave of warm water instead of a beating spray of high pressure.

It was the perfect combination of stimulation from the inside and outside and my orgasm struck hard and fast. I nearly doubled over at first—it was strong and I was balanced on my toes instead of flat on my feet. Suddenly Adam was in front of me and he held my shoulders in place while I came. I leaned into him, letting my orgasm take control. My clit throbbed and my inner muscles massaged the fake cock finding that glorious pressure that made my orgasms even more powerful.

When I was done, Adam let me go with a wicked grin plastered to his face. His cock was so hard that it was red and swollen. It looked damn delicious and I knew he was about to come, too. I slid off the dildo and tossed it onto the floor. Adam was busy rehanging the showerhead so he was surprised when I wrapped my hand and lips around his dick. He gasped, which only turned me on more, while I worked and sucked. As he got closer I tasted the salt at his tip and his fingers tightened in my wet hair. When he came I wasn't surprised. I'd felt the buildup in my hand and the early kick of his cock. He groaned and gasped, massaged my shoulders. I smiled and finished him off when his entire body suddenly relaxed against the shower wall.

"You are constantly full of surprises, you know that?" He gasped.

I stood up and grabbed the showerhead to make

sure I was rinsed from head to toe. "Here's a little something you should know about me: I get really horny when I work out." There was just something about the combination of sweat, endorphins, and tight clothes.

"Duly noted."

I left Adam in the shower while I changed for work. Thanks to my decision to play instead of eat I had to shovel the rest of my breakfast in my mouth as I dried my hair and hastily applied a very light layer of makeup. I mostly avoided Adam as I threw the last of my things into my bag. But he wasn't having it.

"Are you ok?" His eyes searched mine as he ran his thumb along my cheek. He was entirely too good at reading me.

I wanted to tell him everything. That I'd screwed up by letting that fan get too close, that I was miserable and dreading the rest of the day, that all I was looking forward to was being in his arms once it was all over.

But I couldn't. I was too worried Adam would feel responsible. I was even more worried he'd ask to go with me. My life was poisoning his enough already. I didn't want him anywhere near my father. The best thing I could do was fake it for another few minutes, get my ass on the road, and survive the day. "I'm fine. Just didn't sleep too well last night. Weird dreams." I tried to wave him off but my lie only made Adam more insistent.

He tilted my chin up. "Why didn't you wake me? I could have read to you some more or we could have watched a bad movie."

"You can read to me again tonight. Trust me, I'm going to need it." Why couldn't I leave well enough alone?

Adam furrowed his brow. If I didn't get out of there quick, I was going to wind up as the subject of the new Inquisition. "I have to get to class. Enjoy your day!" I practically ran down the stairs and as far away from Adam as I could get. Otherwise I'd wind up in his arms begging him to go with me. And that was something that simply couldn't happen. I needed to do this alone.

Chapter 21

"Roger," I said simply as I sat down on the opposite side of the red booth. I'd chosen a chain restaurant called Bonita's. It was basically a steakhouse with memorabilia plastered to every wall and peanuts on the floor. The servers wore jeans and red and white checked shirts.

"Elizabeth," he replied with a nod. True to his word my father was wearing a Dodgers baseball hat and a rather uncharacteristic t-shirt. Normally Roger wore suits. Sometimes he wore suits. Or occasionally he went wild and wore...suits. So the getup was strange looking on him.

I picked up the menu and scanned the drinks first, doing my best to avoid small talk with my father as much as possible.

"Thank you for coming," he said simply while we waited for our waitress.

"Thank you for not making me fly to New York."

He set his menu down. "That would have been ridiculous considering we were both already in the Carolinas."

Funny how he said that like it was normal. This was the same man who once made me reschedule my dance recital because it interfered with his tee time. "I trust this will be brief." Our last meeting ended with me throwing a full pitcher of water at Roger in Edita's office and our respective security details pulling us out of the room in different directions.

"Your mother and I merely want to know exactly what we're dealing with. You know how difficult it is to manage the press unless you have all the facts. Especially during sweeps."

I closed my eyes so Roger wouldn't see me roll them. "We're a few weeks out."

"Still, you never know how something small in September might turn into something major by November."

So dramatic. They were always so damn dramatic. And liars. There was no way this was as simple as information control. They were being accommodating and sickly sweet. Roger and Cybil wanted something and they were willing to go to extra lengths to get it.

"Hi, my name is Shirley," a sweet, younger woman stopped at the end of our table. Her bleached blonde hair was swept in a loose braid over one shoulder and her eyeliner was far too heavy for the middle of the day. "I'll be helping you out today. Can I get you started off with anything from our bar?"

"Fat Tire," I replied before Roger could open his

mouth.

"Alright, a beer for the lady. And you sir? What can I get for you?"

While Roger asked Shirley several questions, I checked the bar. Sure enough, Andres, my bodyguard, was positioned on the corner, just as Edita had promised when she called to tell me about this meeting. He was a deceptive looking guy. He had a smile that could warm anyone's heart, and eyes that could charm the pants off a nun. His face was so distracting that most people missed the fact that Andres was also six foot three and two hundred and forty pounds of pure hulking muscle. They definitely missed the gun under his arm and the other on his back.

I tucked my hair behind my ear and smiled—my signal to him that all was well. Andres smiled back indicating that he was good to go.

"Do you know what you're having for lunch or would you two like a minute?"

"Turkey club with the fries," I answered automatically.

Roger looked surprised but glanced at his menu. "I'll take the steak fajitas."

"Great, I'll get those in for you." Shirley disappeared and left me alone with Roger. I kind of wished Shirley had stayed.

"Shall we start? There really isn't much to go over." Maybe if we could get this done the tension between us would lessen a little.

Roger frowned. "I'm afraid that there is a great

deal to go over, actually. How long have you been dating Adam Callaway?"

"We're not dating," I answered automatically. My irritation was skyrocketing. I was used to the cold distance of my parents, but it still hit me hard every time we met. There was simply no warmth from the man who was supposed to be my father.

"My sources say you've been spotted with him several times this week."

"Fuck your sources," I replied, leaning back in the booth and crossing my arms. "You'd really rather base your assumptions on the report some jerk threw together in the last forty-eight hours?"

"Frankly, when it comes to you? Yes."

That stung. "We're not dating. He's a friend and he's only in town until the end of the week."

"Then why is he staying at your apartment instead of his? Why is he paying for your food and drinks? And why, if you aren't dating, is he buying you jewelry?"

Jewelry? For fucks sake. What was Adam up to? "One, he's staying at my apartment because we're having sex. It isn't the same thing as dating. You are the last person on the planet I should have to explain that to. Two, he's paying for *some* of my food and drinks and I'm paying for some of *his*. It really depends on who has their credit card out first. And three, I have no idea what jewelry you are talking about."

"He purchased it today." Roger had that sick look on his face he always got when he thought he had an advantage. "He had a long conversation with the jeweler and my undercover investigator about the woman he was purchasing it for."

My heart thudded in my chest. I really wish I'd heard about it from Adam and not my father. *Jewelry from Adam...* "If he purchased it today then you know damn well I have no idea what you're talking about. But thanks for the heads up, asshole." Roger was such a manipulative jerk. He managed to put me under the microscope and ruin a beautiful gift all at once. "Jewelry or not, it doesn't change the fact that we're not dating and he's not my boyfriend."

"He said you were. He called you his girlfriend."

I waved it off. "It was probably for convenience. There isn't exactly a nice word for 'woman I'm casually fucking on vacation'."

My father raised an eyebrow and leaned back as Shirley returned with our drinks. He waited until she was back out of earshot before resuming his questioning. "So you have no plans to continue seeing him after today?"

His choice of wording took me back. Plus the idea of not seeing Adam after today did something ugly to my insides. "I plan on seeing him for the rest of the week. Until his vacation is over." I left it there since I wasn't sure if or when I'd see Adam again.

"With the media interest in your story, seeing Adam any longer will only fuel the fire. You haven't been photographed in months and the video...well, the stories have already started."

By the tone in his voice, I could assume the stories

weren't reflecting well on Roger and Cybil. More than likely one of the entertainment outlets had run with something along the lines of, *"Estranged Lawrence daughter resurfaces in bar brawl, troubled past still haunts family."* Cybil's reality show was built on the crap she sold the world about being reborn into a newer, better person.

Served them right for feeding me to the entertainment wolves. I held in a smirk of satisfaction as I imagined their greed for the spotlight backfiring on them. "We are laying low. I don't see any problems with continuing my arrangement until Adam leaves town."

While Roger stewed over my answer I drank half my beer hoping that our conversation was basically over. When the food arrived, I'd scarf it down and leave.

Unfortunately my optimism was misplaced.

"Adam Callaway is a stumbling block for us. His name puts yours back in the spotlight at a difficult time. Your mother's show is struggling this season and the questions being asked about you and him are not the kind that help boost ratings."

I fought the urge to smile. "I don't see how this is my problem."

"Per our agreement, all things that put your name in the spotlight are everyone's problem. We demand a plan of action."

Every once in a while the amended agreement bit me in the ass. Mostly it kept me safe while providing clear lines that defined my complicated relationship with my family and our family legacy. It dictated that all publicity—intentional or not—triggered a meeting to handle the potential ramifications. It also outlined when and where my parents were allowed to see me. I'd agreed to the amendment for Lily and the relationship I wanted to maintain with my sister. But at the moment, I wanted to light the damn thing on fire.

"Well, *per our agreement*, I agree to stay out of the public eye until Adam leaves. Deal?" I knew it wouldn't be good enough despite being perfectly reasonable.

Roger stared me down. I swear there was no feeling inside that man's heart. His eyes were a testament to that. "We have a proposal for you," he said just before Shirley plopped our plates down in front of us. It took her a minute to deliver all of Roger's sizzling food and condiments.

"What kind of proposal?"

"One photo shoot and interview with your mother and we'll look the other way on Adam Callaway for the rest of the week."

I coughed on my French fry. What kind of crazy train was Roger on? "Why on earth would I agree to that?"

"Because," he replied quietly, "if you don't, we'll release this." He slid an envelope across the table.

I stared at it without picking it up. "Why?"

"Because he's *Adam Callaway*," Roger said Adam's name like it was a sports car he wanted to possess. That was when I realized there was more going on.

"If we release the information in that envelope your relationship with him will be over." Roger was betting that Adam meant something to me. "There is no way the McKinley's will allow him to associate with you. It will smear his good name, his family, and everything they stand for. *Adam won't want to touch you.*"

I struggled to keep my face neutral as realization finally dawned on me. *Adam McKinley Callaway.* Adam was a fucking McKinley. Senator Thad McKinley's gorgeous grandson.

The McKinley's were American political royalty. The Callaway's owned one of the biggest restaurant chains in the country, not just Green Hills and three local restaurants. *Thousands of restaurants.* Adam was the sole heir and partner in a billion dollar corporation, *and* part of one of the most famous, rich, and brilliant political families in America.

Roger and Cybil had an unprecedented opportunity in front of them: they could finally make me pay for what I'd done to them, all while getting a level of publicity they hadn't managed in years. It would mean ridding themselves of the pall I'd put on the family and line their pockets at the same time.

Adam was their golden ticket.

All because I couldn't walk away from him.

I picked up the envelope and glanced inside. It was a single photograph from a night I'd tried to forget for the last twelve years. A stupid, desperate mistake I'd made in an attempt to feel like more than a pawn in someone else's game. I thought it was private, I thought Max loved me. Shit, at the time I'd thought it was fun. But I was young and stupid. And very, very wrong.

"How did you get this?" No one should have that photograph. *I* didn't have that photograph.

"I very recently came across it." That was all Roger said, and I knew it was all he was *ever* going to say.

So I had two options. I could agree to their terms: do the photo shoot and interview in exchange for silence. Or I could take my chances. Play the publicity war games and hope I won in the end. I didn't have the strength for another public war with my family. I didn't know what I wanted from Adam, but I knew I wanted the chance to explore it.

"I pick the photographer, the location, and the reporter," I said, sealing the envelope and putting it in my bag.

"Deal. We want it done by Friday."

"And this stays between us?"

Roger nodded once. "If the photo shoot and interview go well, then Cybil and I will have no reason to seek any new publicity or to manage the existing bad publicity."

"Fine," I spat back. "I'll have Edita send you the details. After this, we're done. We're even. I never want to see you again. Our agreement is off."

Roger's face was stone except for a tick in his left eye. No one would notice it, but I did. I knew the tick well. I was an expert at setting it off. "Goodbye, Elizabeth."

I slid out of the booth, tucking my hair behind my ear to let Andres know I was leaving. And pissed. He met me at the door. "Everything ok?"

"I didn't throw anything at him, did I?"

Andres chuckled. "You look like you should. Want to turn around and throw a fork? I can handle you both."

I shook my head. I didn't want to throw anything. I wanted to cry. A good long cry. That was what scared me. No matter what happened in the past, I always left in a ball of fire. The fight surging through my veins, the anger taking on a life of its own.

I didn't feel any of that right then. I was deflated and very nearly broken. My fight was gone...and I didn't know what that meant. Andres held open the heavy wood door and I slid on my sunglasses as I stepped into the burning bright September afternoon. "Thanks for flying down for such a short meeting."

Andres shook his head. "My girl came with me. We decided to make it a vacation and rented a condo on the beach just down the road from your apartment."

Vacation my ass. "Edita told you to stick around for a few days, didn't she?"

Andres folded his strong arms over his wide chest and smiled. "Maybe. She thought there might be a need for me again this week. Sure beats the hell out of flying back and forth."

I shrugged and kept walking toward my car, desperately wishing it were Adam's AMG instead of my sensible Camry. The AMG would get me back to Calhoun Beach in a fraction of the time...as long as I didn't attract any legal attention. "Well thanks. Looks like I'll need you for a photo shoot on Friday."

"Send me the details," he paused and held open my door for me. "I'll be five minutes away. You need anything, you call." I hugged him. My affection caught him by surprise at first but then he hugged me back. "Go home, Elizabeth."

I nodded quickly and slid into the driver's seat. Good people were hard to find and I appreciated having Andres on my side. "Enjoy the beach with your girl," I winked and slammed the door.

My drive home was eventful. It started with a phone call to Edita that involved a lot of arguing. She hated my decision to do the photo shoot. She quoted a lot of legal jargon from the modified agreement with my parents. She told me over and over the law was on my side. But I'd made up my mind. This was what I needed to do. I would give them one last crumb and I could walk away from it all with no regrets.

I didn't want any more regrets.

Then I called my sister. She was very upset with me, as expected. She tried to talk me out of ending the agreement. *You only get one family. Don't throw us away all over again.* She still didn't understand and that hurt. It hurt more deeply than I was prepared to comprehend. But she agreed to skip her classes on Friday and fly down for the photo shoot.

After that I bribed my favorite photographer, Ronoldo, to fly in and deal with us. He was sad and excited. Then asked if I was really dating Adam and if he could meet him.

Then I called Adam. "Meet me at my apartment in ten minutes."

"Long day?" he drawled. I could hear the chuckle in the background.

"Unbelievably."

"I'll be waiting."

I finished the drive into town, parked my car in the little public lot down the block from my apartment, and practically ran up the sidewalk. Adam was waiting with the door open, nothing but his boxers on, and a wicked grin.

A shiver of desire ran over my skin and heat surged between my legs. I was wet just at the sight of him. He must have seen something because his eyes narrowed, his smile fell away, and his jaw flexed.

"I need you," I whispered as I threw my bag on the floor inside the door and yanked my shirt over my head.

Adam didn't say a word. He just wrapped his strong, warm, comforting arm around my waist and pulled me inside.

Chapter 22

"Thank you," I gasped as I collapsed against his chest. We hadn't made it past the door. Adam's feet were propped up against the base of the front door and his head was the only thing on the rug. The rest of his gloriously naked body was pressed against my cool (and hopefully clean) wood floor.

He was panting just as hard as I was. "You're welcome." He brushed my hair over my shoulder and began to massage away the knot I didn't even realize was there. "You know, I seem to be noticing a pattern with us..."

"A pattern?"

"Mmmm..." he kissed the top of my head and I shifted a little as his cock began to recede. "We appear to be getting closer and closer to the door with each passing day."

I looked up at him, grinning. "Are you upset by this fact?"

"Not at all. Just surprised. I thought we'd be slowing down by now."

I froze. For some stupid reason his innocent comment made me feel weird. *Slowing down?* What was that supposed to mean? I sat up and pretended to brush off his comment. "I think we better get to the bathroom."

Adam grinned. "On the count of three?"

I nodded and jumped off of him, running a few steps ahead, and into the shower. Adam went to the toilet and divested himself of the soiled condom. "I may need to start keeping these in my socks. I go through them like candy."

Again, his comment made me feel weird. Maybe it was the day and everything that had happened. But my head was interpreting things far more deeply than normal. I was overanalyzing every comment out of his mouth.

I shook it off and stepped out of the shower, wrapping myself up in a towel as Adam kissed me on the cheek and took my place under the water. I'd let Roger into my head. Posturing and looking for meaning and angles in everything was his M.O. It was how he manipulated people and used them. It was constant—every single person was out to get him and Roger needed to know how and why. It had to be exhausting to constantly analyze everything everyone ever said. Move, countermove. Bait, switch.

I grew up with that being the norm and had to learn as an adult that it wasn't common behavior. It had taken years of relearning how to view people and their motivations, and I still fell back into old habits from time to time. After my emancipation from my parents I acted just like them, except my motivation wasn't to use and manipulate, it was to protect myself. I analyzed everything said to me. Every look. Every whisper. Were they talking about me? Were they going to use me? Pretend to be my friend and then ask me for favors? It was part of what led to my disastrous early friendship with Allison. She genuinely wanted to be my friend, but all I saw was danger. It was her unflagging friendship and patience than ultimately taught me that some people were good.

Like Adam. I knew he was good. I'd told myself that over and over during our time together and yet, all it took was one meeting with Roger to make me backtrack and question everything.

I really, really hated that man.

I was so lost in thought that I didn't hear the shower turn off or see Adam, towel wrapped around his waist, come up behind me. Not until I felt his lips on my neck. "I didn't mean anything," he whispered, looking up at me in the foggy mirror. His hair was damp and wild.

"I know," I whispered back. He was reading me again—sensing my moods and thoughts better than I could.

"I don't think you do. All I meant was that after a week of daily sex I expected us both to feel satisfied."

"You don't?"

He shook his head slowly, his eyes locked onto

mine. "I don't think I'll ever get enough of you."

My heart skipped a beat and my skin heated. "I'm trying to store up as much of you as I can before you're gone."

He kept his eyes on me as his hands rubbed up and down my bare arms. "Is the haunted look in your eyes because I put you back in the news?"

"You saw that, huh?"

He chuckled and pulled my back flush against his firm front, wrapping one arm around my chest and resting his chin on the top of my head. "It was a little hard to miss. My phone rang most of the day. And I had someone tailing me."

I closed my eyes, remembering the jewelry Roger mentioned. "You can thank my parents for that one. Sorry."

He shook his head. "Doesn't bother me. I don't have anything to hide."

I swallowed and took a deep breath before saying what I knew needed to be said, but still scared the crap out of me anyway. I had bigger problems than how vulnerable the adoration of a wonderful man made me feel. I would deal with the consequences of letting Adam into my life after I was done managing the chaos of my past. "I think we need to talk."

Adam nodded, moving my head along with his. "We do. But not naked, wet, and starving. Let's get dinner and come back up here to get whatever we need out into the air."

Part of me wanted to bare my soul while naked in

the bathroom with Adam. It seemed right somehow, but I also knew these types of confessions changed things. It might be best if I were clothed when I offered Adam my heart—just in case he rejected it. "Downstairs?"

"I can go down and grab takeout. You look tired."

I shook my head. If I stayed home in a t-shirt cuddled up on the couch I would get stuck in my head. The isolation and darkness would start to creep in on me. I needed to get dressed and get out. It always helped me bounce back from a day like this if I could see the world still moving. Seeing people, even strangers, somehow forced me to put one foot in front of the other and keep going.

I wouldn't if I stayed here. Even with Adam. "No, let's go eat. I could use the fresh air."

He watched me carefully as I dressed. I could tell he was worried by the soft look in his eye and tick in his jaw, but he didn't ask any questions.

My hunger got the best of me and I pulled Adam behind me on the way down the stairs. Apparently my half-eaten lunch, followed by exhausting phone calls and fabulous floor sex, wasn't enough to get me through the day. At the landing I heard a strange sound. Something in the back of my mind went on alert. The sound wasn't normal and I needed to pay attention. But I was hungry, so I ignored the quiet little warning.

It wasn't until I opened the door to the street and was greeted by a wall of photographers that I fully registered the sounds of paparazzi. I, brilliantly, stood there like an idiot with my mouth hanging open and the door in my hand, before Adam stepped in front of me, removed my hand, and slammed the door before anyone could push their camera inside.

"What the fuck is that?" Adam ran his hand through his hair and then guided me backwards from the door.

I swallowed, still staring at the door, as I fumbled for my phone. Roger was making sure I followed through on my plans. He'd called in the press. He was going to make my life hell until the interview and photo shoot were done. "Andres, I have a situation at my apartment."

"I'll be there in five. Go back inside and stay there." I slid the phone back into my pocket and looked at Adam.

"Who is Andres? What the hell is going on?" He looked so confused.

"My security."

Adam jerked his head back. "Why do you have security in town?"

Only my eyes moved as I tracked Adam's movements. "I told you we needed to talk."

He stopped in front of me and put his hands lightly on my arms. "Elizabeth, I know we hit the news hard, but this... we shouldn't have twenty photographers waiting outside your door. We're not that big of a story."

"Unfortunately we are, thanks to Cybil and Roger."

I swear I saw steam come off of Adam's head. His eyes widened and lips thinned as he grappled with how to reply. "Your parents are doing this to you?"

I nodded once. It was a little easier confiding in Adam now that I knew who he was. His easy confidence with security and publicity came from a lifetime of his own experiences. I briefly wondered if anyone ever tried to drag his name through the papers and realized that being a McKinley and a Callaway was completely different from being a Hope or a Lawrence. Just as rich and famous, but totally different worlds.

Adam let go of me and pulled out his phone. "Hannah, this is Adam Callaway. I need dinner delivered to Elizabeth's apartment...yes, I'm sorry about that crowd. You can use the service entrance at the back of the stock room. I'll meet you there."

I raised my eyebrows. "Service entrance? How do you know about that?"

He shrugged. "My mom's restaurant, remember?"

Among many. "Still..."

Adam shuffled around the foyer and slid his hands into his jeans pockets. "Like you said, we have some things to talk about." The shouting outside got louder and Adam grabbed my hand, pulling me back upstairs. "We need to get away from that door."

Just as we reached the second floor the door below opened and the sounds of the crowd echoed through the building. It made my skin crawl and memories I didn't enjoy or want came flooding back. Adam shuffled me behind him as I unlocked the door and Andres appeared on the stairs. "Is this your security?"

"It is," I assured him. I felt Adam relax and a layer of tension seemed to dissipate from the air.

"Adam," he said, putting out his hand.

Andres took it with a nod. "Andres." He followed me into the apartment while Adam closed the door and locked it. "You've got quite a crowd out there. Roger is a piece of work."

I walked directly into the kitchen, opened a cupboard and pulled out my favorite Templeton Rye whiskey. Situations like this called for hard liquor, straight so it burned on the way down. I poured a small glass and walked away, leaving the bottle open for either man to join me. "So what's the plan? Move me?"

Andres stood with his hands clasped at his front, watching me as I wandered back and forth in front of the windows. "I think that's wise. They'll be there waiting for you to leave in the morning. They'll follow you to work. And most likely they'll still be waiting to follow you home."

Fucking stupid paparazzi. I wanted to blame myself for all of this, but I didn't have the energy to hate myself that much. Not yet. "There's a hotel just across from campus. It will be obvious, but easy to manage."

Andres nodded and pulled out his phone. "Name?"

Adam cleared his throat. "I have another idea. Come stay with me at Green Hills."

He was looking right at me with that beautiful intensity I loved so much. "Adam, I..." the words evaporated on my tongue. As much as I wanted to say no, I

TEASE

didn't seem to be able to actually do it.

He stepped toward me. "Seriously, this makes good sense. Green Hills is a large piece of property, it's gated and we have our own security and protocols for dealing with..." this time it was Adam searching for words. "With situations and important guests," he finally finished. "The photogs won't be able to get near either of us."

"But," I tried again and failed. I didn't want to continue dragging Adam into my circus.

"Don't say no." Adam took my hand in his, turning it over so he could look at my palm. He traced the lines with his thumb, never looking up. "I want you there with me," he said quietly. "My family would want you there, too." I wasn't breathing. I couldn't. Right after Adam stole my words he stole my air. He was so sweet and sincere. He took my hand and placed it on his heart, holding it in place. I could feel the heavy thump of his heart in my palm and wondered if this gesture was as intimate to Adam as it felt to me.

He finally looked me in the eye. "I think it is the smart thing to do." He was appealing to both my emotions and my intelligence.

Green Hills was out of town and further away from work, but I'd be able to think and actually get some sleep out there. A hotel wouldn't be much better than my apartment. It would be close to work, but would I actually be able to work if I was exhausted? I wanted to be with Adam. That was what put me in this mess in the first place. Refusing him now wouldn't help. "Al-

233

right."

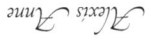

Adam's eyes lit up. "Really?" Clearly he'd been expecting me to retreat back behind my lines, but I was done hiding and compromising. Adam was offering a good solution and I'd be stupid to reject it simply because it put me on the same property with his family.

"Really. As long as Andres agrees."

"I think it sounds perfect," Andres answered immediately and I got the impression he'd been hoping that I would say yes. "Let's get you packed."

Chapter 23

An hour and half later I was wearing my t-shirt, leggings, socks, and a comfy sweater, sitting in the middle of Adam's bed while eating an enormous tray of food sent over by his mother. I was happily hiding away in the little apartment and purposely *not* thinking about the fact that Adam's family, and whole life, were a few hundred yards away.

I was alone while Adam introduced Andres to the property manager and the security team for Green Hills and I was using my time to field phone calls from campus police and a very angry best friend.

"Why did I learn about your weekend online?" Allison hissed.

I shoved a puff pastry stuffed with some sort of cheese and jam into my mouth and shrugged at my laptop. Allison and I were in a Google Hangout catching up while I ate.

"I was testing the waters on living without you."

She shrieked at me. "I can't believe you just said

that."

"Well, you were going to tell me that you're moving to London permanently, weren't you?"

She stuttered, her mouth hanging open so long I thought the chat had frozen. "Maybe. I've been considering it. How did you know?"

"Allison, we've been best friends for ten years. I know you like the back of my hand. First you had the gushing stage, then you had the eating stage," I ticked through Allison's known process of falling in love. "And last week, you stopped talking about how much you loved it there and only wanted to talk about me finding more people in my life. You said, and I quote, 'You wouldn't always be around'."

"Damn it," she pounded her desk and took a swig of her beer. "You know me too well."

I gave her my very best self-satisfied smirk and popped a fried piece of something delicious in my mouth. "Why are you only considering it? Please say it isn't because of me."

I sipped some red wine while Allison looked everywhere but at me. "You're my sister from another mister. I'm not going to abandon you. If it works out for both of us, I'll do it. But the firm is happy to have me in Calhoun Beach or in London. I have a good job either way."

I loved this woman and all she'd done for me. It hurt to hear this. She was considering holding back on her dreams because of me. "I think you should do it. If you want this job, if London is home, then do it."

Her eyebrows shot up. "What happened this weekend?"

"I got a wakeup call I've been needing for a very long time." Being without my support system was eye-opening. My time with Adam was enlightening. But seeing my past come back to haunt me just as I was starting to picture possibilities for my life... well, my options couldn't have been placed in front of me any more starkly.

"How bad is the press? Have you talked to your parents?"

I winced. Bringing Allison fully up to speed hurt. There was some lecturing and a little bit of yelling. "And Friday is the end?"

"Edita is drawing up the paperwork now." I didn't mention any of the other messy details factoring into my decision.

"Good."

Allison loved Lily, but she always hated the agreement. We were grown women now. We didn't need our parents to have a relationship. "So...can we discuss the elephant in the room?"

"And what is that?" We'd covered my parents, my sister, and what happened at the club...what else was there?

"Adam fucking Callaway is *Hottie Pants*?"

"You say that like I hadn't told you who I was seeing." I was being purposefully difficult to rile Allison up.

"You said Adam. You said Callaway. I figured he

was some guy you met in a bar, not *him*."

I shook my head. "I have apparently missed out on the obsession."

That got a good laugh out of Allison. "Do you not remember the screen saver you gave me shit about our sophomore year? Do you seriously not recall the poster behind my door? Hold on, you're getting an email in a minute."

Fuzzy, decade old images were all I could recall. I did, however, remember giving Allison a really hard time about the hot guy on her computer. She was obsessed and to me, it was disturbing. He was always just floating back and forth, and back and forth…

My email dinged on my phone and I started downloading a string of five images.

"I still had these saved in my college folder I always import when I change computers."

Image after image of a much younger, but still gorgeous, Adam appeared on my screen. They were sexy pictures of him gripping the steering wheel of an Aston Martin, leaned lazily up against the car with a blazer over his shoulder, of him holding a gorgeous model against his hip with shiny sunglasses over his eyes. I did remember these. They were a *Vanity Fair* spread from our sophomore year. The picture of Adam driving was her old screen saver. The poster behind her door was him leaned up against the car.

Allison had been obsessed. Said he was the most gorgeous man who ever lived. "I had no idea."

"You know," she chuckled, "that is actually part of

your charm."

"You can't have him. He's mine," I said more forcefully than I meant. It was supposed to be a joke but instead it sounded more like a threat.

Allison shook her head with a shit-eating grin on her face. "To hear you say that, I'll give him up. That sound right there, is worth it."

The door opened and a very tired looking Adam strode inside, locking the door behind him. I took that to mean things were handled and we were in for the night. "You want to meet him?"

Allison clapped her hands and bounced in her seat. "Is that even a question?"

Adam grinned as he crossed the room, leaning across the bed to kiss me on the cheek. "And who is in bed with you while I'm gone?"

I turned the laptop a little so that the camera faced both of us. "Adam, meet Allison."

"It is very nice to meet you." He settled onto the bed beside me.

Allison giggled like a sophomore with a crush, not the twenty-nine year old architect with an exterior of steel. "I should confess, I had a wild crush on you in college."

Adam tensed and avoided my eyes, looking intently at the computer. "I haven't heard that in a long time."

"I just thought I should toss that out there now. I want it to be on both your radars that I'm going to celebra-stalk you. Not because I'm in love with you, but because I can't help myself." She clapped her hand over her mouth and shook her head. "Oh my god. I'm so sorry. That was a really stupid comment considering you two are actually being stalked."

Adam took it in stride, smiling politely. "Well, I'll let you two finish up your chat. I need a drink." Tension rolled off his heavy shoulders. The day had taken a toll on both of us. For once, Adam truly looked like he needed a drink to take the edge off. I didn't like knowing I was the cause of his smile disappearing.

"Well, it's late for you over there on the other side of the pond, and Adam and I have a lot to figure out so..."

"Yeah, yeah, yeah...you've got sex to have. Rub it in."

"No pieces of meat for you to seduce in London?"

A look, slightly pixelated by our trans-Atlantic chat, crossed her face, making it difficult for me to interpret. "Plenty of pieces of meat, none that I've tasted. Yet."

Well, that was an interesting comment. "I expect a better explanation later."

She nodded. "Have a good night. Try and get some sleep. Update me on the Reign of Terror." Allison referred to Roger and Cybil as the Evil King and Queen of Hollywood, and the crap that followed them as the Reign of Terror. It was fitting and useful in situations where we couldn't use names or explain ourselves fully.

"I will. Good night." I closed the chat and snapped my computer shut.

Adam poured himself a glass of wine and slid onto the bed beside me, picking up a puff pastry from the tray. It was going to be hard to get through the night considering how much we both needed to explain.

"I should meet your parents tomorrow. Properly thank them for the help."

Adam finished chewing and studied his glass of wine. "Only if that's what you want. I've explained the situation and, believe me, they understand. It won't hurt their feelings at all if you want to avoid meeting them."

"Are you politely trying to tell me they don't want to meet me?" I didn't like that feeling one little bit. I was the walking, talking embodiment of hypocrisy. It was ok for me to avoid meeting them, but not the other way around.

Adam chuckled low in the back of his throat. "You're doing it again."

"Doing what?" I turned a little more so that I was facing him.

"The thing you were doing before dinner. Overanalyzing and reading too much into things. You've been very different today and I can't tell if it's just because of the press, or because of something else."

My skin prickled as my blood pressure skyrocketed. Nothing about this conversation was going to be easy. "For someone who's known me a week, you sure can read my moods."

Adam set the tray of food on the floor beside the bed and then moved closer so that his bent knee slid along mine. He ran a finger up my neck and his palm along my cheek, before his fingers tangled in my hair.

I could barely hold myself together. Adam's touch did things to me. Sometimes the lighter touch did more—forcing my senses to reach out, only to be met with the overwhelming intensity of Adam's lust for me. The blood rushed out of my head.

Adam swallowed as he leaned in, his breath dancing across the skin of my cheek, and his eyes burning into mine. "I like to think that the moment I sat down at the bar in Seychelles you and I were in sync. Everything about me tuned itself to you. Your body. Your voice. Your desires."

His thumb swept over my cheek and he tilted my head to kiss me, but stopped just short of my lips. It was torture to have him so close, but holding back. Every cell in my body screamed for Adam to just fucking kiss me.

"When we're together," he whispered, "I can hear every breath, every shudder. I know when you stop breathing and the moment I hit the spot that makes you come. Your whole body tenses when you want more, and you relax the moment you let go of everything that worries you. I know," he kissed me, just barely, "that the only way to get you to forget about the world and trust me, is to let you have the control, but that the moment you *do* let it go, the last thing you want to do is think."

I was quivering now. So wet it was uncomfortable. Adam's body and scent were aphrodisiacs, but his words took me apart piece by piece. He was making love to my heart with a speech. I loved everything he said. Normally it would make me run. Someone seeing that much of me, knowing me so well, would be a threat. They could expose me, use me, and hurt me in ways I had yet to imagine.

But not Adam.

I *knew* he was different. Being exposed to Adam wasn't a threat to my safety. He would never hurt me. His intentions weren't to use me—he just wanted to be with me. It was as simple and as perfect as that.

And that was when I realized how well I knew him, too. I had no doubts about Adam. It wasn't just a gut instinct that he was genuine. I knew his grunts and what the different sounds of his voice meant, but I also saw how he treated his friends. His family was important to him, even when they disagreed. He was kind and generous to the people around him. Added to his easy confidence and intelligence, I knew who Adam was as a person because of what I was able to observe.

He kissed me slowly. His lips gliding across mine until we were firmly pressed together. It was just a simple kiss. Lips locked together, connecting us, almost as if it were a first kiss.

Maybe this was. I'd forced us to keep so much about ourselves hidden. Now that the truth was coming out, everything felt different. I put my hands around his face and tried to pull him into a deeper kiss, but he shook his head. "No. This deal we've had...I can't do it anymore."

My fingers tightened onto him reflexively, like I was grabbing on so he couldn't go. I may be emotionally confused and a little stunted, but I could recognize fundamental feelings. I needed Adam. "No."

He kissed the tip of my nose and then pried my fingers away from his face. "It's not what you think," he whispered as he pressed my hands together inside his. "I want to throw away whatever is left of our no-strings-attached deal. I've got strings and I am fucking attached to you."

I was attached to him, too. It was the scariest and most exhilarating experience of my life. It was a lot to accept and I was glad my hands were inside his. In a way, it felt like he was holding me together when I wanted to fly apart. "What do you have in mind?"

"Well for one, we need to be honest. Lay all our cards on the table—no more holding back."

I nodded. There was no denying the pressing need for details where both of us were concerned.

"And," he continued with a smile, "I need whatever this is between us to happen naturally. No rules, no time limits, no assumptions."

I wrinkled my nose. "You're asking me to trust you."

"I am."

"And what do I do if you turn out to be a lying dirtbag who breaks my heart?" Even though I knew Adam wouldn't, I was still terrified. I didn't know if I had the strength to keep putting myself back together. My feelings for Adam were so strong that I might not survive getting my heart trampled by him.

His eyes narrowed and his breathing evened out. "I propose an undressing."

What?

He chuckled and his eyes softened. "Let me explain. We both have a lot to share. It's gonna suck—for both of us. You don't own the patent on painful history. I have something I've never shared with anyone. I'll give it to you to keep safe. If I hurt you, it's yours to do with as you wish."

I wasn't sure if I understood Adam completely, but I was willing to figure it out. "Alright. And how is this going to work exactly?"

Adam tilted his head sideways, letting go of my hand as he assessed me. "Well, it looks like you're wearing enough clothes."

"Clothes?"

"Mmmm..." he nodded. "Like I said, we're going to have an undressing. One piece of history for each piece of clothing."

Chapter 24

The sexiest, funkiest music played softly in the background. A fresh bottle of wine sat on the coffee table which had been pulled over by the bed. We dragged the couch over as well. Adam raided a cabinet and found a couple of candles and lowered the lighting so that the room seemed to glow. He sat on the couch and I perched on the edge of the bed. For a moment I panicked and wondered if I should put on more clothing or take some off. I had a lot to share, I might not have enough clothes. But then again, I might not make it through the clothes I did have on in one piece.

I took another gulp of wine and blew out a cleansing breath. I'd made up my mind: I was going first. I probably had more secrets to unload—and more clothing. Adam hadn't said anything one way or the other, but I felt like taking the lead would give me that little bit of control I needed to get through this.

I stood up. "Maybe this time I should start at the beginning?"

Adam's eyes followed me as I stood. I knew his sounds far better than I knew his expressions. Maybe that was why I liked making him laugh and moan—they were how I read him. When he was silent, I wasn't as sure of what he was feeling. It added to my uncertainty to see his expressionless face staring back at me. "Start wherever makes sense to you."

I swallowed and took a deep breath, rolling my shoulders so that my sweater fell down around my arms. "Cybil and Roger have an unusual arrangement. They are married and for all intents and purposes, they are a happily married couple. But they do not have a normal marriage. They love how they look together. Hero and Hollywood darling. Cybil has had a boyfriend, his name is Alan," I hated saying his name, "for the last twenty years. Roger has a new mistress every six months. Actually no," I corrected myself, "that's a lie. He keeps one in New York and one in L.A. So he has *two* new mistresses every six months or so."

I paused while Adam absorbed the information. With as much as my parents stayed in the headlines, very little of their actual lives made it into the news. Agents, assistants, and very well paid lawyers made sure of that.

"Do they..." Adam paused while he searched for the words he was looking for.

"Love each other? Sleep together? Spend time together off camera? Yes. To all of it."

Adam balked. "How does that even work?"

I pulled the sweater the rest of the way off and sat

back on the bed. "I could spend an entire weekend detailing the ins and outs of Cybil and Roger. I only bring this up so you can understand the world I live in. It isn't like anything else. It is artificial and focused solely on appearances. Truth can be buried and retold like a fairy tale. Lies can be spun as the truth. Children are conceived solely for appearances." I hated knowing I was a born because it would look good.

"Are you saying they had you and Lily for publicity?"

"Not Lily. I'm pretty sure she was an accident."

Adam shook his head like he was trying to immediately forget everything he'd just heard. "That's fucked up."

"Yes. It is. Welcome to my fucked up life."

He slid to the edge of the couch and took a drink of wine. "Can I ask a follow-up question?"

I nodded.

"Is that what you meant when you said you raised yourself?"

I sighed. Explaining my parents was exhausting and unending. "Basically. They didn't want to be parents. I was raised by a nanny. A different nanny every six months, actually."

"Oh, gross. Roger screwed your nannies?"

I shrugged. "Most of them. I think a few escaped. There was no stability in my life. No one who cared about me." I held up my hand to stop whatever was on Adam's lips. "I'm not pulling the *poor little rich girl* card. I'm just stating facts. It was lonely to be raised like that. It's part of why I adored Lily so much when she was born. I finally had someone to love."

Adam didn't reply. Instead he stood up and kicked off his shoes. "I'm pretty sure you know everything I'm about to say, but it's time you heard it from me." He took a deep breath and cracked his neck. "My grandfather is Senator McKinley, and Green Hills owns three very large chain restaurants all over the country."

"I did hear something along those lines," I joked. The mood in the room was far too serious. "So, what's it like being the grandchild of one of the longest serving and distinguished senators in American history?"

"Like living in a pressure cooker."

I had no doubt. The McKinley family had five members serving in Congress at any given time. Adam had more cousins than I could count—actually, I knew several of them, now that I thought about it. A handful had married into my circle of Hollywood friends. All went to Ivy League colleges, married into impressive families, and were expected to serve either in politics or in public service of some kind.

"What does he think of the ex-pat engineer?"

Adam smiled and sat back down. "He's proud of me, but disappointed. Though, he's not surprised either. There's a reason we live down here. Mom wanted nothing to do with politics. When she was eighteen she staged this whole rebellious phase with drugs and drunken partying, all to distance herself from the Senator. That was when she met Dad—a southerner. It was the end of the world, apparently. Neither family approved, which only made them get married faster. Luckily, they really did love each other. Our relationship with the Senator is strained, but open. He visits from time to time, and we spend every other Christmas at the family compound in Maine."

It sounded like Adam's mother and I had a little bit in common. Maybe they really did understand my situation.

It was my turn again. Adam was lucky he'd been wearing shoes. That was an easy piece of clothing. I opted for my socks. I started pushing them down towards my ankles as I spoke. "So I was in my first ad campaign when I was six months old. As soon as I could understand blocking, I was put in commercials and then later I was my mother's daughter on her series *Pacific Nights*. They were careful to keep how much I was working under wraps, but I worked anywhere from ten to eighty hours a week from the time I was six to fourteen. A few people started asking questions around that time and I took a year off to 'enjoy high school'. It was so normal to me I had no idea what my parents were doing was illegal. I also had no idea they were spending my money."

I pulled the first sock off the end of my toes and tossed it on the floor with my sweater. After a long, glorious sip of wine, I returned to my story. "I was old enough to start putting two-and-two together. Plus I had internet. A few searches was all it took for me to figure out that my parents were using me. I started keeping my own records of how much I was working and how much I should be making. Cybil and Roger were careful that my shows and campaign launches were spread out enough that no one outside of Hollywood would have realized I was working as hard as I was."

Adam frowned. He'd caught my subtle hint. "You're saying no one *outside* of Hollywood would have picked up on it. But *inside*?"

"A lot of blind eyes were turned." *Max's* eyes in particular. "Especially if it was in their best interest. Report my hours or get Elizabeth Lawrence's name on the billing? Hmmm...?"

The muscle in Adam's jaw flexed twice but he didn't say anything else.

I pulled my second sock off and crossed my legs. "So when they forced me to star on *One More to Love*, I called my Uncle Oliver. He hired Edita and the rest is history. Your turn," I smiled wickedly as I hopped up and sat in front of Adam on the edge of the coffee table. "I hear you were in a rather gorgeous *Vanity Fair* spread."

Adam turned a little red. "Before I tell you about that one, can I make a confession?" His hand slid up my thigh and stopped several inches short of anywhere worth anything.

"Ok?"

"*You* also did a *Vanity Fair* spread."

"That's not a confession." And yet it was. I'd been sixteen and it was an homage to my grandmother. They dressed me up to match the character in each of her most famous roles. It was glamorous and gorgeous. One of the few things I'd actually enjoyed because it was about remembering my grandmother. Her movies and career weren't tainted by the roles my parents forced on me.

"I may have fallen in love with you a little bit when the magazine came out. I was already a fan, but that spread...*hot*. My crush was out of control. I hid it under my mattress even though there was nothing to hide."

I ignored the casual "love" comment. "Hot? It was old Hollywood glamour..."

Adam slid his hand the rest of the way up my thigh and pressed his thumb between my legs. "Hot. Very, very sexy, Elizabeth."

Oh. I sighed as blood rushed south to the exact spot where his thumb was circling. "You were pretty hot, too." I may not have been in a place to truly appreciate the beauty of twenty-year-old Adam in gorgeous designer clothes behind the wheel of a powerful car back then, but I was now.

"My racing career was just starting to take off. They wanted to feature the hot McKinley legacy taking a turn toward the dangerous bad boy image. It was the only shoot I ever did."

"Well you did it right," I gasped as Adam took his hand away. The emptiness was always so much more pronounced when he pulled away. He popped off his socks and then he slid a little closer, threading his knees with mine, and took my face in his hands, angling it so he could look into my eyes.

"Your life took a turn after that feature. You were in the headlines for very different reasons and then you disappeared from the spotlight. I forgot all about you."

I nodded slowly.

He ran his thumb across my cheek and cocked his head to the side. His eyes dropped to my lips and stayed there as he spoke. "All that was happening in your life just as mine was taking off. I'd been racing on the amateur circuit off and on for years—mostly for fun. Then I had a great year when I turned eighteen. All of a sudden I had teams interested in sponsoring me, wanting to see if I could cut it on the pro circuit."

Adam's voice was very low as he spoke, as if recalling memories from so long ago required a great deal of effort. I was having trouble imagining this version of Adam. Even in the AMG, with all its power and handling, Adam drove carefully and sensibly. Who was this kid who drove fast for a living?

"Between college and races, I was busy all the time. Exhausted. Ridiculously happy." A small smile pulled at his lips. "I had it all. Girls thought McKinley's were hot, but McKinley's who raced cars? I could have had as many as I wanted."

"But you didn't," I whispered.

His little smile turned into a full-blown grin. "I've always been a one-woman kind of guy." He finally looked back up into my eyes. I held my breath as we connected and red-hot desire pulsed between my legs.

"Even on vacation?"

He shook his head. "I never wanted this to be a vacation-only fling. I've been asking you for more since the very first night."

We were connected by eyes, hands, and knees, but I could feel him everywhere just as if he were pressed firmly against me. I wanted to close my eyes and let myself be overwhelmed by all the things I was feeling and needing, but I couldn't bring myself to break the connection with Adam. He needed to see me, and he needed *me* to see *him*. That was why he was still holding my face in his hands.

"Elizabeth, I have to get this out before I lose my nerve."

It was almost impossible for me to imagine Adam having trouble confessing anything. His confidence was so imposing and unwavering I'd almost forgotten everyone had chinks in their armor—even Adam. I nodded once, "I'm listening."

"I was twenty, shooting up the circuit, making a name for myself, starting to wonder if I needed to finish college..." his fingers tightened and his breathing deepened. "I was in a massive wreck. Upside down, buried behind three other cars, it took them fifteen minutes just to get to me. At least that's what they tell me. I have no memory of anything after I came around the turn and saw the two cars ahead of me flip."

I wrapped my hands around Adam's wrists. It was his story and he was obviously having a difficult time with it, but I needed to feel him. I needed the anchor his body provided. I asked the obvious question. "You were hurt?"

"My brain got a pretty good whack. I was bruised badly just about everywhere, but no broken bones. No cuts or burns. All my equipment worked exactly the way it was supposed to. I had to take six months off and let my brain heal...that's when everything changed."

"Changed?" I needed to be closer to Adam. This 'almost touching' foreplay was driving me crazy. I pushed gently on his shoulders and Adam slid back on the couch before helping me straddle his lap. Despite the heavy subject matter he was sporting a rather impressive erection. It rubbed perfectly along all my swollen and needy parts.

"I got a good glimpse of where my life was going and realized it wasn't what I wanted," he grunted as he settled into place. "Everyone wanted a piece of me. My grandfather wanted me to take the opportunity to change majors and go into politics. Follow him into Congress. The press all wanted exclusives. The paparazzi followed me for weeks. The team called every day for an update on my condition. They wanted me back in the car as soon as possible. I was being pulled in five different directions and every single person doing the pulling wanted something from me. I was exhausted just sitting there. And then..." his voice trailed off and the pain crept back into his voice. "And then I got in the car and realized it was never going to be the same for me. Driving was never going to be fun again. I was one of those drivers who was never going to be the same after my wreck."

"You don't seem to have a problem now." I ran my fingers through his hair as I tried to understand what Adam was telling me.

"It's also been nine years. And it's still not the same. Before the wreck, driving was a game. It was calculations and betting the odds. It was playing the field and out maneuvering the other drivers." He took a deep breath and closed his eyes for a moment. When he opened them he looked right at me. "After the wreck it was..." his voice kept trailing away as he searched for the right words, "being careful, and playing it safe. It was sweating through flashbacks and wondering if I was going to die before I got a chance to do anything with my life. I was still a fast driver, but I'd lost my edge. I quit racing, finished college, and put as much distance between me and everyone trying to use me as humanly possible."

"Except now you're going back."

"On the other side of the car."

"Is that why the decision was so huge?"

He nodded. "I miss racing. I think it's time to go back and this is the right way to do it." He tightened his hands on my thighs, running them up to my hips where he pressed me down on his erection.

It sent an electric jolt of pleasure up from my core to my entire body and I tilted my head back and let out at a very satisfied groan. "Whose turn is it?"

My answer was Adam's fingers running under the hem of my shirt and his lips at the crook of my neck. "Yours," his breath whispered across my skin.

I found his fingers and took my shirt from there, pulling it very, very slowly up my torso and stopping just before I exposed my breasts. "Two years after our court case was settled I agreed to an amendment to our agreement."

Adam didn't move but the air around him suddenly felt colder. He ran his fingers over the skin of my stomach. "Why?"

"Lily," I gasped as his hand dropped between my legs and massaged. "She begged me to stop breaking the family apart. She was too young to understand. She still doesn't fully grasp it all."

Adam's head was resting back as he watched me. With every circle of his fingers I grew wetter and more anxious to get my last layer of clothing off. But I also liked letting Adam watch me. "How? I don't understand. She's your sister."

"She is, but she's a totally different person. It's almost like we have two different parents. They had me for a reason: to use me. They had her on accident. She's their pride and joy. Now to be fair, they also learned how to do things better after they screwed me over. I am their tool, Lily is their prize. They see us differently and they always have. She's their second chance—the sweet, irresistible proof they aren't horrible people. They treat us very differently and Lily has never understood that."

I pulled my shirt up over my head but Adam stopped me halfway, temporarily immobilizing me with my shirt over my face and my bare breasts exposed to his mouth. It was a vulnerable and rather advantageous position in his hands. He took first one, then the other nipple in his mouth, swirling his tongue and gently running his teeth along them before kissing the tips and letting me go.

I tossed my shirt to the side and shook my head. "You're trouble."

He shrugged and grinned. He liked being that kind of trouble in my life. I could use more of that kind of trouble.

"So what was the amendment?"

Adam was so handsome. The stubble on his jaw was rough against my fingers as I ran them along his cheek before grasping his chin and kissing him. I wanted to be closer to him so I kept my lips only an inch from his as I spoke. Adam wrapped his arms around my bare back, placing his palms between my shoulder blades, holding me against his chest. "I agreed to a minimal amount of interaction with the family. An appearance at Christmas and I would be in the same room with them for Lily's birthday. I would acknowledge them as my family again and any matters that pertained to the family brand would trigger a meeting in Edita's offices to discuss and agree on how to best serve all parties."

"This is what happened this week." He said simply.

I nodded and kissed him, hoping it erased any doubts he was feeling inside about his involvement. "Any time I show up in the press we meet and make a plan on how to handle it. Roger and Cybil still play their games. I still avoid them at all costs. Lily plays her own games in the middle—I assume she has a delusional hope we'll all be one big happy family one day." I can't help the laugh that bubbles out of me. It's not funny, but it's the only response I have for the way I feel. I can barely imagine Roger and Cybil as my parents, let alone my family. "Lily is my sister in blood, Allison is my sister in life, and my Uncle Oliver is all I have left. That is my family and it is a *good family*. I love them all dearly and I'm very happy."

"I would have gotten you out of there instead of holding Kevin down if I'd realized."

I shook my head and kissed him again. Harder. "You didn't know. No one knows this stuff. We're like the CIA or something."

He laughed a little against my lips. "I think the CIA could use your help." He moved his arms around me and his hands up to cup my face and hold me for a deeper kiss. His tongue slid along mine, gently caressing as his fingers massaged in my hair.

I was breathless when I finally pulled away, placing my hands on his chest and physically separating us. "But I need you to understand something."

It took a moment but his eyes focused on mine. He looked like he was fighting through a fog to concentrate on me and my words. "Ok."

"I may not have had a great childhood or the world's best parents, but I have a good, safe life. I'm not the poor little rich girl. I am not a victim. I take care of myself. I'm in control of what happens to me. I don't want you to confuse regret and disappointment with weakness or need." *Regret*. The word twisted like a knife in my heart. I only had one and I hoped Adam never found out about it.

His eyes narrowed and, for a moment, I worried I'd lost him. His jaw jutted out slightly and he took a deep breath before nodding once. "Trust me, I understand." He sat forward a few inches and yanked his shirt up over his head in one motion—far too fast for me to stop him mid-movement and return his favor. "In Germany, at Mercedes, I'm an engineer. I do my job and have a good time with my friends over there. I'm not a McKinley. I'm not a has-been driver. I don't feel that way about myself but I got tired of fielding the questions, of having to qualify my life choices to people I didn't care about. I walked away from everything that was pulling my life backward."

I froze for a moment as I let Adam's words sink in. They sounded so refreshing and a part of me yearned to be able to feel that kind of freedom. What would a complete break from my past look like? I'd always let Lily be my excuse for half-assing my transformation from Elizabeth Lawrence into Elizabeth Filler. But what if it was more than that? What if I was simply afraid of being alone because I didn't think I was strong enough to handle it? I wasn't a kid anymore. I could make the end of my amended agreement with Cybil and Roger more drastic.

As soon as the thought entered my mind I felt the counter-pull of Lily. Her pleas for me to stay close and repair the family. I'd never really be able to walk away from it all. I would always get pulled back, just like this week. There was nowhere far enough for me to run where they wouldn't find me and pull me back. They always found a way.

"What are you thinking about?" he traced a line down my cheek, over my collar bone, and down between my breasts.

"Nothing," I whispered, shaking my head and focusing on the half-naked man in front of me. I had one piece of clothing left. It needed to go.

As I stood and wiggled out of the black stretchy cotton, Adam stood, too. He unbuttoned his jeans and pushed them to the floor along with his boxers. "I think we've had enough revelations for one night."

"You don't want to hear all the nitty gritty details of my torrid childhood?" I laughed as I thought of all the things I could still tell Adam. I'd barely scratched the surface, but most of it was well buried in places I'd rather not go digging. Sometimes the past was better left in the past.

Adam pressed his naked body against mine, one hand around my waist and one in my hair as his lips hovered just above mine—holding his kiss just out of my reach. *The bastard.*

"Honestly, I think I will have to kill someone if you tell me anything else tonight, Elizabeth. I want to erase this weird, fucked up day by putting my cock inside you until you make those noises that make me forget my own name. If you tell me anymore—"

I cut him off with a kiss. He didn't need to say anything else. The truth was out, the foreplay was hot, and his feelings were clear. We both needed a cleansing release. I hopped up and wrapped my legs around his naked waist.

Chapter 25

Tuesday

"Friday at three," I said without any preamble.

"I'm going to say this one more time: you don't have to do this." Edita was still trying to talk me out of the photo shoot. "This story can only have so much to it. If you let it go you might even get a nice quiet weekend with Adam."

Except I wouldn't. If I backed out I'd spend the weekend buried under a shit storm of hell from Cybil and Roger. I knew this was the best course. It appeased everyone, kept my secrets under wrap, and gave me a guilt-free out. "Mariel is doing a video interview with me tomorrow and sending me the copy to approve on Friday. Ronoldo was only available to fly in for an afternoon shoot, so that's when we're doing it. It's better for Lily that way, too."

"Give me permission to bury them. We'll take care

of them forever. I will eviscerate them. They'll never work again."

I sighed and dropped my forehead into my hand as I glanced at my computer to check the time. "And lose Lily and ruin my family name in the process. As much as I can't stand Cybil and Roger, I loved my grandmother. I can't destroy her legacy because her daughter is a nightmare."

Edita groaned. She hated when I pulled the legacy card. "Vivian wouldn't have wanted this for you."

That hurt. Remembering my grandmother's gentle nature always hurt. She died when I was seven, but I clearly remembered her. She was such an opposite to Cybil I often wondered how they were related. "My plan will work. Make the arrangements."

"Fine," Edita replied. "How's Adam?"

"Good," I smiled as I remembered last night. The confessions had been cleansing, but the sex had been mind-blowing. I shuddered slightly as memories flooded my mind of his cock sliding in and out of my mouth and body, his arms as he strained against his building orgasm, and his eyes as he let all his memories vanish. His swearing and grunting were a pretty hot memory, too. I swallowed and refocused on Edita. "He's good."

"You sound good. Better than I've ever heard you, actually. I take it he's a rather invigorating presence in your life?"

Invigorating, comforting, freeing. "Something like that." After sex he'd fumbled around in a cabinet, naked and decidedly buzzed from all the wine we'd consumed. It turned out his promise to share something with me that he'd never shared with anyone, something to keep safe and use against him if he ever hurt me, was the only remaining pictures from his accident. Thanks to the Senator all other photographs had disappeared. I'd barely been able to look at them, Adam certainly didn't. The blood was hard to see and even a quick glance at what remained of his car was enough to give me nightmares.

I'd carefully slid them into a zippered pocket inside my briefcase along with the picture from Roger. I was going to place both sets of pictures in my safety deposit box as soon as I could get to the bank.

"Enjoy it," Edita said softly. "You deserve it."

"I plan to." We hung up and I sighed as Andres stepped into my office and closed the door. "Have a seat."

"Thanks. I'm ready whenever you are, just let me know. We're on your time."

"What's it like out there?" I dreaded seeing the sea of cameras when we left.

"Only about five of them."

Five more than I'd prefer, but not too bad considering the mob at my apartment. "I'm just about done." Since I'd already unloaded my grading for the week onto my graduate assistants I was able to concentrate the time I did have on a presentation I had coming up and the next meeting of the preservation board. All in all, work wasn't suffering from my personal life and I needed it to stay that way. My coworkers were more fascinated than perturbed to discover my secret. They found the media circus amusing and the campus police were doing an excellent job of keeping them away from me while I worked. I even joked with the office staff that I'd move into my office if necessary. At least here it was safe and quiet.

I shut my computer down and finished packing my bag. "Alright, let's get this over with." I said my goodbyes as we walked through the department and out into the lobby of our building. Andres walked out first before allowing me out behind him. A campus police officer was waiting outside to escort us to the parking lot where my five tentative photographers waited.

"I'm sorry about that, Dr. Filler," Officer Bailey called over his shoulder.

"Not your fault. I appreciate the help." He'd accompanied me to each of my classes and back to the department, just to make sure none of the photographers got any ideas about violating the ground rules they'd established.

"That's what we're here for." He moved into the line of photographers while Andres shuffled me into the car. "Move back five paces. Give the car room to leave."

It took us thirty minutes instead of fifteen to get to Green Hills thanks to the extensive circling Andres did to lose our friendly photographer friends. I tried to keep myself distracted by texting with my sister. Unfortunately that just seemed to darken my mood. She was still trying to talk me into making nice with Cybil and Roger.

I must have looked about as happy as I felt because when I stepped out of the car Adam scowled. "What happened?"

He was kind of adorable when he was worried. I kissed him on the cheek. "Nothing. Just a long, long day. I'm ready for a drink."

He put his hand on my arm and stopped me to kiss me properly on the lips. "Does that help?"

I dropped my bag on the ground and wrapped my arms around his neck. "Kiss me again." His one kiss had taken my breath away and I knew exactly what a longer one would do.

He grinned and popped his brows just before fisting my hair in one hand and holding me tight against him with the other. He kissed me deep and slow, erasing each thought and unwelcome feeling one by one. When he started to pull away I held him in place, thrusting my tongue deeper, begging him, in a way, to stay in this little pocket of heaven just a few seconds longer.

Adam groaned when I finally let him go. "You must have had a really hard day."

"Are you insulting my kiss?" I playfully swatted his arm as I finally made my way inside his apartment.

I lost my breath as I was suddenly, forcefully yanked backward against a solid wall of muscle. His breath was warm on my ear. "That kiss was so hot it made me want to strip you naked and spend the night in my shower." He slid his hand down my stomach and between my legs. "I just also happen to know you kiss me harder when you're trying to forget something."

I couldn't think straight right then. Between the kiss, Adam's hand between my legs, and his breath on my ear, my mind was a blank. His words came to me one by one through the fog until I finally understood what he'd said. He knew me too well. "How about sex before dinner?"

"Nope." He replied, kissing down my neck and over my bare shoulder. "I'm not sitting across from my parents smelling like sex."

"You'd rather be horny?"

He shook his head and backed away from me. "I can control myself through dinner. If we have sex right now we'll be late, I'll look like I'm high, and I'll smell like a man whose just had the best sex of his life. Sex is not an option, Gorgeous."

I groaned and started stripping out of my skirt and blouse. "Fine. I'll just tease you all through dinner instead."

He winked at me and then watched every move I made as I changed. "You still sure about this? They won't mind if we back out."

Was Adam asking to be nice, or because he'd rather skip eating altogether and spend the night exercising. In bed. With me. I pulled my shirt over my head and turned to find Adam sitting on the couch, leaned back with one arm along the top. His eyes were soft and contemplative, not focused and needy. He was definitely trying to be nice.

"Nope. I'm going to be polite and meet the parents of the guy I'm fucking."

Adam grinned. "And how does that conversation go exactly? *It is so nice to meet you Mr. and Mrs. Callaway. Your son has an enormous cock and he fucks me good and hard the way I like it. You did a great job with him.*" He said all of this with a raised voice and silly grin on his face.

I zipped up a clean pencil skirt and slid into a pair of ballet flats. "Nope. It goes more along the lines of '*Your son is very generous and knows how to keep me happy*'."

His eyes focused on mine and his expression became very serious. "Innuendo and yet, not so much...because I do care very much about making you happy in, *and out,* of bed."

When had Adam's apartment become so quiet? I swear the air had stopped moving and become charged with some sort of electricity instead. The silence was so deafening I could hear every breath I took. "I've never been happier," I replied with more honesty than I knew I had the confidence to possess.

There was a flicker of something in his eyes as he held my gaze. I couldn't look away. I was too afraid to. If I looked away then this moment might never come again and I knew it was special. Whatever was happening between us, it was the kind of stuff that didn't happen to everyone. Certainly not to me.

And then he blinked. "C'mon," he said softly. "Let's go to dinner." He rose and took my hand in his, threading his fingers between mine and squeezing.

The moment wasn't gone after all. It was still there and I hoped it never, ever left because the way I felt right then was how I wanted to feel for the rest of my life.

Chapter 26

"So you work with David?"

I quickly swallowed the wine I'd just sipped, nodding the whole time. "Yes. Do you know him? He's kind of my mentor in the department."

"Oh yes. David and I go way back. *Way back*," Lydia Callaway replied.

Mark raised a questioning eyebrow. "Should I be acting jealous right now? I'm not sure I like the way you just said 'way back'."

Lydia waved him away and rolled her eyes as she leaned in to me. "Tell Mark about David, would you?"

I shared a mischievous smile with Adam's mother. "Well, David is remarkably handsome. Six foot, dark, smoldering eyes, lean and muscular, just about fifty, am I right?"

Lydia nodded, "Sounds like an excellent description."

Mark's amusement turned quickly into jealousy. "Oh really? And how do we know David?"

"Preservation board. I've known him since we renovated Seychelle's."

Mark was turning red.

"Oh," I acted surprised. "I forgot to mention! David is also madly in love with his partner of twenty years, Shawn."

Mark shook his head and took a sip of wine. "You have got to stop with the bad jokes. You'll kill me one of these days."

Lydia laughed and pulled on my elbow. "Come with me. I want to show you something."

Adam's mother was fun and personable, not to mention very beautiful. She was about my height with toned arms and legs, dark hair she wore in a knot at the nape of her neck, and a very classic, but simple, light pink dress. I could tell she was making an extra effort to make me feel comfortable and I appreciated that.

She led me away from the living room and down a short hallway. She stopped halfway and turned to the pictures on the wall. It was covered in framed, professional pictures of Adam from every stage of his life, but in the middle were giant pictures of the *Vanity Fair* photos and two others of him in his race car.

"We have had our share of the ridiculous in our lives, Elizabeth. It may be a little different than yours, but it's ridiculous nonetheless."

She was leaving the subject open. It was up to me to either take it or dismiss it. I glanced at Lydia as she admired the photos of her only child and felt an unusual bond. "Adam mentioned you had to make a separation from your father." I wanted to test the waters and see what it was like to open up to someone who might actually understand what my life looked like on the inside.

"I did." She didn't look at me. "There was a point where it felt like I had to make a choice. If I kept on the path I was on—McKinley politics—then my life was over. I might as well cease to exist. Nothing I ever did from there on out would be my choosing." She turned and looked me in the eye. "I had too much I wanted to do with my life. I wanted to live in Paris and make the most delicious food anyone had ever eaten. I wanted to make people fall in love over dinner and remember their loved ones over dessert. Food is a language all its own, and I had a gift for speaking that language. If I hadn't taken a step away from my family, I never would have met Mark, I never would have had Adam, and I never would have had the adventures I've been able to have. I chose to have a life instead of a legacy."

"I know exactly what you mean," I murmured and turned back to the photos of Adam in his car. Her word choice was haunting me. "I wish I'd seen him race."

"He was good," Lydia agreed. "But he's a better engineer." Then she chuckled and took a sip of her wine. "And I'm a much happier mother. I always worried about him."

I moved down the line to a more recent picture of Adam with the Senator. Both were dressed in gorgeous suits, hands up and waving to a crowd. "And now? Do you have any regrets about stepping away?"

"No. I'd make the exact same choice in a heartbeat. It was rough but my dad is a good man underneath all his political neediness. He has great ambitions and blinders. It took a long time for him to understand that his life was not the life I wanted or needed. We're able to have a relationship now and he's always been a part of Adam's life. It isn't perfect, but it works."

I studied the smile on Adam's face. It was nearly identical to the Senator's. If Adam aged like his grandfather then he was going to be a very handsome older man.

"And what about you?" Lydia asked quietly. "Any regrets?"

I shrugged my shoulders. "I don't think I was as conscious in my choices as you were. I was just trying to survive."

"And so now you look back and wonder if you could have done anything differently?"

I nodded. Keeping my eyes fixed on Adam's picture. "I know I didn't have a choice, but I still wonder."

She patted my shoulder. "Sweetie, if you had another choice you wouldn't be hiding from the paparazzi right now."

I took a deep, exasperated breath and held my glass up in a toast. "Here, here."

We clinked glasses and took another sip. "We should probably get some food in our bellies to go with this wine."

She started to move back down the hallway but

our conversation felt unfinished. "Lydia?"

She turned back toward me and smiled patiently.

"Thank you for letting me hideout here."

She nodded once before turning back toward the kitchen.

Dinner was fun. Adam's parents were great story tellers and clearly in love, moving closer after they finished eating and holding hands intermittently throughout the post-meal conversation. Everything was going along well until Adam mentioned his job offer.

"What?" Lydia sputtered. "You're moving and changing jobs? When were you planning on telling us? Before or after you got settled?"

Adam didn't look surprised by her reaction. He just shook his head. "Mom, don't overreact. This is a good thing—you hated Germany."

She pursed her lips and crossed her arms as she sat back in her seat.

"I'll be closer to Paris," he tried again.

Lydia's lips twitched and her eyes lit up just a little. "But you'll be travelling a lot more. Right now we get to see you regularly...a racing schedule? We've been there."

"It will be fine."

"At least when you were racing Indy cars you were here. Formula 1 is everywhere!"

Mark slid his chair beside Lydia and put his arm over her shoulder. "We've been talking about handing more of the business over to Tatiana...maybe this is a sign. Maybe it's time to start travelling again."

She glared at Mark, then Adam. "Are you two ganging up on me? All I want is to see my only son. Is that really too much to ask?"

"Yes," Mark replied flatly. "You are being selfish. This is Adam's dream job. It brings him a little closer to home and gives us a very good excuse to start visiting Paris again. Stop worrying and be happy. I have a feeling this is happening whether you like it or not."

She looked helplessly at me and I shrugged. I had no say in this or anything else in Adam's life. Lydia shook her head as if she were exasperated with me and turned back to Adam. "If I see you any less than I already do then I will make you miserable."

Adam laughed and stood up, crossing the room and tapping his father on the shoulder. He took his father's place and pulled his mother into a hug. "You aren't losing me, Mom. You know that."

She set her head down on Adam's broad shoulder and sighed. "I know. I still worry."

"Nothing to worry about."

She nodded and sat back up, looking directly at me. "I guess you'll be travelling more, too?"

That feeling you get when you're dreaming about being on stage naked? Yeah, that was how I felt right then. Adam's mother wanted to know if Adam and I were serious.

Adam spoke when I didn't say anything. "We're still working that out. This was a shock to all of us, not just you."

Lydia pursed her lips and gave both Adam and me a good once over. I had a feeling she could read my thoughts as well as Adam could. "Alright. I'll give you two space to figure things out. Dessert?"

I was so full after dinner that Adam basically tucked me into his bed naked when we got back to the apartment. Between the wine, the amazing food Lydia prepared, and the dessert of crème and chocolate…I was in a food coma. I vaguely remember Adam chuckling about keeping me away from his mother and then lightly kissing me on the cheek as he pulled the covers over my body.

So I was a little confused when I woke up hours later in the dark. It took me a few moments to remember where I was. The sheets were so unfamiliar and the room was facing the wrong way. I was cold. Adam wasn't there again.

I sat up and tried to get my head straight. What time was it and where was Adam? I found my phone on the nightstand and pressed a button to light it up. One o'clock. That ache I only felt when I was missing Adam was back. It was going to suck when he left. There were no two ways about it. *Suck suckity suck*.

That was when I realized there was a sound coming from the garage. I slid out of bed and wrapped a blanket around me like a toga to keep warm. Sure enough there was light coming under the door to the garage.

I found Adam under the Duster, his jean covered legs sticking out, along with his obviously naked torso.

I stood there and admired the view for a good two minutes, taking in every inch of the way his abs rippled as he moved, the way his grease covered jeans hung from his hips, and the way he made the sexiest grunts each time the wrench gave him trouble.

"How long you gonna be under there?"

He jumped, the sound of the wrench clattering to the ground as he dropped it. Then he slid out and grinned up at me. "How long have you been standing there?"

"Long enough." There was grease on his face and chest. He was hot as hell.

"Did I wake you?"

I shook my head. "Nope. I think I just missed you."

He stood up and cleaned himself off, grinning like a fool the entire time. I never, ever imagined working on cars was so sexy...but it was. Especially on Adam. "What?" he asked when he caught me drooling.

"You look good, Adam Callaway."

He reached out and grabbed my hand, yanking me against the hood of the car. "You look better." He slid his fingers under the blanket and along my skin. It was electric to feel his touch. He smelled like sweat and car grease. He smelled like a man. It only made me want him more than I already did. "Ever had sex in the backseat of a classic car?"

I shook my head, eyes locked on his.

His breath hitched and I dropped the blanket, letting Adam push it to the floor. He pressed his half naked body into my completely naked one, cupping my face, kissing my lower lip, then my upper lip, before running his nose along mine and looking into my eyes. I felt him everywhere when he did things like that. It was as if he was lighting me up and turning me on from the inside out. It got harder and harder to breathe until I felt like I *needed* to melt into Adam.

He kept his hand on my face as his other hand travelled down between my legs and began to massage my clit to life. After a few swirls the heat and throb was almost painful and I had to adjust. Of course Adam was still wearing jeans, so if I was going to be hot and uncomfortable, I might as well get him naked. I moved his hand away from my clit so I could unbutton his pants, doing it all by touch since I couldn't bring myself to break eye contact. He was mesmerizing.

When his pants fell to the ground he finally let me go, stepping back to kick away his jeans. "I should wake you up more often."

"You didn't wake me up," I reminded him as he helped me up onto the hood. "I missed you."

He made a sound in the back of his throat, moved between my legs, and practically growled as I wrapped my legs around him and grabbed a handful of his gorgeous hair.

"Careful, I'm horny. This may get rough fast."

Rough sounded good to me. I'd been thinking too much. My feelings were all over the place. "Good," I whispered in his ear. Adam's reaction was immediate. He yanked me back down and spun me around so that I had to put my hands out on the hood to brace myself.

"My two favorite things," he murmured as his cock rubbed along the entrance to my sex. "You and my car."

"That makes you sound so possessive." I kind of liked that Adam was feeling possessive. I wanted to be possessed. To be his, even if it was temporary.

"I know what I like," he replied as he pushed slowly inside me.

I hissed through my teeth. Adam's cock was always a lot to adjust to, even after all the sex we'd had. He withdrew and slid back in, moving deeper. I grew wetter to accommodate him. The pulse of my core and clench of my inner muscles asking for more.

"Oh, babe... the things your body does to mine."

I grinned, knowing just how to play Adam. "You sure are taking your sweet time enjoying yourself, aren't you?"

He grunted and I felt the yank on my hair a split second before he slammed into me, pushing deep, but not quite as far as he could reach. "In a hurry to get somewhere?" he growled, wrapping my hair around his fist.

"Just to my orgasm. Or were you planning on making me beg for it?"

He pulled back and slammed into me again. "I'm pretty sure you'll be screaming my name either way."

"Harder," I gasped and laid myself flat against the cool hood. I wanted him to obliterate every thought in my mind until the only feeling left was the warmth of his cock slamming into my body.

He yanked on my hair as he did exactly as I asked—only this time he stopped when our bodies finally locked together. It was easily the most satisfying moment of sex with Adam, outside of coming around his cock. "Shit," he swore and draped himself over my back while buried inside me. For a moment I worried he was about to come, but then I realized he was simply savoring the moment. He took my right hand in his and threaded his fingers between mine while his other hand moved up my side, caressing the outside of my breast.

He kissed down my exposed neck and between my shoulder blades, leaving a trail of tingles that shot down my spine. His lips on my back and his fingers between mine were strangely intimate even though I was blind to him—all I could see were his arms as they flexed and strained.

He began to move, his fingers alternately relaxing and squeezing around my hand as he held it. I was splayed and used as Adam took what he needed from me—which seemed to be a combination of raw desire for my body and an intimate connection to my soul. The way he combined what his body was feeling with his emotions always surprised me. Was this something unique to Adam?

I continued to be baffled by how much I needed his body. I seemed to react strongly to everything about him. His scent, his cock, the way his muscles moved...I shook as the images flashed through my mind, ratcheting up my pleasure.

There was no two ways about it: I was deeply attracted to Adam. In a raw, animalistic way. A primal way.

But it was more than that. He didn't make me come over and over solely because he was hot to look at and had a dick made to please. He drew out another level of pleasure I didn't know existed before him. He turned me on with a well-placed word or look. He drove my lust up several levels by appealing to my mind and heart. He connected with me so that he wasn't just fucking me with his cock that was currently pounding into me like a jackhammer—he also made sure I felt him inside where his fingers and erections couldn't reach. Sex with Adam was an experience on an entirely different plane of existence. The kind I didn't think I would ever find again.

There would never be another Adam.

"Backseat. Now." I gasped, pushing back and away from the hood. Adam withdrew and had the door open in a flash, climbing in first and holding out his hand for me. I straddled him on the soft black leather, my knees pressing into the pocket where the seat back met the bench, wrapped my hands around the rounded top of the leather seat, and lowered myself down onto his waiting cock.

When we were locked together I felt the pressure inside where he was just a little too long for me to handle. My body expanded around him. I was swollen and so aroused it almost hurt. I didn't just *want* to come—I *needed* to come so I could relieve the overwhelming need pooling between my legs and around Adam's cock.

I rode him. My legs burned from the exercise and my fingers hurt from holding onto the seat so hard, but I didn't care. Adam ran his hands up and down my bare back and the added sensations from his fingers skating along my skin felt amazing. I slammed down onto him hard, locking us together, and took a moment to enjoy the pulse of my body around his. My swollen clit heated as it sat against Adam's warm skin, and there was a flutter inside me where my orgasm would start soon. A shiver ran over my sweaty skin as I fought to bring air into my lungs.

Adam wrapped his large hands around my hips and encouraged me to move. He picked me up and pulled me down until I took over again. It felt good to give him control for a moment—then take it back. He kept his hands on my hips, directing me and encouraging me, as I felt the jolt shoot through my body. I cried out as the heat suddenly built at the spot where his body met mine. My toes curled and my nails dug into the leather. My orgasm started as a flutter, then became a wave that never seemed to end. I buried my face in Adam's neck. I yelled and moaned. He took over, moving me when I lost all sense of what I was doing. His skin was salty on my lips and I licked him, loving the taste of pure, sweaty Adam. I wanted him inside me anyway I could get him.

I was just reaching the euphoria stage when Adam began grunting. His muscles jerked and his fingers dug hungrily into my hips. I was a ragdoll on top of him as he came inside me. "Fuck," he grunted. "Oh, god...Eliza—" my name caught in his throat and he pumped into me harder, a moan escaping from his lips as a whisper. "*Beth...*" It was a mess of syllables and noises. I loved the sound of his slurred words.

When he was done he relaxed against the seat, letting his hands fall away. He laughed and sucked in breath after breath as I bounced on his chest. "You ok?" he asked.

I nodded, half asleep again. I was spent. Whatever energy I'd had from my few hours of sleep were now drained away.

"I'm sorry I came inside you. I got carried away." He kissed the top of my head.

I shrugged and mumbled, "That's what birth control is for," as best I could.

He wrapped his strong arms around me and held me tight against his slick chest. He stayed like that as we came down from our sex-high. The world was a foggy mess, but finally started to clear. I ran my hands along the black leather. "What do you call her?"

"Who?" Adam sounded as sleepy as I felt.

"Your car. What do you call her?"

He laughed a little and brushed my sweaty hair back from my face and tilted my chin up so he could look into my eyes. "I never named her. But I think I just named you."

I was confused by both his statements. "What do you mean?"

His eyes searched mine for several eternal seconds and I think he was debating whether telling me what he meant was a good idea. "Beth. I couldn't say your whole name when I came. All I could get out was 'Beth'. I liked the way it sounded."

I think my heart actually stopped. He was looking at me so hard and so sweetly. His voice was soft and tentative—so sincere I could *feel* his words. I could feel my name on his lips. He told me the first time we had breakfast that I would never be Liz to him and he was right—I wasn't the same person around Adam that I was with anyone else.

When I didn't respond he swallowed and took a deep breath. "Did I just freak you out?"

I shook my head, still too stunned and overwhelmed to form words.

"Do you like it? I love your full name. It's beautiful and it's *you*, but I like knowing there is something I can call you that's just mine. I'm feeling very selfish when it comes to you."

I looked into his beautiful eyes and nodded. He released my chin and cupped my face, running his thumb over my cheek. "Beth?"

A tear formed and rolled out of my eye. *What in the hell was that shit? I was crying now?*

Adam brushed the single tear away and smiled. "Beth it is then."

I nodded and forced a little smile. I was speechless, but I loved it. I closed my eyes and relaxed into his chest for a few more minutes, letting everything sink in. I couldn't quite put words into what I was feeling towards Adam but I was coming to terms with the idea it was more than friendship and sexual attraction. Adam meant more to me than any friend I'd had before.

"Why haven't you named your car? Didn't you say you'd had this one for a while?" I needed a distraction—even if it was only for a few minutes.

"I usually name them when I'm done. I'm not done with her."

I looked over the perfect interior and frowned. "She looks done to me." And then Adam's words from came flooding back. *She's a project I'll never finish.* "You're never going to finish this car, are you?"

I sat up so I could look into Adam's eyes. He shook his head and laughed a little. "Probably not. There will always be something else I can modify or fix."

"Modifying and fixing are different from being renovated. She's a complete car, Adam."

He frowned and cocked his head off to the side. He really didn't like my questioning. "I like knowing there is always something else for me to do on her. I don't want her to be finished."

I balked. I was being stupid and ridiculous, making more out of Adam's red and white Duster than there actually was. "So you can always have something to fix? Do you like fixing things?"

"Umm...yeah. I pretty much make a career out of finding solutions."

That statement hit me in the gut like a punch I didn't see coming. Adam was a fixer. He got off on fixing problems. I didn't like the way that realization made me feel at all.

I needed some air.

"We better get cleaned up and to bed." I started looking for the best way to extricate myself from Adam but we'd left the blanket and clothes on the garage floor. There'd be a mess in his backseat to cleanup. I scrambled off his lap and out the door, throwing his boxers in the window for him to wipe down the seat.

"I'll clean the car, you go get ready for bed, ok?"

I nodded and wrapped the blanket around me. I was shivering but I wasn't sure if it was from the cool air or the cold blood running through my veins.

I got cleaned up and into bed as fast as I could, pretending I was already fast asleep so I wouldn't have to talk to Adam again. He kissed me on the cheek when he got into bed and fell asleep with his back pressed against mine. I waited, keeping up my ruse, until I heard his soft snores.

I was an idiot.

I was convinced Adam and I had all these crazy connections and that he cared about me. I'd been drawing conclusions based on a fantasy I hadn't even realized I'd been harboring all my life. Despite knowing people were users, I still believed deep down inside that some people were different. Some people fell in love.

But I wasn't some people. I was another project on Adam's list. I was something he could problem solve and fix. I was a challenge for his intellect and a prize to win.

I needed to stop fantasizing about love and a life free of complications. I was being impractical and this was a time when I needed all my wits about me. I was about to survive a small war with my family—one that might end up with my name being dragged back through the media with mud all over it. The last thing I needed to be doing was letting my head get lost in some clouds.

I tossed and turned all night, finally hopping out of bed at dawn. Adam stirred soon after, making me coffee and watching me silently as I threw myself together for work. His eyes were hollow and a little harder than normal. I couldn't tell if he was angry or disappointed that I was pulling away from him. It didn't matter.

Adam doesn't matter.

I kept chanting that to myself hoping it would eventually sink in, but inside I was dying. I was quietly shattering into millions of pieces.

Nothing my parents had done had ever made me feel like this. If I could barely survive my family then there was no way I'd ever be able to survive Adam. If ten days had done this to me...well, I needed to start ending things with Adam now. I'd let myself get too close. It was time to pull back while I still could.

"Have a good day at work. I'll see you for lunch?"

I nodded and grabbed my bag. Andres took me to my office where I worked for the first hour of my morning before my first class. With five minutes to spare I grabbed my USB drive with the PowerPoint for the lesson, my coffee, and my badge. For the next hour I'd be Dr. Filler, a teacher. I would focus on my students and my lesson. It would be a nice break from the heavy reality of my surreal life.

I was so lost in my thoughts about class that I wasn't paying attention when I stepped out of the main door of our department and into the foyer of the building. Andres was waiting for me on the bench outside, reading the paper and enjoying his own coffee.

"Elizabeth." A familiar voice called to me quietly.

I froze where I was and very nearly lost my breakfast in the potted tree beside me. *My mother*.

I turned on my heels and met her gaze. She was standing three feet away. Her hair was perfectly bobbed, her clothes expertly tailored. Her face was more nipped and tucked than the last time I saw her and for a brief moment I allowed myself to laugh at the thought that Cybil was more plastic than human these days.

"Cybil. It isn't Friday. You shouldn't be here."

"We need to talk."

"No, we don't," I laughed and started to turn, but she reached out and grabbed my elbow. Her fingers were cold and I wanted to wrench my arm away from her and run screaming out to Andres. But I didn't. I really don't know why I didn't.

"Yes. We do."

I stared at her hand on my elbow as if it were the strangest thing I'd ever seen. In a way it was. My mother rarely touched me, even as a child. "Friday," I repeated.

"Now. We have private things that cannot be discussed in front of lawyers or sisters. Certainly not photographers."

"We have nothing to discuss ever again."

Cybil let me go and pulled herself up to her full height, which in heels was a good two inches taller than me. She was trying to intimidate me. In a way it was working. I didn't have much fight in me at the moment and while the hallway was quiet, classes were about to change and we would be surrounded by students—many of which were Cybil's adoring fans.

"What do you want?"

A triumphant smirk pulled at the corner of her inflated lips as Max Vettel stepped up beside her. "Hello, Elizabeth. It's been a long time."

My heart stopped beating as I looked into the steely blue eyes of the one man who held the power to truly destroy me. "Not long enough." I replied.

Chapter 27

Wednesday Night

"That's how you're going to play this?" Adam was really, really not happy with me. His eyes had this hollow edge to them and his forehead was creased with frustration.

"I'm not playing anything," I lied. I'd been lying through my teeth for the last two days. I was a damn fine actress but not even the best performance of my life was enough to convince Adam that I wasn't pulling away and hiding things from him.

He shook his head a little, like he was holding in an enormous amount of fury, and then spun away, running his fingers through his hair and let out an exasperated breath. "Fine. I can't force you to talk to me. I just..." He turned back and looked me in the eye. "I just thought you trusted me."

God damn that man knew how to hit me in the heart. "I do trust you."

He stood there, silently staring at me for what felt like an eternity. Adam was studying me, trying to figure me out. He was probably completely confused by the fact I could both trust him and want to keep things from him at the same time.

I was crazy like that.

But it was so much better this way. If I told Adam everything that was happening in my so-called fucked-up life, it would just complicate things. It would ruin what little bit of paradise I had left with Adam. I'd already pulled away—something he was fighting tooth and nail. I hadn't told him yet, but I wasn't going to meet him in Russia. I wasn't ever going to meet him again. The only reason I was still seeing him at all was because I knew he'd just hound me. He wouldn't take no for an answer. He'd want reasons and he wouldn't stop asking for those reasons until he got on his plane. It was much easier to simply play out the last few days of our arrangement, but at a slightly safer distance.

Plus, I couldn't seem to walk away—despite knowing I needed to. Every time I tried to pack my bag, I started crying. This crying bullshit needed to stop. I wasn't a crier, and yet in the last week I'd lost track of how many times water had come out of my eyes. I was suddenly a damn fountain.

"Are you ok?" he finally said something, but it wasn't what I was expecting.

"Of course I'm ok." I looked down at myself wondering what prompted Adam's question. Did I have blood running out of a cut or something?

Adam shook his head. "With whatever it is you're not telling me. It's your right to keep things to yourself if that's what you want—I just need to know that you are ok."

Oh.

No, I wasn't ok with that. Not with any of *that*. I wasn't ok with being blackmailed by my family. I was most definitely not ok with my ex finding me and helping with the blackmail. *That* was a giant cluster fuck that was destroying me one piece at a time.

I couldn't answer Adam truthfully so I blatantly (probably too obviously) changed the subject. "I have a friend in town tomorrow. He asked if he could have drinks and meet you."

Adam's eyebrows shot up. He blinked twice and then yanked me against his firm body. His lips crushed mine and he kissed me hard, holding my head in both his hands with an almost painful grip. It was like he was trying to crawl inside me.

Or maybe it was to shield me.

Because his kiss quickly turned into more. He was wrapped around me and I felt like I was being slowly hidden away from the world beneath a protective blanket of Adam. One hand moved down my back to my hips and pressed me into his firm erection. He didn't say anything—just grunts and sounds of frustration as he stripped me and then himself. He picked me up and set me on the bed, spreading my legs as he kneeled in front of me on the floor and kissed quickly up my thighs. Then his tongue was on my clit and I threw myself onto the sheets, arching my back and gasping for air as my legs tightened around his head. I had to force myself to think enough to keep from crushing Adam but, *damn*, he had a seriously talented tongue.

He was insistent and didn't give much room to make suggestions. I was just along for the ride, holding on for dear life as Adam drove me fast and hard toward orgasm. His fingers began to work me, gliding in and out, curling and coaxing. I was yelling and moaning for my climax when he stopped, stood up, and rolled on a condom.

He took his dear, sweet time, watching me with hooded, dark eyes. Haunted eyes. My core throbbed painfully—needing to orgasm and wanting something to fill it. I arched and gyrated while I waited. All I could think about was Adam and sex. I was consumed by my need for him.

"Scoot back."

I slid backward into the middle of the bed as Adam climbed over me. I was thrilled and terrified by his dark mood. It meant sex was going to be hard and fast, just the way I liked it when my emotions and stress were more than I could handle. But it also meant Adam was being driven by his feelings. Feelings I put there. *I* was the reason for his confusion and unhappiness.

And that realization sucked.

He hovered over me, his elbows beside my shoulders and his cock just out of my reach. He wasn't looking at me and I could feel the tension that was rolling off of him. This was an Adam I'd never seen before, and I suddenly wished I could go back and fix things. I was absolutely certain I wouldn't survive falling in love with Adam. I knew without a shadow of a doubt loving him would consume and destroy me. But seeing what I was doing to him was destroying me anyway. There was no way to win with Adam. I was already in too deep. Pushing him away was hurting us both.

He locked eyes with me a split second before he slammed into me. His cock only making it part way inside. I cried out in pain and relief, digging my nails into his shoulder as I wrapped my arms underneath his. He reared back and slammed into me again, grunting and dropping his forehead to mine, but not breaking the eye contact that was almost as penetrating as his cock.

He was at least halfway inside me now. My core pulsed around the invasion, sending licks of pleasure up through my body, clenching around his cock in search of more friction. Adam shuddered and panted, his jaw going slack as he pulled back again, this time pushing all the way inside me until he was buried to the hilt.

But he didn't savor the moment like he usually did. Instead, he got right to work, moving hard and fast. My orgasm quickly built back up with the friction from Adam's dick moving in and out of me, but it was how his body slammed into mine: so hard and completely. He was rolling his hips so that with each thrust his body made contact with my swollen clit. It created a burst of pleasure with each stroke, and I climbed higher and higher, gasping for air, arching for more. And then it hit. I yelled and shook as wave after wave of my orgasm washed through me.

Adam never faltered. He kept up his rhythm, only grunting with appreciation at the height of my climax. At the rate he was going, I would be sore for a week. I liked knowing I would remember this moment every time I ached for the next few days. I'd remember the feeling of Adam lost inside me, of the complete satisfaction he always gave me, the release from my troubles. It made me want to give him something in return.

I reached up and grabbed his hair between my fingers, pulling until he looked at me. "I want to be on top."

He stopped and stared at me before nodding furiously and pulled out. I directed him to the pillows—I liked it best when he was sitting up a little. His cock was twitching as I mounted him, my hands on the headboard and my knees on either side of his hips. My breasts were in his face and Adam smiled appreciatively. "Mind if I taste?"

I positioned his cock so that it was sitting just inside the entrance to my sex and nodded. He grabbed a breast with each hand and sucked one nipple into his mouth while his other hand massaged. I cried out and panted, while little flutters raced deep inside me looking for something to ride. I slowly—very slowly—sank down onto his cock. It was still wet from being inside me, and I was a river from coming so hard after such fantastic foreplay. His size almost didn't matter—until we were locked together and the tip of his cock pressed at the top of my core. I could never decide if it hurt or just took my breath away to have something so large inside me.

Either way it felt damn good.

Adam was shaking and moaning against my breast, but he didn't to pull away. His hips rolled but I refused to move. Adam wanted rough, fast sex but I *needed* to tease him first. I needed to see that look in his eyes when he was lost in me—completely out of control and willing to do anything I asked.

God, I was so addicted to him... and the inflated high *I* got from pleasuring him into madness.

I moved slowly up and down his shaft. Adam groaned and ran his teeth along my nipple, trading one breast for the other. His tongue and teeth took my breath away and I faltered for a moment. I moved my hands into his hair, running my nails along his scalp and tugging.

He looked up at me and shook his head slowly. A silent warning that I'd pay for my playing. He pressed my breasts together so that my nipples were side by side and took them *both* into his mouth simultaneously.

Every muscle in my body clenched and I froze. I was unable to think or do anything else as long as Adam's tongue was swirling and sucking on both my nipples at the same time. My inner muscles tightened around Adam's cock and he grinned, pulling one of my nipples between his teeth. "It feels an awful lot like you enjoy what I'm doing to you right now."

I nodded. I was doing my best to keep my breathing even, but it was taking everything I had. I was supposed to be driving *him* crazy—not the other way around. He'd already given me an orgasm. And yet, I was pretty sure that the pressure building at that spot where Adam's erection was pressing into me was another orgasm.

I slid up and down a few inches. Adam's hands tightened. "Oh fuck me, that feels good."

And so I did. I rode him hard. Pulling up until his dick was just barely inside me, and then slamming down as hard as I could. I shifted my hands back to the headboard for leverage, moving harder and faster as the heat between us built. Adam was straining, his hands helping me move, his hips rocking in rhythm with my thrusts. He was coming apart, but not undone, and I didn't know what it would take to push him over the edge.

And then suddenly, he flipped me onto my back and drove into me with a long, slow, firm thrust. When we were locked together his hand turned my face to his so that he could look into my eyes. "I need to see you come," he whispered like it took everything he had in him.

He withdrew slowly and I fought for air like I was hyperventilating, but I wasn't. He slid just as slowly back inside me. The sensation was exquisite. His cock was skating along the inside of my body, but it was sending a current of electricity to every inch of my skin.

In and out so slowly I could savor and enjoy every single inch of his dick and the way it felt as it glided against every inch of me.

The head of his cock popped out just a little, and the added sensation of taking all of him back inside me nearly drove me insane. "Don't look away," Adam gasped when my eyes rolled into my head and I arched my back.

I looked back into his eyes and saw something I hadn't seen all night. *Peace*. Adam looked peaceful. And he hadn't even come yet.

I'd made him hurt, but now I'd also made him content.

He slid all the way back, deep inside me, and stopped. His body was pressed up against mine. It was warm and firm in all the right places. He rocked against me with his cock buried and his thumb running along my cheek. With each roll of his hips, the pressure of his body against mine spiking and changing, my orgasm climbed a little higher. I started to shudder even though I'd just barely felt the first flutters. I was overwhelmed and spent from such rigorous sex and my body was coming undone as another powerful orgasm began.

Adam kept doing exactly what he was doing. His breathing quickened right along with mine, his jaw was thrust out as he watched me, and the muscles of his shoulders strained to maintain his position. I started moaning and yelling before I actually felt my orgasm and Adam began grunting right along with me.

He shuddered and I shuddered. We were completely in sync.

And then it hit. I came so hard that I yanked Adam down and he had to fight to watch me come. I wasn't in control of anything I was doing. I wrapped around him, my legs tightening and arms squeezing. My hips bucked.

"My god you are so beautiful when you come, Beth." His new name for me was more than I could handle and I closed my eyes, riding out the last waves of my orgasm.

Adam kissed my neck and reared back. It only took a few long, hard strokes for him to join me.

Chapter 28

I was draped across Adam's chest while I listened to him read. His voice was deep and rough from reading in the cool, but humid, night air. The back windows were all open and a beautiful fall breeze drifted through his apartment. The moon was full and high and an army of crickets was playing background music for us.

This time Adam was reading from his iPad so he didn't have to shift to turn the pages. Why couldn't life always be like this? This was simple and very nearly perfect. I was lying on a gorgeous man who was reading me poetry. *Poetry* for heaven's sake. E.E. Cummings, to be exact. My favorite. It was just the two of us. I was content and so was Adam.

But sex was a Band-Aid. We were fooling ourselves into believing the connection during orgasm had magically brought us back together. It hadn't. I still had major family obstacles to overcome and Adam was still a dangerously tempting taste of a life I couldn't have. He seemed helpful and caring—and he was—but he was also a fixer. There was no room in my life for any form of manipulation or control. Not even for sexy men with good intentions.

I didn't want to be used and I didn't want to be someone's project. This was *my* life, not theirs. My ever-important control was seriously lacking and I wasn't happy about that. It was frustrating to feel like so many outside forces were influencing my life without my consent.

I sat up and sighed, needing to clear my confusing thoughts and hopefully find a way through the mess of my heart and my head. I knew what I wanted…I just also knew what I had to work with, and it wasn't much.

Adam traced his fingers lazily down my back. "What are you thinking about?"

I panicked when he asked questions like that. It was an instinct I still couldn't shake. "I'm thinking about tomorrow."

His fingers didn't falter as they continued to trace some invisible design across my skin. "Who's this friend I'm meeting for drinks?" I'd asked him to meet Ronoldo and me for drinks after the shoot—but I'd also conveniently left out all the messy details about why he was in town.

"His name's Ronoldo. He's an old friend."

Adam set his iPad down and turned onto his side, facing me. "Why's he visiting?"

I shrugged. "Work." *Liar.* I was a big fat liar. It was true he was here for work, but only because I'd hired him. *I* was his work. "He's flying out tomorrow night so it will just be drinks before he heads out." I was going to lie until I turned blue. I didn't want Adam anywhere near that photo shoot, my family, or my crazy.

Adam nodded and studied his fingers as they traced loops on my hip. The look in his eyes was clear—he didn't believe a damn thing I was saying. "I'm not sure what to do right now, Elizabeth. I feel like my hands are tied. There is something wrong and you won't tell me what it is. When I asked if you were ok, you changed the subject, which tells me you *aren't* ok."

I wanted to ignore his questions or make up better answers—anything to keep Adam at a distance. "What do you want me to say?"

He sat up, crossing his legs and dropping his hands in his lap. "My instinct is to crush anything that makes you 'not ok'. I can't do that if I have no idea what or who my enemy is." His voice dropped to a murmur and his eyes narrowed, "But I have my suspicions."

"I'm taking care of things."

Adam scowled. "You don't have to do everything alone."

"I also don't need a knight in shining fucking armor to swoop in and save me." Damn, I sounded angry. Maybe I was.

Adam went white. "Because I care about you and want to help you I'm automatically a controlling asshole who wants to take over your life? Is that what you're saying?" He was angry and surprised. His eyes were wide, but the corners were also crinkled like he was trying very hard not to lose his temper.

I cringed. "It's not like that."

"Then tell me what it's like. One minute we're happy and the next I feel you pulling away. Any time I mention helping, a curtain goes up between us. Your eyes go blank and cold...*I can see it.*"

"Why do you want to help?" This was the question I'd been trying to ask for days, but couldn't seem to find the right way to ask.

Adam looked at me like I'd lost my mind. "Why *wouldn't* I?"

"Am I a project?" I yelled before I lost my nerve. "Do you like being with me because you can help fix me and my problems, like I'm a car you can restore?"

His eyes narrowed and his jaw hardened. A vein I didn't know Adam had, started to throb in his temple. "How can you say that? How?" He was angry and shocked.

Which gave me a small amount of relief, but it didn't answer my question. "This is what you do, isn't it? Find solutions to problems? You said yourself that you like the challenge. You like knowing you'll always have something to come back to." I was pointing and gesturing like a crazy person. "I can't be your project, Adam. I can't be someone else's toy ever again. I'm a fucking person and I just want to be treated that way."

"Where is this coming from? You are not a car and I don't see you that way at all." Adam put his hands up in frustration and shook his head. "I care about you,

Elizabeth! I care so much about you." I felt like he was holding back. That he actually wanted to say more but knew he couldn't.

Because if he really said everything he was thinking it would truly push me away once and for all.

My heart twisted. This was too much. Too complicated. What had happened to my simple little two week fling? "How? How can you *care* about me already?" This was insane. "You don't put yourself on the line for people you barely know." I didn't understand Adam or his motivations and that scared me. It was too fast. Things were happening too quickly for him to know what he felt.

He grabbed my ankles and yanked me flat on my back, crawling on top of me so that his hands were on either side of my face and his knees were around my hips. This positioning was as deliberate as any other Adam used. He wanted my full attention and he wanted me to hear him loud and clear.

"Elizabeth Filler," he shook his head and a little smile curved his lips as his eyes wandered all over my face. His anger had evaporated and in its place was a look of complete wonder and confusion. Of all the things I expected out of Adam, a smile was the last. I'd been yelling at him. I was angry and ready to run out the door. Why in the hell was he smiling at me? "I feel like I'm beating my head against a wall getting you to understand this."

Understand what? Things seemed pretty simple to me: this was a fling gone too far. We had separate lives and needed to reign ourselves in. We'd gotten accidentally tangled up in each other's lives. I was eating dinners with his family and essentially living in his apartment. Adam was helping me with the press and getting pulled into the mess with my family. It was far too much for what was supposed to be a simple vacation fuck. This was supposed to be fun.

He brushed his thumb along my cheek and kissed me lightly on the lips. Adam had a soft, almost giddy look in his eyes. "I've dated girls the Senator set me up with. Politicians, lobbyists, daughters of politicians." He ran his nose along mine. "I've dated women my parents have set me up with. We're talking everything from trust fund babies to executives."

"Are you flaunting your conquests in front of me for a reason?" I had a sudden urge to hunt down these women and punch them in the face—which made absolutely no sense whatsoever.

"Be quiet and listen," he smiled and kissed me again. His eyes were boring into mine with a look I didn't know how to name. A look I was *afraid* to name. "I've dated women I picked up in bars in four different countries. In bookstores. And friends of friends."

I frowned as his list kept growing. If Adam didn't get to his point soon I was going to lose it. This jealousy crap wasn't fun at all.

"Do you know how many of them understood me?"

He was genuinely asking and that pulled at my heart in a way I couldn't ignore. I thought through the list and there were a few prime possibilities in there. "A couple?" I shrugged.

He shook his head. "Not one. Not a single one. None of them have the life I have or dreams for the future I'm building. There is a very small pool of women who come from anything like my family. They understood the whole celebrity aspect and the high profile life—but they never understood my desire to leave it behind. None of them got why I picked up and moved to another country to find my own life. None of them appreciate why I have the fears and hopes for my life that I have."

I touched his face. I didn't think about it—I just did it. I needed to connect with him when he looked at me like that.

Like I was a lifeline. *His lifeline.*

"A couple tried really hard to empathize." He kissed me again, running his nose along mine and deepening our connection. "The accident changed me. It made me see the world differently. I tried to explain it to them...but," he looked into my eyes and shook his head like he was having trouble believing what he was about to say. "...I don't have to explain anything to you."

I tightened my grip and pulled him down for a kiss. I didn't know how to say that I understood exactly what he meant. It felt too raw and real to say it out loud—I needed to push him away, not pull him in closer. But I didn't.

"Elizabeth, I knew the minute I sat down next to you at Seychelle's that there was something different about you. I don't know if it was the fact that you were reading alone at the bar, or how gorgeous you were, or what...but there are some things that people like us do to survive, and you were doing them." His voice roughened as he spoke, growing deeper and far more lustful. *Desperate.*

I knew exactly what he meant. "You keep to yourself because it's easier and safer."

"Yeah." He ran his thumb across my cheek and got lost in my eyes. I got lost in his. "I could feel it. The vibe you were giving off was cautious. I saw all the signs of someone who viewed the world like I did and it made me want to get to know you. Immediately and at any cost."

He kissed me again, but this time it was a deeper kiss. My lips parted and his soft tongue stroked mine. Adam slid his knees down so that he was lying on top of me instead of hovering. I liked having his weight on me. It made him feel real. "I think that's why I let you in, even if I didn't understand any of it at the time."

He smiled. "I care about you, Beth. What we have can't be defined by a timeframe. I could spend a lifetime getting to know those other women and they'd never know me like you do right now. I'm being selfish. I want you in my life because *I* need you. I hope you need me too."

Oh god, how I needed him. I needed Adam like I needed air. That was what was so terrifying.

"So I want you to listen carefully to what I am about to say. Ok?" He waited for my nod. "*You are not a project.* Do you hear me?" He pressed his forehead to mine and stared into my eyes. He was too close and my vision went a little funny, but I didn't dare move. "I admit I have a problem with stepping in to help, especially with you. But it's because I care about you and it kills me to see you unhappy. There's a difference between manipulating and assisting. I am not here to manipulate you or to feed my own need to fix things."

I traced my fingers along his cheek. Adam needed to understand that there were things he'd never be able to fix. "We might need to get you into some 'Helpers Anonymous' meetings."

He suddenly rolled off me and sat up. "C'mon, sit up and look me in the eye."

He waited impatiently while I moved. He took my hands in his. "I, Adam Callaway, do solemnly swear to stop trying to fix everything."

I let out a long breath of relief.

"Ah!" he shook his head. "I wasn't done yet."

Of course he wasn't.

"I promise to drastically reduce my need to fix things as long as you promise to let me help when you need it. You're not ok, Elizabeth, and that's not right. If you expect me to sit back while you navigate complicated things alone, to watch you deal with your pain without anyone to lean on, then this isn't going to work. I can't be that guy. It's a fundamental part of who I am. I will not sit around while you are in pain."

It was part of what I liked so much about him: he was genuinely a good guy. But that didn't change things. "I don't know how to do this, Adam." I honestly didn't. It felt like weakness to let someone else manage my problems. It wasn't his family to deal with—they were my bag of crazy and no one else's.

His face hardened into a mask I couldn't read. "Please don't do this."

"This was a fling, Adam. A simple way to have some fun without complications. *I can't have complications.* I was clear about this."

"Damn it, Elizabeth." He spun off the bed and stood up. I followed him. "You're scared, I get that, but pushing me away with excuses—saying I'm a fixer—isn't the answer. You see bad guys everywhere but *I'm not the bad guy*. I'm not perfect. I make mistakes and overstep my bounds, but it isn't on purpose and it isn't to hurt you. If you're waiting for someone perfect to let into your life, then you're going to be alone forever." He grabbed my hands and dipped down to catch my gaze. "Everyone makes mistakes and you need to learn that sometimes those mistakes can be forgiven."

I automatically jerked my hands away and wrapped them around me. I was suddenly very cold and exposed. Adam's words shook me down to my foundation. He was babbling about mistakes and forgiveness like those were simple things—but to me, mistakes were intentional and forgiveness was for the weak.

What he was talking about was something else entirely.

He was right. I *did* see bad guys everywhere because I was usually surrounded by them. "And you need to learn that some things can't be managed or *fixed*," I bit out the word. "Or *manipulated* simply because you want it to be so." It felt good to lash back. Whether Adam was pushing his way into my life with good or bad intentions, he was still pushing too hard. And I didn't know what else to do but push back.

He winced. Then he reached up and brushed my cheek with his thumb. "I wish this wasn't so complicated. I wish this wasn't just vacation. I know I'm putting pressure on this because I leave on Sunday. But it doesn't make it any less true, Elizabeth. I have deep, complicated, life-changing feelings for you and I am willing to do anything to keep feeling this way."

"I can't do this right now." I took his hand from my face. His eyes looked so hollow it broke my heart. It was like taking away his hand took away his light. "I need some time to clear my head." I grabbed my clothes and pulled them on while texting Andres. Adam stood completely still, like I'd stunned him into silence. "I have some work I've been putting off because of..." my voice drifted as I waved my hands in the air. "All of this. I'm going to go work and clear my head." I paused with my hand on the door and my bag on my shoulder. "We can talk tomorrow after work. If you want." And I walked away without looking back. I knew if I looked back I'd see a look on Adam's face I'd never be able to erase from my mind.

I was breaking his heart just as sharply as he was breaking mine.

I walked quickly, my feet moving faster than I knew they could, and somehow I didn't stumble. My heart was about to beat right out of my chest. I wanted to get to the car and back to my office, collapse into my chair, and cry. Why did Adam make me feel this way? How was it possible to feel so good and bad in a matter of moments? The highs and the lows of knowing this man were so drastic and I felt completely out of control—the one feeling I hated more than anything else. Maybe that was the problem. No matter how good he made me feel, or how much I cared about him, being around Adam also made me feel crazy. I couldn't do this relationship crap if that was what it meant.

I was foolish to think I could.

How could someone make me feel so hopeful and hopeless all at the same time?

Or maybe that was me.

Maybe I was the one giving up my control, not Adam taking it from me. I was the one who'd forbidden myself from seeing anything but the next day. I was a survivalist who hadn't yet understood that I was safe. I was so convinced the next round of pain was waiting for me around the next corner that I refused to see the possibility that I was fine, and whatever lay around the next corner was easily manageable.

Andres pulled up just as I stumbled outside.

Chapter 29

Thursday Afternoon

I felt numb sitting in front of Adam. The day had drained everything from me. Between fighting the night before and work (which I was trying desperately to keep as separate and normal as possible), I was exhausted. It was the first night I'd slept without Adam since we started having sex. It sucked. And it took an enormous amount of effort to smile and act happy when inside I felt like I was dying. Like pieces of me were wilting and turning brown, receding into myself. I was starting to wonder if I would ever feel free again.

At least I didn't have to pretend with Adam. I could look as exhausted as I felt.

He looked exhausted, too. His eyes were darker than normal and his face lacked any discernible expression. He was stone. Immovable, emotionless, stone. "I didn't know whether you'd come."

"I said we'd talk after work," I replied. It took more

power than normal to push the air out of my lungs and say a simple sentence.

"You walked out on me. I wasn't sure." He sounded defeated. Like he'd finally resigned himself to the fact he couldn't force me to be in a relationship with him.

"You said some pretty huge things. I needed time."

I was sitting on the couch and Adam was sitting on the coffee table. His shoulders were straight, but more forward than normal. He held his hands in his lap, one inside the other, and he wasn't quite meeting my eyes. He was looking at my nose or forehead when he spoke. *At* me, but not *into* me.

I sighed. "I think you brought up a very important point." His eyes flicked to mine, finally. "Forgiveness. I hadn't thought of things like that before." My family and Adam were cut from two different cloths and it was unfair for me to expect them both to behave the same way. "I deal in absolutes, probably to an unhealthy level. People are good or evil. They cause harm, or help. I don't see people as living anywhere in between because that has never been my experience."

Adam watched me carefully. His expression didn't really change but I saw something in his eyes. "There's a lot of gray between the black and the white."

I nodded. I'd done a lot of good thinking alone in my office. In the silence I was able to go over each word and the meanings behind them. I was letting my fear color everything I was seeing. I was turning Adam into a villain because I was scared, not because he'd done anything wrong. I wasn't sure how long it was going to take me to really understand that. It was like putting on glasses for the first time and realizing how much you'd been missing. "I didn't understand that you might make mistakes, and that you could learn from those mistakes to make different choices in the future. It was easier for me to believe that you would always behave a certain way, no matter what."

He shook his head slowly, the lines on his face softening. "I'm not like those other people in your life."

"I'm trying to believe that."

"Believe faster." It wasn't a command—it was a plea. His voice cracked at the end and disappeared.

I wanted to believe him, right then and there. To trust with wild abandon and live in the moment. But it was too soon for that. "You want to know why I've been pushing you away and keeping secrets. And I understand. If you were doing the same thing, I'd be losing my mind. But there's a reason, Adam." I looked down at my hands and picked at my thumb nail. Anything to keep my mind distracted from all the thoughts racing through it. "I don't want to be that old Elizabeth when I'm with you."

"I know that," he whispered. "Don't you think I know that? I want you to be whoever you want to be when you're with me. There aren't qualifications on my feelings toward you."

I knew he believed everything he was saying. There was an honesty in his eyes that nothing could ever erase. "But," I hesitated, "*I* have qualifications on my feelings for *you*." I let him have a moment to digest my words. He blinked a few times, but didn't say anything. "I told you in the beginning, I don't do relationships. I let myself get pulled into this fantasy vacation world with you, and I've had an amazing time, but it doesn't change things. I can't be with anyone else who will use me or control me in any way. It's a deal breaker."

"Elizabeth—"

I cut him off before he could launch into a speech. "I know that's not your intention, but the results are the same. If I told you everything that was happening behind the scenes right now..." I tried to find the words to explain without inciting a riot. "Because of who you are, Adam, you wouldn't sit still and let me handle it. You'd want to help. You'd want to hurt people and get involved. It's better that I don't tell you. Because then I get to pretend there is some sort of hope for us."

"No," he replied immediately. "That's not fair."

"Excuse me?"

"Now *you're* manipulating *me*. If I screw things up, at least it will have been *my* choice. If we can't work through this I'd rather know it now—not down the road when I've already fallen so hard for you I can't get back up again. I want to know now."

I'd be lying if I didn't admit part of me wanted that, too. But I also loved holding onto what was left of my fantasy. I still had Adam for almost forty-eight hours. If I told him the truth there was a very real chance I would have to end things immediately.

"Please."

He shook his head and that was when I knew it was over anyway. Adam wasn't going to let this go. Either I told him and took a chance, or *he* was going to be the one to walk away.

"Alright. Then what you need to know is in my bag."

He raised an eyebrow before standing up and crossing the room to where I'd left it on the counter. "Inside?"

I nodded. "Zippered pocket. Your envelope is in there, and so is mine." I hadn't looked at the picture since Roger slid it across the table at lunch. Seeing Max and Cybil in person was just about all the reminder I could handle.

Max had looked visibly older than the last time I saw him—graying around the temples and creasing around his eyes. But he was tan, fit, and as handsome as he ever was. Also just as much of a manipulating asshole. It was a miracle I didn't claw his eyes out. The only thing that had stopped me was my intense desire to get them away from my office and students before anyone recognized them.

Adam shuffled around, finally pulling out the correct envelope. Before he opened it he looked back at me, locking eyes and holding my gaze for several long seconds. I saw his hesitation and his resolve. Then he flipped open the flap. I braced myself for his reaction.

"Oh my god." Adam's voice wasn't more than a whisper. When he looked up his eyes were on fire—

angry and hurt, mixed with confusion and rage. "What is this?"

The air was eerily still and there was a distinct lack of background noise—like everything had been sucked out of the room except us and that damn picture.

"That is my biggest regret."

"Be more specific," he said firmly.

"That is a photograph of me having sex with Max Vittel, the executive producer of my television show. Is that specific enough for you?"

Adam dropped the envelope like it was suddenly on fire, and stared at it lying on the ground. "How old were you? Oh my god, Elizabeth. What the hell? How old was *he?*"

The look of disgust on Adam's face was precisely what I'd been hoping to avoid. It was one thing to regret my past and lock it away in my memories, but it was an entirely different thing to see Adam's reaction. It ripped open my invisible wound, forced all my memories out of hiding, and hurt me more than I'd ever hurt before. Maybe it was because I'd never really let myself absorb everything that happened. I moved forward so fast for so long, never looking back. And now here I was, forced to stop and come to terms with everything I'd run away from.

"In that picture? I had just turned sixteen."

Somehow Adam turned whiter. "You were sleeping with him when you were *fifteen*?"

I nodded, but just barely. It was hard to admit. "Max is twenty years older than me. It went on for about four months. Until I figured out what was really happening and asked to leave the show."

"What was really happening?" Adam's voice dropped to a low, angry rumble.

I wasn't sure there was much blood left in my head. I kind of felt like I was floating just above myself. My hands were tingling and my knees felt like jelly. "Max prefers young girls he can manipulate. He's a classic predator. I didn't realize that until after the night that picture was taken." A night that had gotten out of control and gone too far. "But what I didn't realize at the time was that he was also helping my parents fudge my working hours and splitting my paycheck with them. He was pretending to be in love with me."

Adam stared at me with his mouth open before shaking his head, locking his eyes on me and crossing the room. He knelt in front of me, grabbing my hands in his. "What does this have to do with now? What is going on?"

Adam wasn't overreacting like I expected. I'd been prepared for anger and demands...but instead he was being incredibly calm and gentle. "When we hit the news last weekend, Max decided it was a great opportunity to help Cybil and Roger blackmail me in exchange for an executive producer credit on her show. They jumped at the opportunity. And I'm pretty sure Max is thoroughly enjoying watching me squirm." He'd probably been waiting years to get back at me for walking out on him. "I agreed to an interview and photo shoot with Cybil and Lily. Good publicity to squash all the rumors running around. In exchange, I get to walk away from all of them."

Adam balked. "What?"

"It's a good deal."

"You've got to be kidding me. How is this 'a good deal', Elizabeth?"

I balled my fists. I did not have to explain myself to Adam, and yet I felt like he needed to understand. "I know how to manage my family. This is the easiest way to get what I want."

"And Max? I don't understand...you were a kid and he...*wasn't*. You're not at fault. Let's nail this bastard to the wall and make all of this go away."

"What do you think will happen, Adam? That he'll be arrested?"

"Yes. It's statutory rape." His hands tightened around mine.

"No, Adam. That isn't how the world works. Guys are always awarded for sex, no matter what. The headlines won't read '*Hollywood Executive Abuses Power*'. They'll say '*Young Hollywood Starlet Sleeps Her Way to the Top*' or '*Elizabeth Lawrence Used Sex to get Roles*'. Somehow the underage sex part will get lost and *I* will take the blame for this."

"No," Adam said so forcefully it shocked me. I looked into his eyes for the first time and realized how much pain *he* was feeling. That seemed so...odd. "No. We will not let them slant it like that."

"You won't have a choice. Trust me, I've watched the headlines my whole life. The facts don't matter."

"No," Adam repeated, shaking his head. The pain in his eyes deepened, but he was also very focused, like his mind was moving a million miles an hour. He wanted to act.

"Can you handle this, Adam? Can you handle knowing you can't pull some knight in shining armor shit?" I took a deep breath because I was about to say something and I didn't know how he was going to take it. "We are alike enough that you think you understand my world." I leaned forward and dropped my voice to a whisper. "*But you don't.*"

He stared a hole through me, his jaw flexing, but he didn't say anything.

"There are rules at play that you don't understand." I didn't know how else to explain Hollywood. They operated in a totally different plane than anyone else—even politicians.

"I can handle it if you tell me one thing."

I nodded.

"Did he hurt you?"

I didn't know how to answer that. It was a complicated question with a lot of possible answers. "He didn't physically hurt me."

Adam turned my hand over and kissed the inside of my wrist. It was a long, gentle kiss. His lips softly touching my delicate skin at the exact place my blood pumped so hard. It was like he was trying to replace each of my words with a kiss. Exchanging something bad for something good. It made it easier to talk.

"He was my producer and one thing led to another. At first it was just sex in my trailer. He was sweet. He sent me secret flowers and jewelry. I thought it was 'a dream come true'. A mature man who wanted to sweep me off my feet. I was so desperate to be loved that I didn't notice how he was manipulating things. Or how the sex got more demanding. It became expected. And then one night he convinced me to take pictures with him. He said it would be sexy and fun. I let him..." I swallowed and held back a shudder. "I let him," I repeated. I didn't know what else to say. "The next day he showed me one of the pictures and said if I ever left him he'd make sure everyone knew what a slut I was. That I'd slept my way to the top. He promised to ruin me."

"Beth," Adam whispered. He ran his hand over my cheek and tilted my chin to look at him. His eyes searched mine, looking for the rest of my story.

"I flipped. It really sank in how demented my whole life was. That was when I started getting all the evidence on my parents and called my uncle."

"But you didn't tell him about Max?" Adam looked so confused. To him it probably seemed so simple. Max was in the wrong. It was illegal. There was photographic evidence. If Max did anything with it, he would be the one in trouble.

And maybe that was so. But there was just as likely a chance it would take me down with him.

"I was mortified, Adam. Max and his pictures were proof of my stupidity and that I didn't matter. I wanted to forget Max ever happened, but I also knew he wouldn't let me simply walk away. I made sure that once I sued my parents I stayed in as many headlines as much as possible. It meant Max couldn't risk getting near me." I sighed. "More than anything, I wanted to forget it ever happened."

Adam sat on the couch beside me and scooped me up, depositing me in his lap sideways. "I know I'm being controlling right now," he sighed, "but I want to hold you. I hope you don't mind."

I nuzzled into his chest and relaxed. I didn't mind. This wasn't controlling. Sure he'd picked me up without asking, but it was to hold me. Not against my will, but to be closer. "What are you thinking right now?"

He squeezed me closer. "That I just want you to be happy."

It was so simple.

"I would probably kill this Max guy if he were here right now. And yeah, I want to *fix* things. But," he cocked his head down to look at me, "I just want you to be happy. I want to help, if you'll let me. I'm here, I'm willing, I *care*. Please let me help."

I sat quietly in his lap, listening to his heart and the sound of each breath he took. Adam wanted me to trust him and he was doing everything in his power to make me believe it was possible for him to step back, if I asked.

Maybe there were some people who could be trusted.

Maybe sometimes people made mistakes and could be forgiven.

Maybe it was time for me to forgive myself.

"I want to bury Max under a pile of dirt so thick he doesn't see the sun for years."

Adam grunted with approval. "We can do that."

"We?" I looked up into his hooded eyes.

He nodded. "As it so happens, I have some pretty fantastic connections. We can handle this however you want. Use me."

He kissed me. *Deep.* His tongue skated along mine and his fingers grabbed my hair, holding my head in place. I got the impression Adam wanted to obliterate any thoughts of Max I might have lurking in the dark recesses of my mind.

I slid back onto the couch, pulling Adam on top of me. I cradled him between my legs and kissed the hell out of him, all while grinding against his waist. If he wanted me to use him, then I was going to use him. In every way that I needed him.

But first we needed to get rid of the clothes keeping us apart.

Chapter 30

Thursday Night

"What do we do?" I was standing at the dining room table in Lydia and Mark's top floor apartment. Adam was standing beside me and Andres and Lydia were on the opposite side. Mark was out for the night on a business trip.

"What do you want us to do?" Adam was joking, but I was being serious.

"What *can* we do?"

He looked me right in the eyes. "You want my opinion?"

I nodded.

"I think someone like Max, who thinks he has enough power and money to do whatever the hell he wants, needs to be stripped bare. His money needs to disappear, his job prospects eliminated, and his hidden life exposed. He needs to be ruined. That way, no matter what happens legally, his life is still over."

"You can do that?" I asked, my voice dropping low. What Adam was talking about was full scale destruction.

"Let's talk logistics." He waved at Andres who laid out a paper file.

Over the course of the next thirty minutes Andres and Adam quickly detailed Max's life and the most effective ways to dismantle his world. Lydia watched silently while I asked questions. It started with getting Max fired and his money frozen. Somehow (I had a feeling it was Lydia's connections through the Senator) they traced his secret accounts and some sort of illegal activity associated with them. I didn't care about most of it, just whether it would work.

"Now this is the hard part." Adam threaded his fingers through mine. "We're going to leak to the press some very vague details about Max and his young stars. We're hoping that will be enough and the press will take it from there. But..."

"But," I sighed. "If push comes to shove, someone will need to step forward with actual details and a real story."

He squeezed my hand and gave me a tight smile.

This was part of my problem. I'd always hated that I ran. All I'd done was save myself. I let Max off the hook and probably (most certainly) made it possible for him to continue about his life. "I'll do whatever I need to do. I don't want Max to be able to dangle this over me any longer."

Andres flipped the file shut. "I'll get to work."

Lydia waved her hand. "Why don't you help him, Adam? Elizabeth looks like she could use a drink."

Or five. Hell, I wanted the whole bottle. I caught Adam's eye and gave him a thumbs up. "I really do need a drink."

He kissed me on the cheek and followed Andres out. "How're you holding up?" Lydia asked as she handed me a glass of red liquid courage.

"I've been better and I've been worse."

She clinked her glass against mine. "Here, here." We each sipped slowly and silently for a minute, only commenting on the wine, before Lydia finally got around to asking the question I knew was on her mind. "What are you going to do when the shit hits the fan? Will you stay in Calhoun Beach?"

That was a very good question. One I didn't have an answer to. "I hope it doesn't come to that."

She nodded and swirled her wine. "I hear history is big over in England."

"That's not a very subtle hint."

She grinned. "I've never been known for my subtlety. You and Adam are very good together."

For some reason my heart started racing. I didn't know what to say so I didn't say anything.

Lydia chuckled and set down her glass. "I have connections at some of the colleges over there. I could put in some calls. If things between you two worked out..."

I choked on my wine. "That is a very generous offer Lydia, but I can take care of myself." Part of me wanted to hug her and part of me wanted to run away. Was Adam's mother blatantly pushing for me to move in with her son?

She smiled. "I had a feeling. You've done a great job so far."

"Thank you." I let her compliment roll through me. It left a very pleasant wake. Or maybe that was the wine—I wasn't entirely sure. And honestly, I really did have my own connections. If I wanted a job closer to Adam, I could have it in a heartbeat. I'd actually turned down a position at Oxford earlier this year. Something I kind of regretted. My decision hadn't been based on what was best for my career—it had been a knee-jerk reaction made out of fear. I was scared of upsetting the balance, and of losing Lily. Moving to another country had seemed impossible.

Looking back now, with fresh perspective, I realized how many of my decisions were made out of fear instead of hope. That wasn't a smart way to build a life.

"He's been hard to reach since his accident."

My heart stopped. "Excuse me?"

"You're wondering why I'm pushing you and Adam together. Yes?"

I nodded.

She smiled tightly. "Adam changed after his accident. He wasn't unhappy or distant, but...I don't know. Not quite whole? Like he lost a piece of himself that day that he couldn't find to replace."

"And now?" I wanted to hear this. I desperately wanted to hear this.

"And now he has a purpose again. A renewed interest in living his life to the fullest. He's throwing caution to the wind and taking chances. I didn't like seeing him hold back, but I can't live his life for him. Ever since he met you, Elizabeth, Adam has been a different person. I will do anything for my son, and I want to help him live a happy and fulfilling life. If that means cutting out the barriers blocking *you* from living *your* life, then I'm happy to help, *or push*, in any way that I can."

I opened my mouth to reply—to thank her for caring—but instead all I could feel was a lump in my throat. It was hard to ignore my feelings for Adam after hearing that.

"You've done enough on your own. Just because you *can* do it all alone, doesn't mean you *should*. You're stronger with a team around you. Let us help you."

I nodded. "Lydia, I..." The door opened and Adam stepped inside. Whatever I was about to say vanished. Adam was changing my life, and I was changing his. It felt so good to hear how I was affecting him. It made a lot of my fears disappear.

He stood beside me and smiled. "C'mon. Let's go to bed."

"Go on. I think we're done talking anyway," Lydia waved. She shook her head and took her wine with her out of the room, leaving me alone with Adam.

He rested his hand gently on the small of my back and pulled me against him. "You ok?" He looked down into my eyes and the world started to fall away.

"Yeah," I nodded.

He brushed his other hand along my cheek and cupped my face. I automatically pressed into his palm, closing my eyes. Even though I didn't see it coming, I wasn't surprised when he kissed me.

Softly.

Taking my breath away.

Chapter 31

Friday

The drive out to the gardens Ronoldo chose for our photo shoot was quiet. Usually Andres had stories to tell, but not today. His mood was as dark as mine. A lot of things were in play and I'd asked Adam to stay away from the photo shoot. Neither of them had been happy about that but, seriously? Having Adam around would be a nightmare.

I was dressed in the pencil skirt Ronoldo had requested, and beside me was a dress that was delivered to my office that morning. I hadn't peeked inside, but by the size and shape, I was pretty sure it was some sort of over-the-top ball gown.

The car stopped and I stepped out before Andres could unbuckle his seatbelt. Everything looked perfectly normal aside from the box truck parked in the lot and the scurrying of a crew moving items from the truck to a location beyond the hedges. It looked like

Ronoldo had gone all-out, even on short notice.

Andres escorted me into the gardens and to the white tent where my hair and makeup would be done by Ronoldo's handpicked stylists. Cybil was already in her chair, chatting away with the team working on her. Her eyes shifted to meet mine in the mirror, but she never once broke her cadence. It was like I wasn't there, which was the way I preferred it.

Lily hopped up and gave me a hug. "It's good to see you." Her hair was in curlers and her eyes were half done so she looked a little like a clown instead of a glamorous daughter of Hollywood.

"Good to see you, too. When is your flight?" Having my sister around made all of this worth it. Sort of.

"Seven. Sorry I couldn't stay for the weekend." She squeezed me again. "I miss you."

"Miss you, too." I sat down in the chair beside her and let the circus begin. Andres stood off in a corner. I noticed as he took a few phone calls. I assumed they were from Edita and his girlfriend, but he never lost track of his pattern of watching and waiting.

Lily babbled about her classes and a guy she was sort-of seeing. Apparently he was star struck so she wasn't sure if she should put too much effort into it. The hairstylist made a comment about my "virgin" hair and how she'd love to put some color in it. I smiled politely and declined.

"How did the interview go?"

I shrugged. "Fine. The usual—where have you been, what are you doing, why aren't you acting anymore?"

"I took a role."

My eyebrows shot up and I looked at Lily with surprise. Obviously she'd had her share of acting jobs growing up as well—she was gorgeous and talented—but she was usually content with appearances and being famous for "being famous". She hadn't taken a role since she started college.

"Really? And what are you doing?"

Lily had a shy smile on her delicate lips. Whatever it was, she was excited about it. "It's an indie film." Her eyes suddenly widened as her gaze shot over my shoulder. "Is that *him*?"

I turned just in time to see Adam shake hands with Andres. My heart skipped a beat and the breath in my lungs disappeared. He had such an intense effect on me. Just the sight of him made the world come to a stop.

But what was he doing here?

I swallowed and turned back to Lily. "It is."

"Liz, he's even more gorgeous in person." She turned her head sideways as she sized him up.

I put my hand in front of her eyes. "You're too young to look at that."

She busted out laughing and swatted my hand out of the way. "You didn't tell me he was coming."

"I didn't know he was."

Her eyebrows popped and she smiled as she looked from him to me. He'd locked his eyes on me. They were absolutely smoldering and I wondered what in the hell I'd done to put sex in his eyes.

"Oh my god," Lily whispered. It was a shocked sound. A pleased sound.

I snapped my head around and found Lily staring at me with wide eyes. "What?"

She shook her head and a smile slowly pulled on her lips until she was absolutely grinning. "Nothing. I'm just really happy right now."

She was lying—sort of. I could tell she was happy, but it was not "nothing". "Tell me."

She chuckled under her breath and closed her eyes before sitting back in the chair so her hairstylist could finish. "Can't a girl just be happy to see her mother and sister...*and* her sister's new boyfriend?"

I highly doubted that grin was simply contentment at having her family around her for a change. But then again, I didn't have time to care. Adam was walking my way and nothing else in the world seemed to exist anymore.

"What are you doing here?" I sounded breathless. I *was* breathless. He shouldn't be here. I should be angry. I should feel like running away or crawling inside myself. I would normally get defensive and push away someone who did this. But that wasn't how I felt at all. I was relieved and excited to see him at a time I was feeling so tense and vulnerable. He made me feel stronger just by being here.

It was like he was moving in slow motion as he stopped beside me, kissing me lightly on the cheek and whispered in my ear. "Being supportive. You don't have to do things alone—I keep telling you that." He cupped my face and ran his thumb along my ear, out of the way of the makeup I already had on.

It's possible I actually swooned a little, because his breath on my ear and his words...well, I had to close my eyes to stem the rush of blood to all sexual parts of my body. The change was so fast and hard I think I temporarily blacked out. Luckily he had his hand on my face and held me in place. When I opened my eyes he was watching me with that same intensity I'd seen from across the tent.

Adam was up to something.

"You shouldn't be here," I suddenly whispered as I realized Max would be here, too.

He shook his head and my heart dropped into my stomach. Adam *knew* Max was going to be here. That was why Adam was here.

"Please don't."

"Don't what, Gorgeous? Stand beside you? Wild horses couldn't drag me away."

Before I could answer, he straightened up and walked around me to Lily, who was staring at us with her jaw hanging open. And damn it all, I had fucking tears in my eyes again. Adam was too much.

"You must be Lily. I've heard a lot about you." He bent down and hugged my stunned sister. "How's college?"

She blinked several times and took a deep breath, finally looking away from me and up at him. I didn't miss the appreciative glint in her eyes as she took him in.

Adam looked good, as always. Fall was making an early appearance this year and the air had a cool breeze to it. Adam was dressed in gray slacks and a white button up—just like our first real dinner at Seychelles. The top button was undone and I desperately wanted to unbutton the rest, wrap myself around his bare chest and stay there forever.

"It's good. I'm having a great semester. It's almost a cakewalk at this point."

He laughed and stuck his hands in his pockets. "I remember my last year a little differently."

She grinned and shrugged her shoulders. "Well, I'm not an engineer."

"That does make a difference, I hear. Hey," He leaned forward a little, not looking at me, "Mind introducing me to your mother real quick?"

Lily froze for a moment and then slowly nodded, glancing at me out of the corner of her eye. "Of course."

My heart had leapt out of my chest and into my throat, lodging itself there rather permanently. It was weird to see Adam with my family. I had hoped to never see my past and future together in the same room—and yet there they were, right in front of my eyes. It was like an out of body experience. I was too stunned to process everything I was seeing so I simply watched as Lily took Adam over to my mother's chair. He kissed her hand and worked her over with every ounce of charm I knew he had in him, plus some extra special stuff I could only assume came from some training he got from the Senator. He had that special touch that came from an ingrained, early training in the public eye.

Cybil was just as trained. She countered each of his moves with one of her own. The smile, the compliment, the giggle. God, how I hated that giggle. It was like watching two professional chess players in the game of their lives—except I got the feeling the prize they were playing for was me.

The conversation ended and Lily brought Adam back to me. My makeup was done and they were just finishing up my hair. "Well that was delightful," Adam said. His voice was dripping with sarcasm.

I wanted to kiss him for that.

"Now you've met everyone but Roger."

"Where is he?" Adam asked with just as much sarcasm. Maybe his voice was stuck in fake-mode.

"New York," Lily rolled her eyes which meant Roger was with Mistress New York for the weekend.

"Ah," Adam replied, catching the same hint. He squeezed my shoulder.

"Welcome to the fun."

"You look beautiful." He changed the subject.

I blushed. The things this man did to me... "Thank you. You don't look so bad yourself. I like the outfit."

"You remember."

"I do."

He leaned down and whispered in my ear again, "I wore it on purpose. To remind you we have a new deal. That I can make you come in foyers and that I like to bring you coffee in the morning."

I swallowed as memories of that dinner came flooding back. *If I can fuck you, I can certainly enjoy hearing about your day over a glass of wine.* He'd done that and so much more. I hadn't let anyone in for so long. I was protecting myself—and that was the right choice for me—but Adam had shown me that I was ready and strong enough to let some people back in.

"And," he continued, "That you can't push me away or keep me behind a wall. I'm not going anywhere."

I wrapped my hand around his wrist and held onto him like an anchor. I loved what he meant but it also reminded me of one very real fact: he was leaving in just over twenty-four hours. I think he realized that, too, because he stiffened under my hand and gently laid his forehead on mine. His eyes were screwed shut and his breath faltered.

"It's time, dolls!" Ronoldo's voice pierced the air and cut the moment I was having with Adam.

He swallowed and faked a smile before standing up and checking my makeup. "Didn't ruin a thing. You're still gorgeous." He meant that in more than one way.

I shook my head and stood up. "I don't know what to do with you, Adam Callaway."

"I know. I like it that way." And I did too.

Lily took me by the arm and walked with me out of the tent and into the garden. "I love him," she whispered in my ear. She had a ridiculous look on her face—like she was a kid at Disney for the first time.

"I already told you he was off limits."

She rolled her eyes. "I love him for *you*. You two are perfect for each other. It makes me so happy to see you like this."

Tortured and love sick? "Don't jump to conclusions."

She patted me on the arm. "I'm not jumping anywhere. I'm observing and what I see is as plain as day. He loves you. Desperately. And you love him."

I stopped. *Love*. I knew what we had was special and intense, but hearing that word from my sister made it all much more real. "I can't do this right now."

"I know," she pulled me toward the bench Ronoldo set up under a massive oak tree. "This is good, Lizzy. This is really good. I'm happy for you."

It hit me, suddenly, how worried I was about my choices. I was desperately worried about losing my sister. "Please don't hate me for ending the agreement." I'd agreed to the three-ring circus modification with my parents solely to help ensure my relationship with Lily stayed intact.

"I don't. I don't understand everything and I *know* that I don't—but you're my sister. You're smart and if you think this is the best thing for you, then I am behind you, no matter what." And then she grinned. "Especially if it means you keep looking like this."

We silently ended our conversation as Cybil joined us at the bench and Ronoldo started directing. We were doing a quick run of shots in the outfits we arrived in, then changing and doing most of the shots in the gowns he'd sent us. Apparently these were our serious pictures that he was juxtaposing with more whimsical, ethereal photographs. When it came to photography I gave it all over to Ronoldo. He'd never taken a bad photograph as far as I was concerned. I just showed up and did as he asked.

He kept Lily between me and Cybil, then sent us off to change. It felt like a triathlon and we were entering the third stage. I could see the finish line, but it was still so damn far away, and there were a lot of hills between me and that line.

Adam and Andres left the tent while we changed, as did Cybil's security. Andres kept on the opposite side of the tent from the other man, clearly not liking him. I didn't blame him—I didn't like him either. He had a vibe that screamed "asshole" from a mile away.

The mysterious gowns were gauzy yards of chiffon in three different shades. Lily was in a strapless blush-pink gown with gold accents. Cybil was in a white (which made me giggle at the irony) halter top. And I was in a one-shoulder gown of a very soft shade of light blue. They were beautiful, glamorous gowns that echoed our old-Hollywood heritage.

When we returned to the garden Adam was gone and only Andres followed us out to the oak tree. I gave him a questioning glance and Andres waved me off, telling me not to worry. Maybe Adam had gone to the bathroom or something.

This time Ronoldo, all tiny power in a trim Dominican body, was barking orders left and right. He often got tense and dramatic in the middle of shoots, his creative mind working overtime and getting frustrated with crew members who couldn't move as fast as he was thinking, but this was different. He was mad.

"Cybil, I want you standing behind the bench. Lily, lie out and prop your head up with your hand. Liz, stand next to your mother."

Black-clad photographer's assistants manipulated our hands and chins, shoving us into the poses they wanted as Ronoldo fussed and took test shots. By the time they were done I was standing arm to arm with my mother, facing just slightly away from her. "So this is it?" she finally said.

"It is."

"No going back?"

"Nope," I replied simply. Sometimes I wondered if Cybil spent so much time in her fantasy world that she was incapable of seeing anything else. To her this was probably just a little spat that would turn into another dramatic chapter in our lives.

"I'm sorry about Max."

"Really?" I tried desperately to hold the pose I'd been given. "If you were really sorry you wouldn't have brought him here."

Lily gasped from below. "Mom. What in the hell is wrong with you?"

"It's not my business. It's yours and his, Elizabeth."

"Smile, for heaven's sake." Ronoldo muttered and

we all fell silent for several minutes.

When he paused to change out memory cards and reposition us, I turned to Cybil. "If it's my fucking business then why the hell are you butting in at all?"

"Max and I have our own deal. It just so happens to somewhat involve you. The two are not related."

In crazy world, maybe. "The two are inextricably linked. You are helping him blackmail me."

Lily gasped again.

"Stay out of this," Cybil put her hand in Lily's face which only made things worse.

"Stop lying to me," she shrieked.

Suddenly we were having two separate fights between the three of us.

The assistants started shoving us into a new configuration, this time with Lily sitting up on the bench and Cybil and me with a hand on each shoulder. "And Adam Callaway? Really, Elizabeth? Your grandmother would roll over in her grave if she knew you were dating a southerner. And from a political family? Really?"

She was trying to redirect the conversation by insulting me. A classic Cybil maneuver.

"I'm fairly certain Adam's southern *and* northern roots go back just as far as ours. Grandmother wouldn't have been upset at all. As for his family and politics… get over it." It pissed me off that Cybil was trying to insinuate that my grandmother was so much of a snob that she would be upset by her granddaughter dating a man with southern roots—it wasn't 1950 anymore. And for heaven's sake, she was an *actress*.

The family had been mortified until she won her Oscar.

"Still, you could date anyone. *Anyone*, Elizabeth."

It was at that exact moment that Max appeared. He smiled at me and waved to Cybil as he took a seat behind Ronoldo and made himself comfortable. An assistant ran over with a bottle of water. I glanced at Andres. He was watching everything.

"What in the hell is going on?" Lily asked, her voice much harder than before. She knew about Max. In my big-sisterly duties I'd cautioned her about predatory producers, directors, and executives. After a lot of questions and pushing on her part, I finally started divulging details. She knew it all.

"He's here to make sure I smile pretty for the camera."

"No," Lily said firmly. "Get him out of here now. If you don't, I will."

"We're almost done. Elizabeth will be fine for fifteen more minutes. Let's not cause a scene."

Because Ronoldo, his team, and our security had never witnessed a scene before. I rolled my eyes. Lily glared at me. "Why are you just standing there? Have Andres kick his ass back to L.A."

"In fifteen minutes, I will," I replied with a fake smile and as much sweetness as I could muster. Maybe my little sister would finally get it through her thick head that I didn't have the same relationship with Cybil and Roger that she had.

Ronoldo got back to work. He was looking angrier by the second and there was a permanent scowl on his lips. I started silently counting down the seconds in my head. My lips hurt from smiling and my arms were getting tired from holding the different poses for such long periods of time. Not to mention I kept wondering where Adam had wandered off to. He was taking far longer than a bathroom break and I had to wonder if it was because of Max.

Maybe he was waiting until Max left, but I didn't have much confidence in that hope. It seemed to run counter-intuitive to pretty much everything about Adam—despite my demand he leave this for me to handle.

"Done. That's a wrap." Ronoldo called and handed off his camera. He came straight for me and pulled me into a hug. "I can't believe this is my last shoot with you. Please let me do all your personal photographs in the future."

As if I'd let anyone else take my picture. "You know there is no one but you."

He lingered, hugging me harder, and then whispered in my ear. "Please get all this trash out of your life, my dear. Now."

"As fast as I can. Drinks in an hour?"

"I'll meet you there."

I ignored Cybil completely, leaving her to deal with Lily's tirade, and marched right up to Max. "Done. Photo shoot complete, interview approved. You got what you wanted—now leave me alone and never, ever come back."

He smiled up at me from his canvas director's chair. I wasn't sure what I'd ever found attractive about

Max's icy blue eyes or his jet black hair. He looked horrible to me now. "Kitten, it doesn't have to be like this."

"Yes, it does." I waved for Andres. "What do you still have on me? Are they digitized?"

"You'll never know."

Sometimes I hated the digital age. Photographs and videos lasted forever. There was no envelope for me to burn. Copies could be made by the billions. All he had to do was hit an upload button. I leaned closer. "There is nothing for you to get from me. I'm done. If you want revenge get it now. Get it over with."

He stood up as Andres came to a stop behind his chair. Andres placed a hand on Max's shoulder "You might want to check your phone before you say anything else, Mr. Vittel."

I shot Andres a look. Had they been able to move that fast?

Max smirked and pulled out his phone. A moment later his eyes widened and the color drained from his face.

"I suggest you leave and take care of your business. It seems you're having some trouble."

Max cut me a look "You'll regret this."

"Somehow I doubt that." I murmured as he pushed away from us with Andres following closely behind.

I had the perfect opportunity to slide away unnoticed and without drama, so I quietly walked into the tent and grabbed my things, barely catching a wayward glance from one of the assistants breaking things down, and then made a break for the parking lot—just in time to see Adam pick Max up off the ground and shove him into a shiny black Town Car.

Andres waved at the driver and the car took off.

I stood frozen at the entrance to the parking lot. In a ball gown. Trying to rectify everything I'd just seen.

And then I smiled. A giant, genuine smile that I couldn't stop if I'd wanted to.

I'd waited a damn long time to see someone knock the crap out of Max.

That was when the giggles started. I was relieved. Walking away from the past wasn't as horrifying as I'd imagined and letting someone in wasn't nearly as terrifying as I feared.

It was actually kind of nice.

But it was all a huge shock to my system.

Adam locked eyes with me and cocked his head to the side. I grabbed up the front of my dress and ran up to him, taking his hand, and turning it over to inspect it. His knuckles were red, but he otherwise seemed fine. Apparently Adam knew how to throw a proper punch.

He closed his fingers around mine and pulled me closer. "You're laughing."

"I'm happy." I tilted my head up and kissed his chin. "Thank you."

"Even though I pulled some 'knight in shining armor shit'?"

I leaned back and frowned up at his handsome face. "It's true. You did hit my ex without my permission...but in this one particular case, it was actually kind of hot." Seeing Adam all mad and defensive with Max crumpled and defeated was a much bigger turn-on than I'd ever imagined. I kind of wanted to jump Adam in the backseat of his car with yards of chiffon all around us like a blanket.

"Hot, huh?"

"This time," I said with a shrug. "Now kiss me like you mean it and take me out for drinks."

"Yes, ma'am." And then he kissed me so hard and deep I forgot about everything but him for the rest of the night.

Chapter 32

Saturday

I woke up to an erection digging into the small of my back. It actually hurt a little. Adam was rock hard and still asleep even though the rest of him was quite clearly awake and ready for action. He'd fallen asleep wrapped around me and hadn't moved all night. I was surprised, but not upset in the least. I'd only get to fall asleep with him around me one more time. If that meant hard-ons waking me up and soft snores tickling the bare skin on my back, I could take it.

The early morning light was filtering in through the soft white curtains that covered the bank of sliding glass doors and I realized this was probably the latest Adam had slept since I met him. Is this what mornings would be like with him if we could be together? Sleeping in with him wrapped around me? Spending half the morning tangled in the sheets, reading, talking, and fucking? What would his new apartment or house look like in Brackley? Or would he be on the road so much it wouldn't matter?

I liked that so many things were in flux. I felt like there were more possibilities and more opportunities to escape, if necessary. There wasn't too much pressure to decide on my future immediately.

"What are you thinking about?" Adam's voice was rough.

"How did you know I was awake?"

He kissed the spot between my shoulder blades and spread his large palm across my belly, holding me firm against his erection. "Your breathing, Gorgeous. I know all the sounds you make."

I closed my eyes and let out a slow breath. I never thought I'd love having someone know me so well. I always thought it would make me feel vulnerable and scared, but it didn't. Adam made me feel content and safe. I liked knowing someone out there knew me without explanation. "I was wondering if you were going to like your new job."

He adjusted so that his cock slid between my legs, instead of digging into my back. "I'm going to love it. I've known Raif for a long time and I've been trading emails and phone calls with the team for months. It's a good fit." He kissed up my shoulder and neck, then whispered in my ear, "Come with me."

"To Russia?" Adam had no idea how many times I'd cancelled and reinstated that trip in my mind.

"To the UK. Leave all of this behind. Run away with me." He nudged the head of his cock against the entrance of my sex. "I've never regretted leaving it all behind. I think you should give it a try."

I gasped as he slid a little inside me. My entire body roared to life and suddenly all my thoughts focused solely on how to get Adam's cock fully inside me. "I spent a summer in Oxford once. I like it there."

Adam froze. His body was completely still and he was holding his breath. Only his cock twitched in protest to the sudden halt in friction. "Is that so?" I'm sure the last thing he expected to hear was any form of acceptance on my part.

I opened my legs and propped my foot on top of Adam's calf, giving him more access and room to move deeper inside me. "I'm happy in Calhoun Beach, Adam. But I'd be lying if I didn't admit that I was curious about us. I think I've been jealous of how easily you left everything behind and started over. I don't know if it will be right for me—or if I'll even like you in a few weeks—but I want to look into my options."

Adam thrust harder, sliding deep. It shocked me and took my breath away. It hurt a little, but not too much. He massaged my hip. "I'm sorry. I didn't mean to do that. I just..." his voice fell away and he groaned as I pushed back. "Fuck, Beth. I was ready to fight you all day on this."

"Why fight when we can fuck?"

He chuckled and kissed the sensitive skin behind my ear. "That wasn't exactly the answer I was looking for."

"No?" I asked innocently. "I'm not picking up and

moving after two weeks in the sack with a great guy. But I'm done with this life and the drama. If I never get tailed by another photographer I will be a happy woman."

"That's all I can ask. I don't want you to pick up and move for me. That isn't fair. But I also don't want to end this. I want you to be happy and I think as long as you live in the States you'll be haunted. If it just so happens that you find a new job and a quiet happy life in the town of Brackley, then I'll thank my lucky stars and never ask for anything else for as long as I live."

For someone who was "hopeful" about our future, Adam was certainly talking in grandiose absolutes. He wanted more, he was just too worried saying so would scare me off. "This is too serious before coffee."

"Well, then. Let me finish waking you up." He reached around and found my clit as he fell into a rhythm from behind. I was thrashing and moaning and a couple of minutes later, coming undone to his lips, hands, and cock. Nothing in my toy bag could possibly compete with a wakeup call like that.

After naked breakfast we actually got dressed and snuck over to the main house. I was in a simple sundress and sweater for the shade. The fall air was chilly again today, but in the sun it was beautiful. Adam left me in the library while he raided the kitchen for a picnic lunch. The room was quiet and filled with the comforting smell of old books. I ran my hands over the spines. I had no idea what I wanted to read, but I had my pick of just about anything.

I came to a stop in front of a section of paperbacks that looked old and loved. I stopped at one called *Woman Without a Past* and pulled it free of the other books. The corners of the cover were bent and the pages were yellowed. This was a book that had been read multiple times. The back blurb described the story of a woman who accidentally discovers the truth about her past in a whirlwind trip to Charleston. Romance, danger, inheritance... it sounded like a book I needed to read.

"Found something?" Adam was standing in the doorway watching me. A basket hung from his hand. He was wearing a white short-sleeved button-up with large pockets over a pair of grey shorts. He looked relaxed and sexy as hell standing there.

"I think so. You?"

"I've got enough food and wine to get us through an apocalypse. I'm pretty sure we're good to go." He walked up to the shelf one over from where I was standing, scanned the titles and smiled. "And now I'm good to go." He pulled a black covered novel off the shelf. *Jurassic Park*.

"In the mood for mutant dinosaurs and idiot scientists?"

"Action, danger, and dinosaurs? Sounds like a fun way to spend an afternoon to me."

I shook my head and kissed him on the cheek. "Let's go."

We took the pickup truck out to the same field he'd taken me to the first time I visited Green Hills. It was nice that we could have a day outside without fear of being hounded by photographers. We walked hand in hand out to the ruins and set up under a massive oak tree that shaded most of one side. Adam spread a thick blanket out along the wall. He really did pack a feast and we nibbled all afternoon while lying in the shade and reading.

Adam massaged my foot, ran his fingers over my back, and through my hair. When he moved to my lap, I ran my fingers along his scalp as he talked. "I loved it out here when I was kid, but now I *really* love it out here."

I put my book down and looked out at the rolling hills and clusters of oak trees. The sky was bright blue and white clouds dotted the sky. "We're so far away from everything. It's like we're the only two people in the world." The only sound was us and the wind. No cars, no voices. Nothing. "It's peaceful."

"It's perfect."

My chest constricted a little. I didn't know why it hurt a little when he said that. "It is."

"Did I ever tell you about my side job when I was a teenager?"

"Besides building cars and racing?" What else had Adam squeezed into his life?

He chuckled and looked up at me. He looked funny upside down, but still so handsome. "Well, it goes hand in hand. I used to troll the junk yards, but I also used to drive around the countryside looking for old cars just sitting in people's yards or garages. I found a few really cool cars that had been sitting unused and unloved for years. I'd buy them for nothing, get them towed back here to the garage, and restore them. Some of them I barely made my money back on, but some were true classics with original parts. They just needed someone who knew what they were doing to restore them."

Adam got this faraway look in his eyes when he talked about cars. His face softened and his hands moved with each word out of his mouth. He became animated. Cars were in his blood and his love for them extended to every level. "That sounds pretty cool."

"I loved it. I always thought one day, once I retired, I'd go back to doing that."

"I think that's a great idea." I could see an older Adam spending his days in the garage transforming cars from trash to treasure. It suited him perfectly.

"What about you? You said you traveled a lot looking for old buildings." He knocked the stone foundation beside us. "Like this baby, for instance."

I frowned. "Well, not quite like this. There isn't anything to renovate or preserve. She's already gone."

"But that's what you do, isn't it? Preserve and restore old homes and buildings?"

I nodded. "I've never done it personally. I help make sure the laws are followed and codes are maintained. I advise other people how to properly restore things."

"Ever wanted to do it yourself?"

I stared at Adam. He was opening a tiny little door

I never dared open before. I never even looked at it. I knew it was there, hidden inside me, but I also knew I wasn't ready to see what happened if I let myself see what was on the other side.

"What?"

I shrugged. "Nothing. It was just an unexpected question."

Adam grinned and I suddenly got the distinct impression I was in for trouble. He sat up and spun around, separating my legs and pulling me into his lap so that my arms were around his neck. In this position we were nose to nose, it erased the ten inches he normally had on me. "You want to renovate a house. I can see it in your eyes. There was a glint—I know I saw it. Don't hide it from me."

I let out an exasperated breath. "Ok, so maybe when you said that I got a little excited. *Maybe* there are some projects I want to tackle one day. I'm not sure. I've never really thought about it."

"Oh baby..." Adam groaned and ran his hands over my body. "You should do it. Practice what you preach. You'll love it, I promise. I do."

Maybe. It would take time to let myself see the future. I was excited to open myself up to the possibilities and stop living in hiding.

But one step at a time.

In fact, if we were going to go crazy and talk about wild ideas, I had one of my own. One that, normally, would have flashed through my mind a split second before I squashed it. I never realized before how that made me feel. It hurt a little—to have a wonderful dream for the future and demolish it almost immediately because I couldn't allow myself to be foolish.

But I was changing that.

"Will you build me a house?"

Adam's eyebrows shot up and his eyes softened as a smile pulled at the corners of his lips. "What kind of house and where?" He was playing along spectacularly.

I loved him for that.

"Right here. In the middle of this field. Far, far away from everyone and everything. A little cottage just for us to hide away from the world."

He studied me and I studied him. It was kind of a huge statement coming from me. "To hide?"

"To find peace," I corrected him. I couldn't imagine a time when I wouldn't want a quiet place I knew, without a shadow of a doubt, I was safe to be me. "Hiding, but for a different reason. I don't want to run away from my problems and pretend they don't exist. I just want somewhere peaceful to rest."

His hands tightened around me. "Right on top of the old house?"

I glanced at the crumbling stone foundation and shook my head. "Definitely not. Something new."

"Just like us," he replied with a kiss.

A kiss that turned into so much more. We weren't ready for plans or even the words to explain what was happening to us. So instead we were acting it out. I couldn't tell Adam that I loved him—I still wasn't entirely sure I was capable of loving him the way he deserved to be loved. But I could show him how passionately I felt about him.

My fingers tangled in his hair as I kissed him deeper and deeper. His hands wrapped around my hips and pulled me down against his erection. "Thank god for sun dresses," he groaned.

"Mmmm...I may never wear pants again. You make them seem so constricting."

Adam pulled back and balked. "You *will* wear pants."

I laughed and stood up, sliding my hands under my skirt and dropping my panties. "Oh I will?"

Adam nodded and laid back on the ground, divesting himself of his grey shorts and boxers and rolling on a condom—that was *not* hidden in his socks. "You will. Every day that I'm gone."

I sat back down on his lap, wrapping my legs around his naked waist, his cock pressed between our bodies, as I slowly unbuttoned his shirt. "I will," I agreed with a smile and seductive raise of my eyebrows. "And only skirts when we're together."

One button, two buttons...gorgeous muscular chest. I ran my index finger along his skin and Adam sucked in a breath. Three buttons, four buttons. I opened his shirt and pressed his naked chest against me. His skin and warmth were electric. One of the most comforting and arousing things I'd ever experienced. "Please don't back out on Russia. I'll come here if you do. I can't go that long without seeing you."

Thinking about being apart made me ache inside.

So I raised myself up and let Adam position his erection at my entrance. We moved together in short, quick strokes, lubricating his cock and stimulating my body, until he began to slide inside deeper and deeper. "I'll be there."

Adam let out a slow breath—both because he was relieved *and* because he was finally, completely, inside me. "I'll be moving the next week."

"You'll be busy." It was getting harder to talk. I was panting and aroused and words seemed so pointless.

"I'll be here for the US Grand Prix."

"I'll come see you." He thrust up and into me hard. I called out and saw stars for a moment. His cock was a work of art. A true, genuine work of art. So large and long. Perfect. And the way it fit inside me—stretching me almost to the point of pain—with maximum friction in all the right places. I ground against him.

"I won't be home again until Christmas. That's too long." He wrapped his arms around my back and hooked them on my shoulders so he could pull me down harder.

It was mind-blowingly good. So much stimulation in so many places, I was about to lose my mind—or just come really hard for a long, long time.

"You're in luck. I already have my flight booked to see Allison in London for Thanksgiving break. Lily is going, too."

I don't know if it was my trip or the fluttering of my inner muscles, but Adam jerked, his hips suddenly moving with urgency to find his release. It lit me up from the inside, the heat and the sudden need throwing us both over the edge. As his cock pulsed and kicked, so did my core. It drove my orgasm on, lengthening it to the point I wondered if I'd ever stop coming.

Adam started laughing and panting, forcing himself to keep moving despite being done and spent. I kept calling out. I was wrapped around him—my legs holding his body to mine—my arms around his neck. He kissed me up and down until I finally relaxed. "Damn we're good together." I dropped my cheek onto his shoulder and let out a breath.

"You better believe it." He started stroking my hair and running his other hand up and down my back. "And I'll be here for Christmas."

I smiled. "Sounds like we're going to be seeing each other a lot over the next three months."

Adam let out a long, sad breath. "And it's still not enough. What are we going to do after that? You're here and I'm there. Eventually, this back and forth is going to hurt a helluva lot more than I can handle."

Adam was chatty after sex. Way too chatty.

"We both have busy careers. I'm sure we'll make it work while we figure out what this is." I sat up and waved between us. I couldn't define it yet. I knew how I felt about him, but I couldn't give him more than that until I had my head on straight. It wouldn't be fair.

"I don't say this to put pressure on you. I just want you to know how I feel about us. A trans-Atlantic relationship isn't going to be enough for me. I want all of you as fast as I can get it."

Normally a statement like that would have scared the pants off of me. But not now. Not from Adam. "We'll figure it out. I know we will."

That made him grin and I realized that Adam wasn't actually looking for definite plans—just the guarantee I wasn't running away. "Now *that* I can live with."

Chapter 33

Saturday Night

We had a quiet dinner with Lydia and Mark on the back porch of the main house. There were no events that weekend, thankfully, and we had the gardens all to ourselves. Lydia created a feast of seafood and pasta and served it with the smoothest white wine I'd tasted in years. After a dessert of strawberry shortcake on steroids, Adam took me on a walk.

The gardens seemed to go on forever. Twinkle lights were strung above and some of the stones in the walkway actually glowed. There were rose bushes and topiaries, arching willow trees, and small beds of pink and yellow flowers. There was a slight breeze but I wasn't cold. I was never cold around Adam. He seemed to keep my blood pumping at all times.

"Over here," he murmured, pulling on our entwined fingers. There was a bench under a large oak tree with an antique looking lamp post beside it. I leaned into him and he wrapped his arms around me. Neither of us said a thing. We just sat there, absorbing as much as we could of each other. I tried to memorize the pattern of his breathing—the way it sounded when he was calm. It was so different from the rough, rich sounds he made when he was excited. His heart thudded in my ear and I swear mine slowed to beat in time with his. Like we were syncing up all over again.

Adam was right, every time we were together I felt like everything around us changed. The air, the speed of time, the sounds of the voices around us. It all slowed down while Adam and I felt each other out and settled into a rhythm.

Then he cleared his throat and his heart started to beat faster. "I have something for you," his voice was low, but not quite a whisper.

I'd been waiting for this moment ever since Roger spoiled my surprise. "Oh yeah? What's that?"

He ran a hand through my hair. "Promise you'll just take it and enjoy it without making a big deal out of it."

"I promise."

He wrapped his arm around my waist so that he could use both his hands without letting go. It was a little awkward but I wouldn't have it any other way. "I bought it hoping you'd understand what I meant and not read too much into it." His voice was rougher now. Adam was more excited than he'd been a moment before.

Something gold appeared in his hand, as if by

magic, and he slid it onto my wrist. It was a bracelet. Basically a cuff, but much more elegant that that. It was clearly an expensive piece of hand-crafted jewelry. There was delicate scrollwork and engraving. "It's beautiful."

"Like you. I saw it and I immediately thought of you. I had to have it."

There was a hesitation in his voice. A catch. There was more to this than a simple gold bracelet. He was too worked up and worried I'd freak. Maybe there was something to the scrollwork, a symbolic meaning or story behind it. "I love it. Now I'll always have you with me."

He kissed the top of my head and tucked me back into his side. "I checked your jewelry and saw you usually wear gold. I was hoping it would go with most of your stuff."

"It's perfect," I assured him.

He was quiet again as I turned and twisted my wrist trying to study the bracelet in the faint light of the lamppost. It was very delicate, but I couldn't find any special meaning behind it. Maybe I was looking to make more out of it than there needed to be. "I think I'm ready to get into bed and spend the rest of the night there." Adam had insisted that I stay at Green Hills until the paparazzi left me alone—even if it took all month. I wasn't planning on staying that long, but at least a couple more nights. The photographers had been dwindling by the day and only the desperate and die-hards were still hoping for some sort of shot of me.

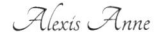

Once Adam was gone I had a feeling they would give up.

"Sounds good to me."

The walk back was slow and filled with lazy groping. The kind that was fun and arousing, not weird and selfish. By the time we shut the door to his apartment we were kissing and stripping. I wanted to soak up every minute I had left with Adam. Absorb and store it inside so I wouldn't forget what it felt like to be this content.

Being with Adam didn't just make me happy—it made me feel accepted. But it wasn't only knowing him—I couldn't give all the credit to him. I think I'd been waiting for the right time to step into myself, I'd just been scared to move until Adam shook the foundation I was standing on and made me realize I could do it. He never pushed me. He always laid out the challenge and then stepped back to see what I did with it.

For once in my life, I wasn't trying to claw my way out of my own skin. That was why I put up so many boundaries and hid behind so many walls. Everything felt out of control—including me—without some sort of structure to live inside.

But it was false control. Smoke and mirrors. Just enough to give the impression of control while still allowing myself to be pushed and manipulated by outside forces. What I had now was *actual* control. The confidence to stand in my own shoes and refuse to be moved. The power to say no and the strength to endure the storm that followed. The satisfaction of knowing (instead of hoping) that none of it mattered. All that mattered was me and what made me happy.

Cybil and Roger didn't matter. My name didn't matter. I wasn't tied to any of it, and it was up to me to decide where my path went from here.

And at that exact moment, it meant thoroughly enjoying a man who made me happy to be alive. No strings attached to anything other than being happy.

"Lady's choice," Adam growled as he nipped at my ear and pressed his erection into my belly.

Oh, how I loved being in charge, but it was so hard to choose when it came to Adam. I wanted *all the things*. I always wanted everything. And so many things had changed in the last two weeks.

I had an idea.

I peeled the last of Adam's clothes off and walked around his gorgeous, naked body. I wasn't going to see him for quite a while, and even when I did see him, it would be brief. I needed to memorize as much of him as I possibly could.

His sounds.

The shape of each muscle.

Every single way that he liked to be touched.

I wanted an encyclopedia of Adam to keep me occupied with dirty dreams for the foreseeable future.

"What are you doing?" he asked with a smile.

I stopped in front of him and tapped my chin as I sized him up again. "I need equipment."

He frowned. "I don't think we grabbed your boxes in our mad dash out of your apartment."

"Not that kind," I murmured as seductively as I could manage. "Do you trust me?"

"Without a doubt."

"Excellent." I turned and found my bag. It took me a moment or two to arrange everything the way I wanted it, and Adam watched from the middle of the room with barely restrained curiosity. He clearly wanted to jump in and help. He kept opening his mouth, then snapping it shut. He took a step toward me and I waved him back. Finally he just raised an eyebrow and grunted.

By then I had my iPad opened to the note-taking app I liked to use for work. It combined all kinds of wonderful things: like notes, pictures, and recordings. I snapped a full-body picture of Adam and grinned. "I'm making myself an Adam Manual."

His face was blank for a full three seconds before a sly smile replaced the look of shock. "Really? And do I get to make one as well?"

I shrugged. Max had used pictures of us having sex to blackmail me and control me, but I was a teenager and that was part of another life. I was a consenting adult now and, despite my own issues with trust, I had faith in Adam. I wasn't ashamed of anything we were doing and I knew he'd never share my pictures with anyone. Adam wasn't the sharing type—especially when it came to me. "Do you want one?"

He shook his head like I'd just said the single most ridiculous thing he'd ever heard. He strode over to his own bag in three steps and produced his own iPad.

While he got his own notes on me ready, I added basic information to the page beside the naked picture of Adam.

Name: Hottie Pants
Likes: coffee, wine, bacon, football, fast cars, and me
Hair: tuggable
Eyes: panty-melting
Body: totally fuckable

"What are you grinning about?" Adam asked.

"Nothing!"

He shook his head and popped his eyebrows as he got to work, tapping away at his screen with as much enthusiasm and as big a grin on his face as I knew was on mine.

I pulled up the second page and typed a big "A" at the top. Where did I want to start? I pranced over to him and sat on the coffee table, holding the iPad up in front of his face and snapped a picture of his luscious lips. Then I opened the picture editing software and changed it to a soft black and white that accentuated the shadows I loved to trace around his full lips.

I added the edited photo to the app. *Soft, talented, insistent.*

What next?

Adam took a picture of my boobs while I studied him. "What do you like when I touch you there?" His voice was deep and dark. Not quite rough, but not smooth either.

I set down my iPad and caressed myself. I didn't

think Adam had ever gone wrong where my breasts were concerned. "I like it when you swirl your tongue around my nipples." I had a feeling he was doing a voice recording so I did my best to sound aroused and sexy as I spoke. "When you first suck it into your mouth it feels almost exactly the same way your cock feels when it slams into me. I get so wet and it hurts to be empty, so I grind my hips looking for you." I rolled my hips as I spoke. "When you use your teeth and gently pull my nipples, it hurts, but I usually like it. It makes me want to ride you until I hear you panting."

Adam swallowed and nodded, tapping the screen and shuddering.

I took a picture of his shoulders. God how I loved the way his muscles bunched and moved when we fucked. It constantly reminded me that I was with a man. And not just any man—a strong, confident, capable man who was willing to do whatever I asked in bed (or out of bed, for that matter).

I had to close my eyes before I typed that note. I was so wet I was probably leaving a mark on the surface of the coffee table.

"Turn slightly," Adam pushed my crossed legs to my right and leaned back on the couch to get a shot of them. "I love it when they're wrapped around me."

"My legs?" Holy crap my voice was so raspy it barely sounded like me. I knew making this memento was going to be fun, but damn I was horny as all hell now.

"Oh yes. They are gorgeous in a skirt or with my

arms wrapped around them while I suck and lick you until you scream, but my favorite is when they are wrapped around my waist and I'm buried inside you."

I swallowed. Yep. I liked all of those things, too. Maybe I should have him take a picture of my legs and repeat all of that. I wanted that memory, too.

Adam was more than happy to oblige and even added a few extra lines to my voice recording. Somehow licking and sucking sounds even hotter when the man who enjoys doing it to you adds in how much he loves tasting you on his lips for the next two hours and that you're better than any dessert he's ever had.

Oh yeah.

Speaking of desserts... "I need you to stand." I was too close to him so I had to move to the other side of the coffee table. It took a few different angles to finally capture the beauty of Adam's erect cock, but the moment I snapped the last picture—the one highlighting the rounded perfection of the head of his dick and the smooth length of his shaft against the palm of his hand—I knew I had what I needed.

I turned that one black and white, too.

So large he fills me completely. It takes my breath away. Every inch of me is touched—inside and out—when he's buried as deep as he can go. His breath tickles my skin. He moans and growls. His hips press into me and his chest crushes my breasts. Inside I am so full that he forces me to expand. It hurts and it feels so good. I love knowing that with Adam I will always be full and he will always give me what I need.

I swallowed and took a deep breath.

Damn. That was a diary entry for the ages.

I set the voice recorder to start as I sat back down in front of him, his cock right in front of my face. He wiggled his hips and took a picture of me looking up at him.

"Now, I want you to tell me how you feel. I want to hear everything you're thinking. Tell me what you want."

He dropped his iPad on the couch and stood facing me with his hands on his hips. "I want your mouth on my cock."

"I *know* that..." I teased as I took him in my right hand and slowly—torturously slowly—licked up his length.

"Shit. It feels like... a tease. Kind of the way it feels to be inside you, but different. I like it, though."

By the way he was grunting in the back of his throat, I had no doubt. I swirled my tongue and took him in my mouth. He moaned and grabbed my shoulders. "I want to grab your head and thrust in your mouth. It makes me insane when you do that. I lose all control and this crazy part of me wants to go wild."

I sucked up his length until his cock popped free. "You never grab my head."

"I know," he gasped. "I'm too afraid I'll hurt you if I do."

I shrugged and looked up at him. "A quick thrust here and there wouldn't hurt me..."

He shuddered and shook his head. I sucked on his

cock some more. Eventually his hands started massaging my shoulders, creeping up my neck, guiding me in a way he'd never done before, until his fingers were in my hair at the base of my neck. It was a little scary to have such a large cock in my mouth and Adam's hands on my head, but then again, I was an adrenaline junkie from time to time and kind of got off on the thrill.

He thrust a little harder and gripped my hair a little harder, then let me go with a gasp. "Yep. Best feeling ever. And too much power for me to handle, baby. Suck harder and moan for me."

So I did.

"Again."

Moaning wasn't hard, in fact it was a relief, but I never knew how hard to suck. He sounded like he wanted more, so I sucked harder. His hands tightened on my shoulders and he grunted as he started to come. I wanted to smile, but didn't, instead I concentrated on finishing him off. My recording was going to get me off so many times while he was gone. I loved hearing him talk and groan and ask for more.

So hot.

"Shit, fuck, damn." He collapsed on the couch, panting and grinning. I ended the voice recording and took a picture of the look on Adam's face. He was completely relaxed with the most ridiculous smile on his face. I wanted to remember how he looked when I pleasured him.

But it only lasted a moment. Two seconds later he was sitting up and eying my naked body. "Lie down."

"On the coffee table?" I hated and loved the idea. The table was hard, but it was sexy as hell to think of Adam pleasuring me while I was splayed on the surface.

He nodded and I immediately complied—hard tabletop be damned. He kneeled on the ground in front of me, flicking his iPad around to snap a picture, then he turned on the voice recorder. "Same rules. I want to hear everything."

Turnabout was fair play. I leaned back and relaxed just as Adam's warm, wet tongue began to explore. "There," I gasped, "it feels so good right there." His tongue was running along one of my folds. He repeated the action several times before his fingers began to move: caressing, spreading, and circling. I was terrible about talking during sex. All words seemed to vanish from my head. It was the one time my mind was quiet. It took a lot of effort to remember to say what I was feeling.

"Suck. Oh, yes!" Adam's mouth closed over my clit and his tongue gently swirled as he sucked.

This was going to be a very short recording.

"My god you have a talented mouth, Adam Callaway." I cried out as he plunged a finger inside, curling it and stroking. "Fuck, how do you do that?"

He didn't reply. He was focused on my pleasure and knew that my questions weren't really questions so much as praise. At some point I gave up. Words and sex didn't go together for me—but I could still make sounds—and I made a lot. I moaned and groaned, panted and cursed, until I was shaking and shattering from another Adam Callaway mouth fucking.

It was mind-blowing how thoroughly he could pleasure me with his fingers, lips, and tongue. He managed to stroke, caress, and suck every sensitive pleasurable spot—all while massaging my breasts and rolling my nipples. It was like he had four arms and two mouths.

And just when I thought I was so satisfied and spent that nothing could possibly compare, he got me hot bothered all over again.

"I need to be inside you." His voice was thick and barely controlled. It was the sexiest thing I'd ever heard. Adam's restrained need for me took me right back to desperate and wanting.

I hopped up and grabbed my iPad as I moved to the bed. If this was the last time we were together for a while then I knew exactly how I wanted him: on top of me and buried as deep as he could go. I wanted him to fuck me senseless so I would remember how it felt to have his cock inside me for weeks.

And I wanted to be able to hear it any time I wanted.

I started a new recording and set it on the nightstand beside Adam's. He tackled me from behind and I fell face first onto the bed with his erection between my legs. There was no preamble or lead up, he just moved his hips until his cock was in the perfect position, and started to thrust. Inch by inch he made his way inside me. I brought my knees up and Adam moved up with me, wrapping his arm tightly around my waist as I got onto my hands and knees.

That was when he finally slid deep inside. I cried out as he tore me in two, loving the feel of my body being forced to accommodate him. He dropped his head onto my back panting. Adam from behind was primal. He was in control—sure I could move and rock, but it was Adam who was in charge of how hard to thrust and how deep to plunge. It was his arm around my hips, holding me in place so he could have me precisely how he wanted me.

It was incredibly erotic to feel his passion. It was a huge part of what attracted me to him. I needed someone who was focused and confident—willing to go after what he wanted. It was like gravity, pulling me toward his center, giving me stability so I could be free.

I hoped I returned the favor for him. I wanted him to feel like this around me.

He pumped wildly, grunting and feeding his need while I pushed back with my own need to please him.

"Fuck, I need to see you. Roll over."

I grinned. "I want you slow, deep, and long."

Adam nodded furiously. His eyes were so dark with his pupils dilated. His cheeks were flushed and his jaw was thrust forward as he grabbed himself and angled his cock to slide back inside me. He did just as I asked, moving slow until he was as deep as he could go. I closed my eyes and savored the feeling. I tried so hard to memorize the way it felt when his warm cock was inside my hot, wet body. The way he felt too big and yet not big enough all at the same time.

He brought up his knees and bowed down over me so he could have both his arms free. He took my breasts in each hand, cupping them and bringing them to his lips one at a time.

I cried out as he sucked one nipple and then the other. I grabbed his shoulders and rocked my hips up and down his cock as he swirled and sucked, nipped and flicked. I was a quivering, shaking mess. Then he slid his knees back out so that he was lying flat on top of me, wrapped his arms under my shoulders, and slowly pulled out as far as he could without withdrawing.

He repeated this type of thrust over and over until I was burning everywhere. I swear anything would tip me over. He pushed deep inside and stayed there, rocking his hips so that he hit my clit. It drove me wild. I wrapped my legs tighter around his waist and clutched his shoulders, pulling as hard against him as I could. He pressed harder and circled his hips.

Every muscle in my body jerked and I yelled out. The orgasm detonated in the center of my core, racing out like an explosion across my body. My skin tingled, my core pulsed, and I couldn't breathe deep enough to catch my breath.

As I started to come down from my sexual high, Adam thrust longer and deeper, totally changing the experience. It was fantastic and it kept my orgasm going, rolling it directly into another, weaker orgasm. That was when he lost all control. His cock pulsed and he thrust one last time.

The movement of his cock inside me as he came was more than enough to keep my second orgasm rolling for far longer than it should have.

Adam pulled himself up onto his elbows to watch, kissing my cheek and whispering how beautiful I looked when I came around him.

When I was finally done we rolled apart and Adam tucked me into his shoulder.

We didn't sleep, but we did doze in and out the entire night—neither of us willing to lose the time we had left together. He read to me while I relaxed on his chest, his fingers raking through my hair. I acted out scenes (naked) from my favorite books. We drank wine and snacked and showered until I thought my skin might never look normal again.

Adam's shower was definitely my favorite place on Earth. Period.

Sometime around four o'clock in the morning we were drinking water while wrapped up in blankets on the back porch. The sliding glass doors were all pushed open—bugs be damned—tiki torches were lit all along the periphery and I sat in Adam's lap while we looked up at the enormous harvest moon and talked about the mysteries of the universe.

Like, *actual* mysteries.

The shape of the universe, the big bang theory, and manned space flight.

I was fairly certain Adam was asleep. He was snoring lightly and his hands were lead weights weighing down my arms, instead of trailing back and forth the way they always seemed to when he was awake. I needed to wake him up soon so he could get dressed and leave for the airport.

I didn't want to wake him.

I was panicking. It was a weird feeling that I'd never experienced. When Allison left for London I was sad, but it was a selfish emotion. I was going to miss my best friend and partner in crime. I didn't want to be lonely. In reality we still talked every day and I could call her day or night to tell her anything. We still drank and ate together—it was just through the power of the internet instead of being in the same room. Our friendship hadn't changed. Distance didn't fundamentally alter anything other than a little more loneliness in my days.

But Adam was entirely different.

I'm quite sure my feelings were selfish as well, but it was more than that. I was dying inside. I knew the moment Adam walked out the door it was going to feel like I'd amputated part of my soul and sent it away. He was part of me and I was part of him…and I didn't know how to live without a piece of me.

This ache was more painful than anything else I'd ever felt. No betrayal or manipulation from anyone had ever hurt like this. It made me willing to do anything to make the pain stop. Climb mountains, board airplanes, abandon my career. Not that I was going to hide myself inside Adam's luggage and run away with him, but I was entertaining the thought.

If we were so good together and starting over somewhere people didn't immediately recognize my name was a possibility, maybe I should stop entertaining the idea and start seriously considering what I wanted. I needed to take Adam out of the equation and look at my life objectively.

If that was even possible.

I liked the idea of leaving all my ties to Hollywood behind. Lily was finally on board with the idea that we were never going to be a happy family. So what did *I* want? Where could I escape my past and build a future? I thought Calhoun Beach was my best shot, but maybe I hadn't been dreaming big enough.

I'd had a job offer earlier this year. It seemed too wild, too complicated to make work with my recent move. But now? Now it might just be the perfect first step in a new direction.

I kissed Adam on the cheek. His skin was so soft against my lips. His eyes fluttered open and his hands tightened around me. "Damn. I fell asleep?"

I nodded and kissed his cheek again. *So soft.*

"I don't want to go."

"I don't want you to go," I whispered back.

"Three weeks is too long."

I shook my head. "It is, but you'll be busy and it will be over before you know it."

"Video sex will be fun." He didn't sound convinced at all.

"I promised you a look inside the second box."

Adam grinned. "That you did. I look forward to it."

"You need to get dressed." Or I could handcuff him to the shower faucet and keep him as my prisoner. That could work, too.

Adam kissed me on the cheek and shifted me to the side so he could stand. Every move was so deliberate, as if it caused him pain. While he got dressed I closed up the back doors and made him coffee. When I heard the faucet turn on I grabbed my computer and opened my email, searching for the message from my friend John. It only took a moment to find it and re-read it. He'd only sent it two months ago.

Seriously Liz, you don't belong in America with your young buildings. Come here where we have really old stone for you to study. Offer stands—just say the word and I'll make you a position.

I hit reply.

Hey John, I'm saying "the word". Tell me where and when. I'm all yours.

Well, in May, after the spring semester was over, I'd be "all his".

Adam stuck his head out while he brushed his teeth, then again when he shoved his toiletries bag in the pouch of his suitcase.

I sipped my coffee and tried to stop the panic. A new email popped up and I held my breath. There was always the possibility that John's enthusiasm was misplaced. But since sending my message I'd allowed myself to imagine what a life at Oxford would look like. I'd given many guest lectures there over the years and had even done a summer semester. John was a good friend and we'd worked together on a preservation project in southern France where we bonded over wine and the Tour de France. In the span of five minutes I'd completely and utterly fallen in love with the idea of taking a position at Oxford.

I clicked on the email and let out a slow breath.

Thank god! We need you. The job is yours. Our next term starts 1st of July, and we'll draw up the paperwork today.

"What's that smile?" Adam was standing near his suitcase.

"Nothing. Just funny how things work out sometimes."

"In ways you never expect," he agreed.

Allison was staying in London, Adam was moving to Brackley, and I was going to teach at Oxford—a city only twenty miles from Adam's new job. Maybe I could convince Lily to take up theater in London. Then everyone I cared about would be in the same place for a while. That idea was a little slice of heaven.

I grabbed a piece of paper and pen from the counter and scribbled a note.

Dr. Filler is the new professor in the school of Archaeology at Oxford starting July 1st. Do you have a room you could possibly rent to her?

I folded it in half and walked over to Adam and his suitcase. I held it up in the air and gave him a wicked, sexy smile. "This is to open on the plane." I slid it into the pocket of his carry on, giving him a nice view of my ass in the process.

"What is it?"

"Wait and see. You'll like it, I promise." Even if Adam and I never saw each other again, I was happy with this decision. As much as I loved Calhoun Beach, it wasn't home. I needed to find "home" and this was the first step. It was a good job at an amazing university with people I liked working with.

"It's time," he murmured.

I took a deep breath. I wanted to run back to the bed and hide under the covers. I wanted to pretend this wasn't happening.

He grabbed my hand and gently tugged until I fell into him. Tall and warm and strong. Being in Adam's arms was the safest and sexiest place to be. He pulled on my hand and brought it up between us. "This bracelet has something engraved on the inside," he said simply, pulling the cuff off my wrist and holding it up so I could read it.

Inside was the E.E. Cummings poem he'd read to me the other night. *I Carry Your Heart (I carry it in my heart)*. The letters were impossibly tiny and I couldn't even begin to comprehend how it had been created.

"You can pull away and hide. You can be scared and worried. Do whatever you need to do, Beth. It won't change how I feel about you. You've gotten deep down inside me and I'll never be the same. Nothing you do or say will change that." He slid the bracelet back on my wrist and pressed my hand to his heart.

"This is yours—without strings or obligation."

I had his heart in my hand. And he'd basically said my heart was inside his heart. We were part of each other forever. I'd never be the same after meeting Adam Callaway.

He leaned down, looking into my eyes. "I love you, Beth. Completely."

This was love. I knew it without question the moment he said it. All doubts I'd been debating about fake feelings and misguided emotions were wiped away by the simple clarity of the words on Adam's lips.

He smiled and kissed me lightly. "Don't say it back," he whispered. "Don't say it until it doesn't scare you anymore. Only say it when it makes you feel like flying." He ran his nose along mine, his fingers in my hair, tilting my head so he could kiss me deep. I kissed him back, hard and desperate to show him all the things I didn't know how to say yet.

That I loved him too.

That I wanted to spend forever with him so badly it scared me.

That being without him was impossible.

Then he released me, kissed the tip of my nose and smiled. "I know."

"What do you know?" I whispered back. I was breathless from my feelings and that kiss.

But Adam just smiled and shook his head. "You'll figure it out. Get some sleep today. I'll call you when I land." He grabbed his bag and turned toward the door. I was frozen and unable to speak. It was like I'd just been bowled over by an avalanche on an icy mountain.

"I love you, too." I clapped my hand over my mouth and stood there with my eyes bulging out of my head. Did I really just say that? Did I mean it?

Adam stopped and spun on his heel, dropping his bag and scooped me up in his arms. He carried me the six steps to the bed and tossed me down, crawling on top of me, grinding against my hips and looking intently into my eyes.

I did mean it. I didn't quite feel free enough to fly, but I was going to run with it. I knew if I didn't tell him how I felt that I would regret it.

No more regrets.

"You mean it, don't you?" he was looking at me with awe and wonder. His eyes were wide and soft, but the smile on his face was full of pride.

"I do. I'll say it again when I'm ready. But I absolutely meant it." And that felt incredibly freeing. Almost like flying—like the feeling you get right before takeoff.

"I'll be waiting." He kissed me deeply one more time and pressed his forehead to mine. "I love you and I will make this work even if I have to work for my parents."

That made me grin, which caught Adam's eye. "What?"

I shrugged, feeling quite full of myself now. "Maybe you can open that piece of paper in the car, instead of the plane."

His eyebrow shot up. "What's on that piece of paper?" He ground against me. Heat exploded between my legs and I pulled on the belt loops of his jeans looking for friction. "Tell me."

His sexual demands worked most of the time, but I was going to hold strong on this. I wanted him to be surprised after he left. At the rate we were going he was never going to make his plane. "Nope. You'll find out when you leave."

He huffed, kissed me, and hopped off. "Well then, I better leave."

He grabbed his bag and grinned. "I'll see you soon, Gorgeous."

I stayed on the bed, letting out a long, slow breath. This hurt. Like really, *really* hurt.

Adam was gone and I wouldn't see him again for three weeks. And even then it was only a quick weekend.

But there was light at the end of the tunnel. I liked knowing that. We just had to make it work until May. I'd get two months to play and move before starting my new job.

Then the damn tears started. It didn't matter how many times we saw each other. May was too far away and Adam leaving before dawn made the whole day feel entirely pointless.

And then I had the piss scared out of me as the door slammed back open and Adam, his eyes locked on me, stalked across the room. "You're quitting your job for me? Hell no. I told you I'd come back and work for Green Hills. We just need time to sort things out." He ran his hand through his hair.

I wasn't expecting this reaction. Adam was supposed to be delighted and happy—and on his way to the airport. Instead he was *mad*.

He let out a breath. "I figure if I get through the end of this season with the team then I can walk away happy. I'll get racing out of my system once and for all. I won't let you quit your job for me. I can't be the reason you change your life."

"I'm not quitting my job, Adam. I'm taking the job I was offered months ago, but was too afraid to accept. It's a good job. A job I desperately want. I'm not quitting anything for you. You can go live in China for all I care." His eyebrows shot up and his eyes narrowed. "I don't *want* you to. I want you to live with me in England. I want us to find some adorable old home to renovate and maybe an apartment in the city. I want to hang out with Allison and watch races with you. I want you to find old cars to tow home and fix up. I want to teach about buildings older than the United States in a country that actually has some." I got up on my knees and put my hands on my naked hips, giving Adam an eyeful. "If you really want to come back to Green Hills one day and build me my cottage in the field, then fine, we'll do that. We can do it all Adam. You're not making me do a damn thing."

He stepped into me and I had to crane my neck up to look at him. "Promise me."

"I swear to you that this is all my choice." Every single bit of it. The truth and the fantasy. I wanted it all, and I wanted it with Adam.

He stared at me for a long, hard moment, making sure I was telling the truth. "Fuck my flight," he whispered, grabbing me and kissing me. His tongue slid along mine, our teeth knocked as we fought for control. I pulled myself up and wrapped my legs around his waist. He crawled onto the bed with me holding on tight. "I'll catch the next one."

"I'll make it worth your while," I gasped, unbuckling his belt and wiggling his pants down.

"You always do," he grunted appreciatively.

I dug inside his pants for his already firm cock. It wasn't as hard as a rock, but he was aroused enough to play with. I guided him to me and rocked my hips. He gasped. I moaned as he slid home.

Two weeks ago I was too afraid to take a chance on anything. It was crazy how one little leap of faith had changed my life.

* * *

Thank you for reading Adam and Elizabeth's story! If you enjoyed it, sign up for my newsletter. Subscribers get information on upcoming releases first!

If you have a moment, please leave an honest review where you bought this book. Reviews help authors be found by new readers.

Want more? Dive into the rest of the series now!

More from Alexis Anne

The Storm Inside
Reflected in the Rain
When Lightning Strikes
Never Let Go

Tease
Stripped
Tempt
Burn
5 Dirty Sins
6 Dirty Secrets

Box Sets:
The Storm Inside Box Set
The Tease Series Box Set

-BE A FRISKY FRIEND-

I'd love to have you join my Facebook reader group! Click on the link of search "Coffee, Whiskey, and all Things Frisky" on Facebook.

About the Author

Alexis Anne is the author of the steamy *The Storm Inside* series and the sexy *Tease* serials. A recovering archaeologist, she loves writing stories about passionate people overcoming mistakes and finding where they belong (amidst some equally passionate sexy-times). Her heroines are smart, her heroes are strong, and her stories are always close to her own life experiences. She lives in Florida with The Sexy Editor, their two super heroes, and a dog who would be much happier in the snow (although he seems okay with the beach).

www.AlexisAnneBooks.com
alexisannebooks@gmail.com

Please visit me online!

Facebook: /AlexisAnneBooks
Instagram: @AlexisAnneAuthor
Twitter: @AlexisAnneBooks
Tumblr: @AlexisAnneAuthor

Printed in Great Britain
by Amazon